Taking Care of Business

He'd done everything exactly the way she'd told him to, and now he was here. She could have pretended not to hear the knock on the door. She supposed she could even have made up a reason not to let him in.

But she didn't want to.

She was going to do this. Her heartbeat pounded in her wrists and the base of her throat and in strange places like behind her knees. Places she wanted to feel his mouth.

She stepped back, one, two, three. He moved inside the room. 'Close the door, Brandon.'

He turned to do it and Leah admired not only his swift obedience but also the curve of his ass. She took another two steps back and waited for him to turn around. It took only moments, but felt like forever.

Taking Care of Business
Megan Hart and Lauren Dane

Published by Black Lace 2008

2 4 6 8 10 9 7 5 3 1

First published in Great Britain in 2008 by
Black Lace
Virgin Books
Random House, 20 Vauxhall Bridge Road
London SW1V 2SA

www.black-lace-books.com
www.virginbooks.com
www.rbooks.co.uk

Addresses for companies within The Random House Group Limited can be found
at: www.randomhouse.co.uk/offices.htm

The Random House Group Limited Reg. No. 954009

Distributed in the USA by Macmillan, 175 Fifth Avenue, New York, NY 10010, USA
A CIP catalogue record for this book is available from the British Library

ISBN 9780352345028

The Random House Group Limited supports The Forest Stewardship Council [FSC],
the leading international forest certification organisation. All our titles that are
printed on Greenpeace approved FSC certified paper carry the FSC logo.
Our paper procurement policy can be found at www.rbooks.co.uk/environment

Typeset by TW Typesetting, Plymouth, Devon
Printed and bound in Great Britain by
CPI Bookmarque Ltd, Croydon CR0 4TD

1

'I expect you to be gone by the time I get home. You have until Friday.' Leah Griffin paused in the doorway to look back at the man she'd been sharing her life and bed with for the past year and a half. 'Don't forget anything, Mike. Because I won't be letting you back in to get it.'

Mike gave her a confident sneer. 'You'll be begging for me to come back.'

Leah's suitcase hung comfortably heavy from her hand. She hadn't packed her whole life inside, just enough to get her through the next four days, but the simple act of taking what she absolutely needed to live and leaving the rest behind had made all of this ugliness seem much easier to deal with. Somehow knowing she had her favourite night-shirt, her hairbrush, her scented soap, the bits and pieces of her life Mike could never take from her the way he'd tried to take everything else, made walking out the door so much more bearable.

'I don't think so,' she said mildly.

Mike's gaze flickered for a moment. He'd grown cocky and complacent. The fact she'd told him to pack his shit and get the fuck out only twenty minutes ago obviously hadn't sunk in yet. And, she had to admit, it wasn't as though she'd never tried to break up with him before. She knew this time was different, but Mike couldn't be blamed for not knowing. Except she did blame him, for everything, even the parts she knew belonged to her.

'C'mon, honey,' he purred, moving towards her with his hands reaching. 'Don't be that way.'

'I'll be at the conference until Thursday,' she said, not moving towards him but refusing to shrink away either. 'But if your number comes up on my cell I won't be answering it, and I won't be returning your calls either. I meant what I said, Mike. Get your stuff out of here and be gone by the time I get home. You have four days. That should be plenty of time.'

Still reaching, his hand stopped in mid-grasp. He blinked. The mouth she'd once thought so sultry turned sullen. 'Where the hell am I supposed to go?'

'I'm sure you can find a couch to crash on. But, to tell you the truth, I really don't care.' Her fingers slipped a little on the suitcase handle. Despite her calm exterior she was sweating. She was, in spite of herself, a little afraid of him. Of herself. Of giving in to his confident charm.

His hands dropped to his sides and the corners of his mouth turned down even more. He looked around the kitchen he'd never cleaned or cooked in, then back to her. 'You don't want to do this, Leah. I'm telling you, you don't.'

'Oh, yes. I'm sure I do.' She flashed him a smile.

He recoiled as though she'd bared her teeth at him. Who knew, maybe she had. Leah gripped the suitcase harder, watching him warily. Mike put his hands on his hips. His eyebrows lowered to match his frown.

'Nobody will ever love you the way I do,' he warned.

'Oh, God!' Leah cried, her composure cracking. 'I hope not! I hope nobody ever loves me the way you do ever again!'

Her suitcase banged the door frame as she turned. The impact jarred her arm and her elbow hit too. Bright sparks of electric shock reverberated all the way to her shoulder and she bit her lip against the small cry struggling to

escape. She wasn't going to give Mike the pleasure of thinking she was crying about leaving him.

He didn't come after her. He didn't even follow her to the door to watch her go. Leah couldn't decide if that made her feel better or worse, but, as she put her suitcase in the trunk of her late-model Volvo and then slid into the driver's seat, she decided she didn't care. He would be gone by the time she came home. She could only hope she wouldn't also be missing anything important.

Belongings could be replaced. Her life could not. She backed out of the driveway and looked carefully left and right before pulling out into traffic, and then she drove away without looking back.

She went to the office first, where she put out a few fires and handled a few disasters, all without breaking a sweat. It gave her something to do, that was all, and Leah appreciated the distraction of a hundred daily tasks to keep her from dwelling too long on what had happened at home.

By midday she had no excuse for hanging around. The Harrisburg Hilton was only a few minutes away from the office. She wished it were an hour. A day. A month's journey. Instead, she found herself pulling into the parking garage before she'd even had time to cycle through a full playlist on her iPod. She didn't get out of the car right away. She sat with her hands folded in her lap and her eyes closed. Listening.

To silence.

Thinking, for the first time in a long, long time, of nothing.

Usually, no matter what else she was doing, she was also thinking of Mike. What to cook him for dinner, what dry-cleaner to use for his shirts, whether or not she ought to have picked up the black lace bra and panty set or the white one. Her world had revolved around pleasing him. At work

she'd been the Empress of Employment, the High Priestess of Human Resources. At home, she'd been a housewife and a sometime-slave.

Her eyes flew open. So much for not thinking about it. The word had never shamed her, but now it felt so ... wrong. Like it didn't fit and, worse, never had. That the past eighteen months of her life had been a lie.

Hell. Longer than that. If she really wanted to turn on the brights and get out the tweezers to pluck out the splinters left behind by the disintegration of her disastrous relationships, she had to admit that Mike had only been the last in a series of mistakes.

Hopefully, she thought as she grabbed her bag and got out of the car, he would stay the last.

She'd made her room reservation just that morning, when Mike was in the shower. Of course, this meant her room wasn't yet ready, though the clerk behind the elegantly polished front desk did offer to take her suitcase while she waited in the Market Street Café. Leah let her take it. She wasn't going back to the office today, and none of the meetings started until tomorrow. She wanted to go straight to her room and have either a hot shower or a good cry. Maybe both at the same time. First though, she had to talk to the conference-services manager about the week's preparations. Leah had emailed the woman for several months and spoken to her once or twice, but now, when she asked to speak to her, the clerk gave her a surprised blink.

'Oh, I'm sorry. Heather is on maternity leave.'

Leah took a long slow breath before she answered. 'I just spoke with her last week. She didn't mention anything about leaving. In fact, I specifically asked her if I'd be working with her on this project.'

The clerk, a tall thin woman with a head of tight braids, gave Leah an apologetic smile. 'Sorry.'

The clerk didn't sound or look sorry, but Leah held her temper. 'Did she leave a replacement?'

'Hmm?' The clerk furrowed her brow and pursed her lips as though Leah had asked her the meaning of life. 'Oh, yeah. Her assistant will be taking over all her duties.'

'Great. Can I talk to her assistant, then?' Leah managed not to grind her teeth. She even managed a slight smile. Not a big one, just enough to make it look like she wasn't ready to say a dirty word. Or three.

'Oh, sure. He's around here.' The clerk looked around as though expecting him to jump out from behind one of the potted palms. 'I can page him for you.'

'That would be great.' Never let it be said that Leah Griffin didn't know diplomacy.

The clerk picked up the phone and spoke into it, but whoever was on the other end didn't seem to have any satisfactory information for her, because she frowned. 'Uh-huh. Yeah. OK. Sure. OK. Well, when will he be back?'

That didn't sound good. Leah wished desperately for a cup of coffee, a can of cola ... a good, stiff drink. Hell. A chocolate cheesecake would have done nicely, too. She gave the clerk an expectant look when the other woman hung up the phone.

'He'll be back soon,' the clerk said with a small shrug. 'I left a message on his voicemail and paged him.'

'And my room's still not ready?' Leah peered across the desk, though the computer monitor showing the room listings was indecipherable to her.

The clerk hit a few buttons on the keyboard. 'No, I'm sorry. You could wait in the bar. I'll tell Brandon where you are.'

At least she could get a drink. 'All right. Thanks.'

The bar was quiet this early in the afternoon, though she spotted a few men in business attire seated at one of the booths along the back. Nobody she knew though. Anyone

from her office would still be at the Allied Packaging corporate centre. Only those from out of town would have arrived already, and she didn't know any of them.

Her phone buzzed in her purse as she took a seat at the bar, and she pulled it out. 'Griffin.'

'Leah, it's Dix. Just checking that you got the latest updates from corporate.' Charles Dixon, the in-house counsel for Allied Packaging, didn't waste any time.

The head honchos. 'Yes. I got them this morning. Jeanette's making the copies for the packets now and will bring them over with her tomorrow.'

'I've got some other addendums,' he said. 'Want me to drop them off on your desk?'

'I'll be at the hotel, actually. Give them to Jeanette, would you?' Leah's assistant was blonde, young and had an immense crush on Dix. Leah was pretty sure he knew it but, if he had any inclination of going against the company policy of dating co-workers, he'd never shown it in front of her.

'Going above and beyond, huh?'

It took her a bare second to realise he thought she meant she was going to be there early. Dix didn't know she was staying at the Hilton. He wouldn't be. There was no reason for him to, because Dix had a nice house only fifteen minutes away. Well, so did she.

'I'll be at the hotel. I thought it would be best,' she put in smoothly, giving away nothing. 'You know. To keep an eye out in case of issues with anything.'

'Right, right. Well, I'll drop off this stuff with Jeanette then and see you first thing.'

'I'll be picking up Katherine at the station tonight,' she added before he hung up. 'So if you wanted to come early tomorrow morning to meet her . . .?'

'Yeah,' Dix cut in. 'Yeah. Maybe I'll do that.'

With that business finished, Leah disconnected. Her phone rang again almost at once. The small view screen showed a simple black-and-white photo of a rose. Mike's icon. She watched as the words 'missed call' appeared on the screen and the phone stopped ringing. A moment after that it buzzed in her hand like a wasp to alert her she had a voicemail.

'I told you,' she murmured, 'I wasn't going to answer.'

She deleted the call without even listening to it.

2

Charles Dixon looked out the window of his office at the trees lining the walk just outside and picked up his phone. He'd promised himself he'd let her come to him this time but here he was, hitting the button with her name on it. When she answered, the sound of her voice shot through him sexually and emotionally as always. Fuck, he was such a sucker for this woman.

'Hiya, Kate, you all ready to finally meet me all official-like and everything?'

He heard street noise, pictured her trying not to smile. 'Good morning, Dix. As you know it's the highlight of my year. Now, what do you want?'

'Just calling to make sure everything was ready at your end. And you didn't yell at me for calling you Kate. Are you feeling well?' He loved that, loved knowing he was the only one other than her friend Leah who got away with calling her Kate during business hours . . . and afterwards.

'It's a losing battle. I give up because you're incorrigible anyway.'

'Where are you? Is that street sound? Kate, darling, are you speaking on a cell phone while walking in public?' He laughed. 'I'm a terrible influence on you. I like that.'

'I told you I'd be in Philly today to do a CLE on non-competes before I head to Harrisburg later tonight. I'm walking from my hotel to the office.'

She'd ducked why she picked up the phone but he knew

8

the reason. Because it was him. And that was enough for now.

'Thrilling.' He quirked up a smile, knowing she was smiling too.

'It is, Mr Dixon. Quite actually. Which is why Allied Packaging pays me and Hargrave and Aaron quite handsomely for my services. And to answer your first question, I've sent ahead all the paperwork I'll need. Leah said she'd take care of getting it to the conference hotel. My assistant won't be coming with me so I'll be solo. Other than that, it's fine.'

Her voice was professional but warm. He'd heard her talk to enough people to know the difference in her tone.

'Good. I've got to talk to Leah again later today anyway to keep her updated. I'll double-check with her on all the paperwork. Have you told her about us?' He lowered his voice. His door was closed but he knew Kate would appreciate his discretion.

'Not yet. I wanted to tell her in person. We can talk later, I'm getting ready to walk into the building now. I'll see you tomorrow, right?'

He wished it was tonight. He'd wanted her in his bed instead of secret meetings in hotels, but she'd balked.

'First thing tomorrow. I'll see you then.'

She broke the connection and he sat back, unable to get her off his mind. From the first time he heard her say hello until that very moment she'd been like a song in the back of his brain and he couldn't shake it. Didn't want to.

Katherine loved the way his voice sounded. The tease layered in innuendo. If any other man had spoken to her the way Charles Dixon did during her business day, she'd have cut him off at the knees. He was that one little bit of dark chocolate she allowed herself in a sea of eating fibre and doing the right thing.

To what extent she gorged on the absolutely sinful man, no one but the two of them knew.

She'd decided to walk from her hotel to Hargrave and Aaron. Normally she would have ignored the call, preferring not to carry on phone conversations on a public sidewalk but she'd seen it was him on her caller ID and picked up. She flipped the phone shut and tucked it into her bag as she approached the glass revolving doors to the building housing the Philadelphia offices of her firm.

The artificially cool air soothed over her skin as she pulled Katherine tight, pushing Kate far away. Here in the midst of $3,000 office chairs and floor-to-ceiling glass and chrome, there was no room for mistakes.

The shiny reflective walls of the elevator showed a confident, cool woman. Feminine, but not too much. Her heels weren't matronly, nor were they sexy. Understated and expensive, chosen with the same deliberate care she put into everything else to do with her career. The suit, a summer weight, was smoky grey. The deep-wine blouse added just enough colour. Not flashy, but it complemented her skin tone and hair. Hair carefully tucked into a sleek chignon at the base of her skull completed the look she wanted to achieve.

Choices. It all came down to choices, and Katherine Edwards made the right ones. The right choices were what it took to get ahead in the savvy and male-dominated world of corporate law. It didn't mean she was a ball-busting bitch, but she'd made her share of attorneys on the other side of the aisle cry, she was sure. A smile touched her lips at that.

Katherine wasn't cold, nor did she hate sex and men. She wasn't a cliché. What she was, was smart and ruthless when she had to be. She knew the difference between how men and women were allowed to act at work. She wasn't one to fret over it, it was what it was so she sucked it up and dealt with it.

She'd nearly lost it all as a result of her wilder days when she was in college. Lost a job, nearly had her future derailed in the aftermath, so she knew the importance of staying on the straight and narrow during business hours.

She saved jello shots and gossip for after six and well away from the office. She kept a firm wall between Katherine, the woman with her eye on the prize of the corner office and her articles in legal journals, and Kate, the woman who wore jeans, ate Doritos and watched reality television while on IM with her best friend Leah.

A flicker of unease shot through her at thoughts of Leah and that stupid fuck she lived with, but she'd have to deal with that later. She'd also have to confess about Dix. Leah would love that one.

The elevator doors opened up to a large reception area and the two women behind the ridiculously large credenza looked up in unison and smiled brightly. Holding her briefcase in her left hand, she approached with a smile of her own and introduced herself.

'Hi there, I'm Katherine Edwards and this is my first day. I'm doing a CLE and I'm supposed to meet someone from HR to get all my paperwork turned in.'

Another surprise she hadn't told anyone about. She wasn't sure how to process any of it. Something big was going to happen one way or another. A sense of expectancy had been building over the last two weeks. Excitement warred with worry deep within her.

Christ, it's bright. A shaft of absurdly golden sunshine heated her arm as she waited in the hotel lobby for her cab. At least the air conditioning kept the space cool.

June in Philadelphia was, um, golden and hot. It had been so easy to forget when she'd headed to the University of Washington to go to law school and ended up staying. How

quickly the rain and mist became normal. Back home it would be nearing about seventy degrees and the sunlight would still be pale. Well, not back home any more. Philly was home now. All her stuff would be delivered the following weekend to move in. How this would affect her arrangement with Dix she didn't know.

They'd begun speaking on the phone when she'd been hired of counsel to Allied Packaging on a contracts issue and the spark had been there immediately. How it had flowed into phone sex Kate wasn't even sure of any more but it had. And then emails.

The first time they'd met face to face was for two days in Chicago when she'd gone to speak at a legal conference and he'd shown up at her door. The sex had been explosive, amazing, so furtive and guilty, nothing had ever been so delicious.

That had been four months before and they'd met once more in San Francisco a month prior. In between the few times they'd been together physically, they'd gotten to know each other, which in retrospect had been very stupid on her part, because she liked Charles Dixon a great deal. The more she got to know him, the more she liked him. Which was, of course, the crux of the issue.

What they had was a nice, part-time, no-strings fling. Had she endangered that by taking a job at the Philadelphia offices of her firm and moving there?

She had a plan, she had goals and she prided herself on keeping her business separate from her personal. And yet, there she sat, majorly muddled with this man at the core. Katherine Edwards and her right choices – only she'd cheated and made a wrong one because he was too delicious not to.

She heaved a sigh and settled in the cushy chair. After returning from her day of meetings, she'd taken a shower

and changed out of her suit and into a sleeveless shirt, Capri pants and sandals to battle the heat. Something she'd be doubly glad of on the two-hour train commute.

Her phone rang. 'Shake It Like a Salt Shaker'.

Leah's voice came over the line and, while she tried to play off her break-up with that ass-hat Mike, the emotion hung heavy in her voice.

In any case, they made arrangements to meet at the train station but there was a moment when Dix came up in passing.

Kate's breath caught at the mention of his name. Leah had been her closest friend for what felt like forever but Kate hadn't told her about him yet. It called for alcohol and lots of it. They had a lot of catching up to do when they met later on that evening in Harrisburg.

They rung off and Kate settled back into the plush faux-comfort of the chair. She stared out the windows to Market Street just beyond and waited.

She could have jotted down her notes. Could have pulled out her laptop and worked. Could have made a few calls and checked her voicemail. Instead she allowed herself to do nothing but think.

3

'What can I get you?' The bartender had waited until Leah's phone conversations finished before asking. He tossed a towel over one shoulder while he put both hands on the bar between them. 'You look like you could use something.'

'That bad?' Leah tried a laugh but it came out sounding more like a sigh.

The bartender grinned. 'We're supposed to say that to everyone. Gets the customers in a drinking mood.'

Now her laughter trickled out of her with more force. 'Really?'

He nodded and grabbed up the twenty-dollar bill one of the suits had just passed to him. He filled two mugs with beer as he talked, then handed them off and made change. 'Not really. But it usually works.'

He wasn't as young as many of the bartenders working at a lot of the new pubs and clubs springing up in downtown Harrisburg. Not that Leah had been out to a club in a long time, but sometimes she had lunch down here with some of her co-workers. This guy, though, looked to be in his early forties with a head of dark hair going nicely silver. He had a sweet smile, too.

'I'll take a glass of Cabernet,' she told him. 'It's too early for anything else.'

'Never too early,' countered the bartender, but he filled her glass with red wine anyway. 'Cheers.'

'Cheers,' she said, and sipped.

'It won't put hair on your chest,' the bartender said with another grin, 'but I guess it'll have to do, right?'

It would have been too simple for her to merely sit and have a glass of wine by herself. No, the beer-drinking suits in the corner booth kept glancing her way. Only a matter of time before one of them worked up the gumption to come over and hit on her, she thought as she sipped and made casual conversation with the bartender.

She was wrong, though. One of them didn't come over. They both did.

One on either side, they flanked her. The one on her right, the blond, wore a wedding ring. The dark-haired one on her left flashed her a grin of teeth so white and straight he could have been in an ad for cosmetic dentistry.

They introduced themselves as Stu and Larry, and she told them her name. They asked her if she was in town on business, and she said yes. The bartender made himself scarce, and, while Leah appreciated his discretion, she had absolutely no intentions of taking up these men on their obvious intentions.

Their flirting was easy, if a little too ... calculated ... for her tastes. After fifteen minutes she felt like a deer being run down by wolves. The tag-teaming was subtle but unmistakable and, though she gave them loads of credit for the effort, she finally had to ask the question.

'Does this usually work for you?'

Stu, the married one, looked faintly surprised. 'What?'

'Sometimes,' said Larry, obviously the brighter of the two. 'Is it working for you?'

Leah smiled. 'Not really. Sorry.'

Stu looked a little confused, exchanging glances with his friend. 'Listen –'

'It's OK, Stu.' Larry shook his head. 'The lady isn't interested.'

'Thanks for the drink, though,' Leah said.

Stu's phone rang and he excused himself to answer it. Larry turned to her. 'What about if I ditched him?'

It was unaccountably refreshing to talk this way, the pretence of flirting gone. It had been quite some time since Leah had flirted with anyone, but she was pleased to discover being courted still made her tingle.

'It's not you,' she said, but added his name, slowly, easing it from her lips, 'Larry.'

He grinned. 'Sure. That's what they all say.'

'I just broke up with my boyfriend today,' she explained.

'Congratulations. All the more reason for you to celebrate.'

'You really know how to work it,' she said, impressed.

He feigned a moment of modesty quickly overtaken by pride. 'Thank you. You're beautiful.'

'What about your friend?' she whispered, leaning towards him as though to share a secret. They both looked over at Stu, still on his cell phone. 'Won't he get upset?'

'Stu? Nah.' Larry shook his head. 'Disappointed. But not upset.'

Leah leaned almost close enough to allow her lips to brush his ear. 'Let me ask you something, Larry.' Again, the name. It added intimacy. This all would have been better in dim lighting with the pound and throb of music around them, but she could work with mid-afternoon and the buzz of construction on the street outside if she had to. 'Do you and Stu do this often?'

Larry murmured directly into her ear, and his lips did brush her skin. 'Yes.'

She leaned even just a teensy bit closer. The satin lining of her skirt slid over the tops of her thighs, bare above her stockings. She'd dressed for Mike every morning for close to two years, but today she'd dressed for herself.

'You both take a woman to bed?' she whispered. Larry smelled good, like expensive cologne. 'At the same time?'

'Sometimes.' His hand had inched forwards, fingers tracing her knee.

'Do you fuck each other too? Or just her?'

The slow circling of Larry's fingertips, which had been inching higher, stopped. He pulled away a little bit to look at her, his smile a little crooked. 'What?'

Leah swiped her tongue slowly along her lower lip, and Larry's eyes followed the motion. 'Do you fuck each other too?' she repeated slowly, so he was sure not to miss a word. 'You and Stu, Larry. Do you suck each other's cock? Does he rim you while you fuck some strange woman you picked up in a bar?'

The words came out mildly, casually, as if she were enquiring about the weather, but she might as well have poked him with a sharp stick. Larry jerked back. He looked past her, presumably at Stu, and when he looked back at Leah his gaze was faintly panicked.

'No,' he said with a shake of his head. 'Hell, no.'

Leah leaned back in her chair and swivelled round to face the bar. She lifted her glass of wine and drained it, then set the empty glass carefully back on the coaster. She licked her lips clean and pulled a five-dollar bill from her bag. She put it on the counter.

'Too bad,' she said with a sweet smile for Larry, who still looked as though someone had hit him on the back of the head with something heavy. 'Because, if you'd said yes, I'd have gone upstairs with both of you.'

The bartender stifled a guffaw as Leah winked at the flummoxed Larry. She headed out of the bar, with a small wave for clueless Stu, and went to see if her room was ready at last.

It was, thank God, and she was already stripping out of her suit jacket as the door closed behind her. She tossed her bag on to the bed and went straight to the bathroom to turn on the hot water. She still wanted a hot shower, but she no longer needed the good cry.

The bartender seemed to think she was joking, maybe just using an excuse to get rid of the too-exuberant suitors, but Leah had told the truth. If Stu and Larry had promised more than just a standard tag-team screw, she'd have gone with them to their room and fucked the stuffing out of both of them.

Steam filled the bathroom as she slid open the buttons of her silk shirt and hung it carefully on the hook behind the door. Next came her skirt, until she stood wearing only the white lace bra and panties, the matching garter belt and sheer nude stockings. The lace between her legs was already damp.

That morning after fucking Mike – and there was no way for her to think of it as making love, because there had been no love to it – she'd wondered if she'd ever want sex again. The thought of another person's hands on her had made her stomach churn. Her relief at knowing she wouldn't have to suck his cock any longer, wouldn't have to suffer him pumping away on top of her, had only strengthened her resolve.

There had been no one thing at which to point blame. The break-up was the accumulation of months of dissatisfaction. But if there was one thing that had tipped her over the edge, it was the toothpaste. He'd left the cap off the toothpaste yet again, left squeezed globs of goo all over the place and expected her to clean it up. That had been the final straw. He'd woken her early with a demand for oral sex, but it was the toothpaste that had stayed with her until she could no longer face a life with him.

Leah had always had a healthy libido and her sex life with Mike had been compatible . . . at first. Over time her desire for him had been squelched by his lack of consideration.

Their games of dominance and submission had become nothing more than an excuse for him to act like an asshole.

Larry's touch on her knee, the purely masculine smell, the look of interest in his eyes: all had triggered something lying dormant in her for months and months. He'd thought he was in control of the situation, but Leah had been the one manipulating and manoeuvring the conversation. She'd been the one in charge, though Larry hadn't realised it.

It felt good.

A sigh whispered out of her as she ran her hands over her body. The woman in the mirror didn't look like the Leah she'd come to recognise: the one who kept her eyes downcast when she was naked; the one who gave in.

Leah slid her fingers into the front of her panties, over her clipped curls. Her clit throbbed under her touch and another sigh opened her mouth. Her finger dipped lower, between slick folds, and she shuddered.

Leah stripped out of her panties, leaving the whole pile on the floor and climbed into the hot water. She hissed at the sting even as she welcomed it. She turned her face to the spray.

'Oh,' she breathed when she saw one of the reasons why this hotel room cost so much. 'Yes.'

She pulled the detachable shower head from its hook and turned the massage setting from spray to jet. Immediately the water pulsed from the shower head in short hard bursts.

She hadn't made herself come in a long time. Mike had been a big fan of orgasm denial as a show of power and, since the less often she came, the more likely it was she would climax when he fucked her, Leah had complied with his commands.

But that was over now. No more Mike, she remind⟨ herself as she centred the pulsing jet of water direct⟨ her clit. She cried out at once, the pressure almost t⟨

Too strong. Her hips bucked forwards and she reached for the handrail.

She thought of the two men downstairs. Of having two cocks, four hands, two mouths on her. Of how Larry's neck smelled and how it would taste if she bit it. How it would feel to have one of them kneeling between her legs, lapping at her cunt, while the other tongued his way down her spine.

A soft muttered curse slipped out as the water pounded her. Already her breath was coming in short sharp pants and her vision was blurring. Leah, shower head still in hand, lowered herself to the floor of the bathtub and opened her legs as she adjusted the spray to a gentler setting.

The water caressed her flesh like a hundred tiny tongues licking her. Her clit, the soft folds, her ass. She moved the water back and forth across her flesh, her back arching as she came so hard a grunt escaped her. Her entire pussy spasmed, clamping down on nothing, and she longed for something to fill her.

Unfortunately, she hadn't thought to pack anything. She had a drawer full of toys that had lost their appeal when wielded under Mike's dominating hand. This morning she'd been sure she didn't care if she ever saw her vibrator again.

Fortunately, she had her hand and she knew exactly where her G-spot was. The water tickled her as she slid her fingers inside herself, stroking. She came again, as hard as the first time.

It was a miracle.

Leah lay back in the tub, the spray now directed towards the wall so only a fine mist came down to cover her, and tried to catch her breath. Her heartbeat slowed. Relief.

'Wow,' she said and then laughed. 'Thank God.'

She'd been half-afraid she'd never want to fuck again. More afraid her body would never demand pleasure the way it had in the past, that somehow she'd allowed Mike to break her.

Well, Leah thought as she got out of the shower and wrapped herself in a fluffy white towel, at least she wasn't broken.

4

'So, I took a job here at Hargrave.' Kate dropped the biggest bomb of her day into the conversation she'd been having with Leah. Her friend had picked her up at the train station and they were on the way back to the hotel. Leah had neatly avoided Mike talk for the time being so Kate let her evade. God knew she'd been evading enough herself.

'Seriously? How long have you known? Why didn't you say anything?'

Kate sighed. 'It's all tied in with something else I haven't told you. First things first though. I closed on a really nice condo yesterday. I'll start full-time next week. It's a pay raise, my moving expenses, a nicer office. I'm a senior partner here.'

'Well, good. Having you two hours away is great. Better than an entire country away. So tell me the big thing.'

Kate braced herself and blurted it out before she could change her mind. 'I've been having a fling with Charles Dixon.'

'Get out! Dix? A fling like how? And you didn't tell me?'

'A fling. An affair. Sex. Guilty, really hot, furtive sex where we both fly in somewhere, fuck for the entire weekend and go back home. It's, oh my God, it's fucking marvellous.'

Leah grinned. 'Wow! How long?'

'We've been flirting since day one, then, um, emails followed. Phone sex, he's very inventive.' A shiver went through her at that. 'We met in person for the first time four months ago. We've only done that twice, first in Chicago and last month in San Francisco.'

'You know I have to ask this, does he make you scream out the "Star Spangled Banner"?'

Kate laughed. 'Upside down from the chandelier. How do you think he is? I'm not a virgin by any means but he's a rock star in bed.'

'I'm totally shocked. Not that you'd have a fling and all, but that you didn't tell me. He has seemed more chipper lately. I guess you're the reason for that. How does he feel about the move here?'

'I haven't told him yet. I don't know what to say, Leah. We've had this no-strings thing, just fun meetings for sex and suddenly I'm here in his backyard. He's got kids and an ex-wife . . . a life. And he hasn't asked me to be part of it in any way other than what we've had.'

'Wow. Well, I suppose you won't know until you tell him. Am I going to have to pretend like I don't know?'

'I told him I was going to tell you today. But no one else knows. I'm already uncomfortable enough with people thinking I got this of counsel job because I know you; I'd be horrified to think anyone thought I got it because I was fucking in-house counsel.'

'Anyone who knows you would laugh at the idea. I expect to hear everything, in great detail. Now that you live here we can actually hang out. I can almost forgive you for not telling me because of that.'

'Well, you're the one who has a string of cute male strippers all lining up to give you attention every time you go to the club. I'm just there to grab your sloppy seconds.' They both snorted and began chatting for the rest of the short trip to the hotel about nothing much but all the stuff that makes you really like someone else. Shoes, Duran Duran, Clive Owen, the newest sci-fi movie they both wanted to see.

Kate had met Leah in the eighth grade when Kate's parents had decided she should try public school. It was love at first giggle and they'd been friends ever since. Leah had seen Kate through a lot of rough times. Leah had stood by her during the whole mess all those years ago and it was Leah who she told all her secrets to. There hadn't been an important moment in Kate's life that Leah hadn't shared in some sense.

Hell, they'd even shared a man once. The summer after high school they'd worked at a horse camp for junior high-schoolers. There'd been another counsellor who worked mainly with the horses and he'd been older. Delicious even. After an evening in the barn, just the three of them doing shots of Jack Daniels, she and Leah had stripped him naked, tied him up and tag-teamed him quite nicely. Kate snorted to herself at the memory. They'd rocked his world and she couldn't even remember his name.

Still, of all the people in the universe, Kate knew it was Leah who'd tell her the truth, even if it hurt, who'd listen to her without judging. It was a huge comfort to have a person who'd keep you honest with yourself and who also gave you safe harbour.

By the time they arrived at the hotel, Leah's spirits had risen. Being with a good friend could do that. Make even the crappiest day better.

'He'll get that,' Leah said when Kate lifted her suitcase from the trunk. She pointed at the bellboy, who'd been lounging by one of the tall marble columns. He snapped to attention at Leah's gesture. 'Take these up to room 223.'

He nodded as the valet stepped up to take her keys. Leah turned back to Kate to continue their briefly interrupted conversation as they headed inside the hotel. She stopped just inside the doors when she saw her friend's expression. 'What?'

Kate shook her head with a small laugh. 'They just do whatever you want. I love watching it.'

Leah's brow furrowed. 'Who?'

Kate waved a hand towards the bellboy carrying her suitcase towards the elevator. He gave them a smile and a nod as he passed. 'Boys. You say jump, they ask how high.'

'Oh, stop.' Leah laughed and led Kate in the direction of the bar.

'I'm serious.' Kate gave her a look. 'Don't tell me you don't notice.'

Leah paused, her smile fading as she thought of Mike. She sighed. 'Not usually.'

They took seats at one of the booths instead of at the bar. A different bartender was on duty, a girl this time, and Leah insisted on paying for the drinks even though Kate protested.

'You can get the next round.'

'Next round?' Kate lifted her glass in a semi-toast. 'OK, if you're talking more than one round, I know you've got a lot to tell me. Start talking.'

Leah hesitated. Not because she didn't trust Kate's judgement, or because she thought her friend would criticise. It was just hard to admit she'd made a mistake – another one. Some things were too personal even for a friendship as long and close as theirs.

'I woke up today with a dick in my mouth,' she said finally.

Kate's eyebrows rose. 'And you didn't bite it off?'

Leah laughed, feeling the knot coiled in her stomach start to ease. 'No.'

Kate took a swallow of her drink. 'Leah. You never talked much about Mike, so I know I can't say too much, but . . . he sounds like an utter asshole and I'm glad you dumped him.'

Leah sipped some of her drink. 'It's not as simple as that.'

'Is it ever?' Kate sighed, commiserating. 'So tell me.'

Leah drank again, thinking exactly what to say. The bar had been mostly empty earlier, other than the two absolutely-not-queer suits, but now as evening wore on it had filled. Mostly young professionals stopping on their way after work or staying in the hotel, she judged by their clothes. Typical for a Monday night.

Kate was waiting and Leah really wanted to tell her. She doubted her friend would be shocked or even surprised, yet somehow her mouth wanted to keep holding on to the past eighteen months like a secret. Like something shameful, when that wasn't it at all. At least not because of what she'd done. Just because of why.

'I really thought,' she said slowly, shaping the words to keep her voice from shaking, 'it was what I wanted.'

Kate said nothing, the perfect response.

Leah looked at her. They'd shared just about everything with each other ever since the eighth grade. 'Do you remember Todd?'

Only one of Kate's brows raised this time. 'I was just thinking about that on the way over here. I'd forgotten his name but it's kinda hard to forget him, don't you think?'

Leah laughed. 'Yeah. I guess so.'

'Mike doesn't sound like Todd, sweetie.'

'He wasn't. But . . . you remember the rope?'

Kate laughed and covered her face briefly with her hands. 'Oh, God. Yes. Of course. He didn't know what hit him. I bet he thinks of us every time he uses rope.'

Leah laughed too, remembering how they'd tied him up in the hayloft and had their wicked way with him. 'I couldn't ever forget that.'

Kate sobered a little. 'And?'

Leah sighed and finished off her wine, wishing she'd ordered something a little stronger. 'You know I've had a few boyfriends since then.'

'You and me both.'

'Well ... I guess I just kept looking for something that reminded me of that.' Leah shrugged, took a breath. Took a chance. 'I always thought it would be so nice to have someone just ... do stuff. For me. To me, I guess.'

Again, Kate only nodded, listening.

'Mike wasn't the first,' Leah continued. 'But he was really into it. Dominating. And, at first, I really liked it, you know? He laid it all out for me. What I would wear. What I'd make for dinner. The sex was great. He knew just what to do. I never had to tell him a thing.'

Leah gestured at the waitress to bring another round. 'But, after a while, he stopped knowing what I wanted and expected me to know what he wanted.'

'And when you didn't?'

'That's the thing,' Leah said. 'I did. I always did.'

Kate smiled. 'Of course you did.'

Leah shrugged. The conversation didn't hurt as much as she'd expected. In fact, the more she talked, the less it seemed to bother her at all. The less important Mike and his demands became.

'He never made me do anything I didn't want to do.' She wanted to make that clear. 'He was just a little more into the whole master/slave dynamic than I was, I guess. And it started feeling all very one-sided. I never felt like a slave,' she said finally. 'And I realised he really wasn't much of a master. He was just a selfish, self-involved prick who liked having someone do everything for him.'

'And getting his dick sucked apparently.' Kate waited until the waitress delivered their drinks before continuing. 'And no, he doesn't sound like much of a master.'

They'd always been open with each other about their sex lives – sharing a boy had sort of broken down any barriers there might otherwise have been. But Leah had never told

Kate about the particular quirks of some of her relationships. Now she wondered what had held her back.

'So that's that.' Leah drank thoughtfully. 'And you know something? I thought I was going to be way more upset about it. Now I'm just relieved. I'm just ... yeah, relieved.'

'Good for you,' Kate said sincerely. 'I mean it.'

Leah grinned. 'And I thought I was going to be completely soured on even the thought of ever having sex again, too.'

She told Kate about the afternoon, Stu and Larry, and how Larry had practically run away at her suggestion.

'But let me tell you,' Leah continued conspiratorially, 'those massage shower heads? Awesome.'

Kate snorted with laughter. 'Glad to hear you're getting back on the horse.'

This set them both off into gales of laughter at the memory of a barn, a boy and a bale of hay.

'I'll tell you what. I'd like to break off a piece of that,' Leah said when her laughter subsided. She discreetly pointed with her chin towards the bar.

The man there had leaned forwards, elbows on the polished wood, to talk to the bartender. From this angle she got a good look at the way his black dress pants clung to the curve of his ass.

He stood, up and up as they watched. He stood at least a head taller than most of the other men in the bar. His dark unruly hair looked thick enough to get lost in. It was hard to see the colour of his eyes from this distance, but Leah guessed they'd be dark, too. His white dress shirt, sleeves rolled up and tie pulled loose, wasn't showy but it flattered his broad shoulders and lean waist.

He grinned at something the bartender said. A true, genuine smile, not a smirk or a seductive, sly quirk of lips. He ducked his head briefly before replying.

'Him?' Kate pursed her lips and spoke in a put-on, deeper

voice. 'Golly gee whiz, ma'am, can I mow your lawn for some extra money? I'm saving up to go to Paris with the band.'

He did have that look about him, just a little. A clean-cut, earnest sort of aura that wasn't entirely out of place in the bar but not entirely in place, either. Leah couldn't hold back the chuckle at her friend's assessment.

'I like that,' she said. 'Like he's just waiting to be corrupted.'

Kate gave her a look, serious even though she was smiling. 'Did it ever occur to you that you've been putting yourself on the wrong end of the leash?'

Something tightened inside Leah at her friend's words. She looked again at the guy by the bar, who was still chatting up the bartender. He looked serious now, his hand tracing something like a list on the bar's polished surface. The bartender was nodding, solemn.

Leah looked at her friend. 'I think I'm done with all of that, Kate. I think I'd like to try something just ... normal for once.'

'First of all, just because not everyone does it doesn't mean it's abnormal.' The lawyer in Kate was coming out and Leah sat back with a grin for the lecture. 'Second, you're so full of shit, because having a fantasy about fucking two guys at the same time and wanting them to also do each other is so not something your average soccer mom is dreaming of.'

'I'm not a soccer mom,' Leah pointed out. 'And I bet more of them than you realise want to have two men.'

'Two men, yes,' Kate replied. 'Boy touching? Not so much.'

'Mmmmm,' Leah sighed, thinking of it happily. 'Boy touching.'

'Admit it, you're a perv.' Kate finished her drink. 'Nothing wrong with that. And if you want Band Boy over there, I say

29

go for it. I doubt he'd know what to do with you, but go for it.'

'I think he'd know exactly what to do,' Leah said under her breath just as he turned and looked in their direction.

His eyes were dark, she could see that now. He'd been smiling again as he turned, and it sent a bolt of sheer desire straight between her legs. She'd always been a sucker for a smile.

'I bet he could trim your hedges, too,' Kate said, and they both burst into laughter again.

'Oh, shit. Shit,' Leah breathed between bouts of giggles. 'He's coming over!'

'See? I told you!' Kate wiped her eyes and tried to force away the giggles but didn't quite manage. 'He's coming to hit us up for a couple of bucks. Maybe he'll p-p-play his trombone . . .'

Leah put both hands over her mouth to hold back the semi-hysterical fit of chortles forcing their way out. He was coming over, weaving his way through the tables with effortless grace. By the time he got to the table, she only managed to get herself partially under control.

He looked back and forth between the two of them. Kate kicked Leah gently under the table and waggled her eyebrows. Leah ignored her, afraid she'd burst into uncontrolled mirth again. She cleared her throat and attempted to take her hands away from her mouth, ready to slap them back at the first sign of an errant snort.

'Hi,' the man said. Though his grin was all 'garsh, ma'am', his voice was anything but. Deep, low and entirely male, it followed the path his smile had taken straight to her centre. 'How's everything over here?'

Kate sat back in her seat but, damn her, didn't answer. She kicked Leah under the table again, a little harder this time. Leah craned her neck to look up, up, up into his face. Damn, he was long.

'Fine,' she said. 'It's fine. How're things for you?'

He looked momentarily perplexed and then, damn. The grin was back, spreading wide and bright across his face. 'Um . . . it's fine. Do you need anything else?'

Ah. He worked here. He wasn't just trying to hit on them, more was the pity. Kate made another small noise and pretended to study her glass. Leah, bolstered by a day that had begun like shit but had ended up being much better and by the alcohol too, looked up at his face.

'Well, yes,' she said and rubbed the back of her neck to prove looking up so high was giving her a pain. 'You're very tall. Sit down.'

And damn . . .

He did.

5

'You're very tall. Sit down.'

The woman with the dark hair spoke like she had no doubt she'd get exactly what she wanted, and Brandon did as he was told. He pulled an unused chair from the next table and sat. He watched the smile freeze on her face. She hadn't expected him to do it, he thought, and wondered why she'd told him to if she didn't believe he'd obey.

'Is this better?' He'd turned the chair around the opposite way so he could straddle it, and now he folded his hands on the back to look at her expectantly.

It wasn't Brandon's job to make nice for the guests, but the hotel manager had talked him into taking some extra shifts and he could use the cash. Taking over for Heather while she was on maternity leave had meant a lot more responsibility but no raise. Besides, it wasn't like it was hard work or he had anything better to do with his time.

'Much,' the woman said while her friend stifled a laugh.

He'd already made sure their waitress was taking good care of them, but their laughter had drawn him. They were having fun. The fact they were both smoking hot had nothing to do with it, he told himself, knowing it wasn't true. Hey, working late had to have some perks, right?

'Well, if you need anything,' he said, 'just let me know, all right?'

'Did you hear that?' the woman on his left said across the table. 'He did say anything, Leah.'

Leah. He let the name play around on his tongue but kept inside his mouth. She had an empty drink in front of her, and he knew he should ask her if she needed another but before he could her friend got up. She used his shoulder to help her get out of the booth but waved him away when he started to get up to help her.

'I'm fine,' she said. 'You stay. Leah, I'm wiped out. I'm heading upstairs.'

Leah looked at her. 'Kate —'

'No, no,' Kate said. 'You stay. Get that grass taken care of.'

Leah put a hand over her eyes briefly, shaking her head, before she looked up with a grin. 'You're so bad.'

Kate flashed him a grin he returned, and she patted his shoulder again. 'Have fun in Paris.'

He waited until she'd gone before turning back to Leah. 'Paris?'

'It's nothing.' She waved a hand. 'Private joke.'

One he clearly didn't get. 'OK.'

Behind him he heard the buzz and murmur of the crowd and knew he ought to make some more rounds. He didn't want to. 'Well, I guess I should get back to work . . .'

'Should you?' She raised an eyebrow and leaned back in her seat. 'What will happen if you don't?'

Not much, probably. Rick wasn't on duty and the front desk knew where he was in case of problems. The bar staff didn't need him looking over their shoulders.

'I could get into trouble,' he said anyway, teasing but not smiling. He wouldn't get into any trouble if he left, but he was hoping to maybe find some if he stayed.

Her smile widened. She had pretty eyes. Dark blue, he thought, though it was hard to judge the colour in the bar's dim lighting. He liked the way her mouth curved, how her lips stayed plump and didn't disappear.

'We wouldn't want that.' Her words were light, a little

teasing, but he didn't mistake the hint of flirtation in them. 'You'd better get back to work.'

He didn't get up, just gave her another purposefully solemn look. 'I just have to make sure you're all taken care of first. Don't I?'

'Oh my,' she said and laughed, ducking her head before she gave him a sideways glance. 'You're very good, aren't you?'

She was good, too. Brandon leaned, not too close but just enough. 'That's up to you to decide, isn't it?'

'I'm Leah.' She held out her hand for him to shake.

'Brandon.'

'Tell me something, Brandon.' She let her mouth linger on his name and it wasn't hard for him to imagine her moaning it. 'Is this part of your job description?'

'Keeping the customers happy?' He was still holding her hand, warm and surprisingly small, in his. He was always surprised by how much smaller most women's hands were than his. 'Yes. Sure is. All part of taking care of business.'

She squeezed his fingers briefly and let go. 'I'm not the only customer here, though.'

He deliberately didn't look around at anyone else. 'They're all OK. I checked.'

'Did you?' She seemed amused.

'Sure.'

Her eyes drifted over his face and he took the chance to look over hers. She wasn't easy to judge, not like half a dozen of the other women he'd already met tonight. The ones he hadn't sat down next to. It had always been pretty easy for him to figure out what women wanted, how to give it to them . . . when he wanted to. Most of the rest of the women were here to get picked up, have drinks bought for them. Be pursued. It was part of the club-hopping game, and he didn't mind flirting with them because it made the time pass faster.

But this woman was different. He wasn't quite sure how. He thought she was flirting, but not in the coy, clumsy way he was used to. He couldn't be sure if he was turning her on or making her laugh. Maybe it was because she was older, he thought, studying her as she looked him over without pretending she wasn't. Older and more confident.

'Besides,' he added with a glance at the clock. 'I'm off duty in half an hour.'

'Really?' Her tone indicated an arch surprise. She turned her glass around and around in the circle of condensation on the table. 'That's convenient.'

Oh, yeah.

He still needed – sort of – an excuse to stay here beyond the simple fact he wanted to. 'Can I get you something else?'

'No. I'm done drinking for the night.'

'A pop? Coke, maybe?'

She laughed. 'Where are you from, Brandon?'

'What makes you think I'm not from around here?' Someone passing behind him nudged him, and he glanced back to make sure he wasn't blocking the aisle.

'You don't sound like you're from around here.'

'What gave it away?'

'Pop.' She dragged a finger through the wet circle, smearing it. 'So, where are you from?'

'Iowa.'

She leaned back to make a show of looking at his legs, all the way up again to his face. 'They grow them big in Iowa, don't they?'

It was his turn to laugh. 'Yeah, I guess they do.'

'So how'd you end up here?' she asked, but before he had time to answer she was looking over his shoulder and that pretty smile had disappeared. The light in her eyes went out, too, just like that. 'Oh, shit.'

Brandon looked over his shoulder, too, but saw only the

crowd. Leah was getting up though, and he automatically stood as she did. The floor of the booth was raised a few feet, so she stood almost level with his eyes. He reached for her elbow without a second thought. He didn't want her to fall. She didn't shake him off. Her hand came down on his shoulder.

'It's my ex,' she said in a low voice.

Brandon twisted to see where she was looking as she got down. He spotted the man she meant. On first glance he'd blended in with the crowd, just one more guy in a suit with his tie pulled loose and a beer in his hand. On second look, though, it was easy to see he was looking for someone and wasn't happy about not finding her.

Brandon had seen fights in some of the clubs downtown, but never here. The Market Street Café wasn't really the place for that sort of thing. Watching this guy catch sight of Leah, though, Brandon thought maybe tonight that would change.

'Leah.' The other guy didn't even look at Brandon. 'Come on. Come home.'

'No.' She didn't shrink away and she didn't put Brandon between them. 'I told you that before. We're over, Mike.'

Mike didn't seem to like that idea. Brandon had seen guys like this before. The ones who thought money in their wallets and a nice car entitled them to anything they wanted.

Mike held out his hand. 'Leah. Come, now.'

'No,' she said again.

This time, Brandon stepped forwards. 'Hey, buddy. She said she wasn't going with you.'

His muscles tensed, fists not quite clenching. He was taller than this jerk, if not broader. Brandon could take him, if he had to. The other guy looked at him, finally, but dismissively.

'Fuck off, junior,' Mike said. 'Leah.'

Brandon didn't move. Leah stepped past him, past Mike. She looked over her shoulder at Brandon, her expression cool and composed, though he'd felt her hand twitching on his shoulder.

'Come with me,' she said to him.

And, of course, he went.

6

'Leah!' Mike's voice turned heads, but not hers. She kept going, out of the bar, through the lobby, without looking back.

Brandon followed.

By the time they got halfway across the lobby, Mike had decided to come after her. He yelled her name again, and her footsteps faltered. Brandon caught up to her. He put a hand on her waist, just above her hip.

'Want me to call the police?'

'No.' She shook her head without looking around. 'He thinks he can make me do what he wants.' She looked at him then, this tall long man with the choirboy smile. 'He can't.'

'I can see that.' Brandon looked over his shoulder, but Mike had apparently decided not to bother coming after them.

She wasn't taking any chances, though. 'Walk me to my room.'

He nodded, gave another glance over his shoulder and seemed satisfied by what he saw. 'Absolutely.'

He let go of her waist when she looked down at his hand. He stepped back. Her guts tumbled and knotted and she tasted sweat when she ran her tongue along her lip. She'd been more afraid than she'd wanted to admit, but she didn't want to show it.

'Four,' she said when they got in the elevator, and Brandon pushed the button.

He studied her as the elevator began its smooth ascent. Leah stared back. They didn't speak, and she liked that about him. He wasn't one of those guys who had to fill every space with words, or tried to impress a woman with stories. He looked at her, though, his stare intent and intense.

She felt naked under his gaze.

Leah leaned back against the elevator's mirrored wall and gripped the brass handrail. Her knees were a little weak, but was it from the confrontation downstairs, or the unaccustomed alcohol . . . or the way Brandon smelled? She breathed in, deep. Fabric softener, that was the scent. Mixed with a bit of cigarette smoke and the fainter odour of the scented candles that had been on the tables in the bar, but mostly the soft, fresh scent of something clean and warm from the dryer. It was a smell she wanted to bury her face in.

The doors opened and she stepped out without waiting for him. She didn't want to think too much about what she'd been thinking of, flirting with him downstairs. Or when she'd told him to come with her. It had all just sort of happened, even if there was no denying she wanted it to.

She pulled her key from her pocket and opened the door. Again, he followed a few steps behind. The door clicked shut after him, and Leah let out a breath she hadn't known she'd been holding. There was a door between her and the hall, and no way Mike could get in.

'You OK?' His voice had just the right pitch of concern.

She looked. His expression echoed his words. Nice guy.

'Yeah. I just didn't expect to see him tonight, that's all.' Her stomach was still twisting. She pulled a dollar out of her purse and handed it to him. 'Would you get me a soda from the machine?'

It was a request, not a command. He took her dollar and looked at it, then at her. His smile made her feel anything but helpless.

'Sure. I'll be right back.'

He was, too, in record time. He handed her the dollar and the bottle. 'My treat.'

He'd bought one for himself, too. She cracked open the top with a 'Thank you', and sipped greedily.

'Have a seat.' She indicated the couch, curious. Wanting to see if he'd do what she'd told him to do with the same lack of hesitation as he'd done everything else since she'd met him.

Brandon sat. He drank. He watched her.

Leah's insides had started twisting for another reason. She was alone in her room with a man she'd just met, and there wasn't a doubt in her mind that she wanted him. It didn't matter that it was too soon, that it was wrong on so many levels, that she'd only be asking for trouble.

'Recent break-up?'

His words surprised her into answering without holding back. 'Yes. Today, as a matter of fact.'

Brandon took another drink. She watched his throat work as he swallowed. He screwed the cap back on his drink and set it on the side table.

'You sure you don't want me to call someone?'

She shook her head. 'No. Just ... wait a few minutes.'

Her breath lodged in her throat when he grinned. No matter what Kate said, this guy was neither a geek nor an innocent. He might not swagger around to show off his testosterone, but then she'd recently decided she didn't really care for that, hadn't she?

'Part of the service,' he said with hands spread.

He settled them on his knees and she noted with no small thrill how big they were. How big all of him was, really. 'How tall are you?'

He tilted his head, thinking. 'Six-four?'

'You don't know?' She was surprised a laugh could escape the tightly knotted tangles inside her.

'I ...' He ducked his head for a moment with an utterly charming shrug. 'I keep growing.'

Jesus. Her cunt actually pulsed at that, the same as if he'd swiped his tongue along her skin. Leah masked her involuntary noise of pleasure by clearing her throat.

'Thank you for coming with me, Brandon.'

He looked straight at her then, without a smile. 'My pleasure.'

Downstairs, bolstered by the booze or the crowd, this had been easier. Flirting had come as a matter of long-forgotten habit and she'd been relieved to learn she could still do it. Here, in the intimacy of her room, innuendo couldn't be misconstrued. What she said, she'd have to mean.

'He shouldn't have talked to you like that,' Brandon said suddenly.

'It's the way he always talked to me.' She sat next to him to curb her impulse to pace.

The couch was large enough for three, but when he turned to face her his legs were so long their knees brushed. Leah didn't jump. She looked at the spot where the dark fabric of his trousers touched the soft peach of her dress, and she wondered what it would be like if his fingers touched her there instead.

She looked into his face to keep from focusing on their bodies touching.

'He was always the one in charge,' she told him, the second person in a day to whom she'd revealed this when she'd said nothing to anyone about it for the entire time she and Mike were together. 'Always.'

Would he get it? Did he understand? His brow furrowed a little. He bit down on his lower lip. He wore the evidence of thinking all over his face, open and easy to read. Leah envied him that confidence to show what he was feeling. When he looked into her eyes with a small shrug, she felt like she could read his every thought. She couldn't, of course. He wasn't nearly that transparent.

'Well. Not any more, right?'

It was exactly the right thing for him to say. She didn't want sympathy. She didn't particularly even want his understanding.

'Not any more,' she agreed.

The air got thicker between them. His mouth would taste sweet. Her fingers would sink into his hair. And he'd make a sound when she pulled it.

Leah got up with one smooth motion on unsteady legs. What was going on with her? First the men in the bar, now this? She'd known there'd be some sort of reaction to her break-up with Mike, but this ... this was just ridiculous.

'You sure you're OK?' The concern in his voice tried to crack her open, but she wouldn't let it.

Without looking at him, she grabbed the glass near the ice bucket on the small table and tossed a few mostly melted cubes into it. It gave her hands something to do.

'So, how did you get into hotel management?' she asked, keeping the question innocuous.

He laughed. 'Oh, I didn't really. I'm not the hotel manager, I was just filling in for him.'

She turned, finally sort-of, kind-of calming down. 'Oh?'

'Yeah. I'm actually the conference-services assistant manager. I just took over for my boss because she went on maternity leave.'

Her mouth opened but all that came out was a tiny hiss of air. Brandon. The clerk had said his name was Brandon, the man she was going to deal with. She hadn't even thought about it.

The glass slipped from her hand and hit the carpet where it bounced and splattered icy water on her ankles. Leah looked down, blinking, glad she hadn't poured it full of soda.

She hadn't made more than the barest gesture towards picking up the glass. She didn't have to. Brandon had moved off the couch immediately to grab it. He knelt at her feet, his fingers sliding around the slippery ice and plunking the cubes back into the glass.

At her feet.

Kneeling.

A tiny strangled sound escaped her and he looked up. He looked as though he meant to say something, but didn't. She hadn't moved. His face was so close to the hem of her dress his breath ruffled the wispy, fringy hem. His hands stilled, full of melting ice.

'I think you'd better go,' she said. 'Now.'

For a second he hesitated, the first time he'd done so. His dark eyes blinked, fast, and he took in a breath. She heard the intake of air and saw his shoulders lift with it. She saw his lips part, as though he meant to speak.

In her mind she backed away, but her body didn't move.

'Now,' she repeated, no less firmly than she had before. Only now she heard herself, really heard it, and that note of command scared her.

Brandon got to his feet, all 70,000 square feet of him. He towered over her, yet, unlike Mike who'd always made her feel small, Brandon didn't overpower her. All she had to do was recall how easy it had been for him to settle himself at her feet.

She gave a pointed look towards the door and his gaze followed hers. He gave a last look at her, but she shook her head. She said nothing. In silence, he put the glass with its clanking contents on the table and, in silence, he left the room. The click of the door was very loud behind him.

She'd always been the one on her knees. Always. She'd always thought it was what she wanted: to give up and give in. Not to be powerless, never that. But not to be the one in control, the one in charge, the one giving the orders.

That was not her.

Except maybe Kate was right.

Maybe it was.

7

When Leah told him to sit and he immediately obeyed, Kate knew it was time to make her exit. It didn't take a genius to see the brewing of something interesting there and Leah may just have found out what it felt like to be on top for a change.

There would definitely need to be a full accounting when they got a break. Kate knew Leah would be all over whatever happened when she and Dix got together the next day.

Kate went back to her room, slightly lonely but pleasantly drunk. She let herself think of Dix briefly as she changed out of her clothes and hung them up carefully.

She showered and, clean, warm and naked, she headed to the bed dominating the room. The cool cotton sheets lulled her a bit. Briefly, Kate entertained calling her parents to tell them she'd arrived and had closed the deal on her condo. But she was too drunk to deal with her mother's attitude just then. One drink less and she'd be perfect, just tipsy enough to ignore the barbs and to deliver a few of her own. At present, she lacked the filters she needed to survive a phone call without calling her mother's behaviour out.

Shuddering, Kate changed the direction of her attention to something much better. The thought of Dix brought her cunt to life. Mmm, yes, that was a much nicer train of thought. Her eyes drifted closed as she trailed her fingers down her belly. And fell asleep.

* * *

'Dude, you totally have to tell me what the hell happened last night after I left the bar,' Kate whispered to Leah as they met on the conference-room floor of the hotel the following morning. 'Was there any lawn mowing or hedge clipping involved? Did you make him stutter, "P-p-please, mistress!"'

Leah blushed but before she could answer she gave Kate a sharp elbow to the ribs.

'At long last, I finally meet my lady face to face.'

Kate turned and tried to keep a pleasant expression, pretending she hadn't ever heard the groan he made at the back of his throat when he came. When really, as she watched Charles Dixon approach, all she wanted to do was fall into his arms and kiss him.

She felt like a teenaged girl. Crap. All the schooling, all the years she'd spent smoothing out any professional edges and it all threatened to slip through her fingers. He was the highway to hell and she suddenly wanted to wrench the wheel and take off. Oh the clichés!

Buck the hell up, Katherine!

Tugging the hem of her jacket down, she straightened her spine, took a deep breath and tried to keep her smile professional.

When their eyes met . . . holy shit, holy shit, holy shit.

She froze as green eyes bored into hers. Unable not to, she ate him up with her gaze. Perfectly cut dark-brown hair, as dark as the sinful chocolate he represented to her, tempted her fingertips. The suit he wore fitted him well enough that she knew it was made for his body alone. When he smiled he showed white teeth, not blindingly so, but perfect enough, and she remembered what they felt like closing over the sensitive skin of her shoulder.

He took her hand and the shake was professional, but there was no mistaking the intent in his eyes. Or her body's response. Utterly mutinous hormones shot through her, nipples hardening, pussy slickening, blooming, cripes, she had to squeeze her thighs together to try to relieve the tension.

'Hello, Dix,' she said, one eyebrow rising as she struggled to get her bearings. She wasn't some newbie. Not to being a woman and certainly not to her job. Tonight they'd meet and have sex. She could last. She'd meant to masturbate the night before to take the edge off but she'd had a few too many tequila sunrises and had fallen asleep before she'd been able to do more than run the idea of making herself come through her head.

'I take it your incredibly interesting seminar on confidentiality agreements went well yesterday?' One corner of his mouth lifted and for a fleeting moment he looked like a pirate in a business suit.

He smelled good. Really good. Dark and spicy. She knew what he smelled like covered in clean sweat after a rousing bout of sex, what he smelled like first thing in the morning. What he tasted like. Inwardly, she took a shuddering breath.

Beside her, Leah shifted and Kate latched on to her friend's presence to bring her back to shore before she lost it and sniffed at him for real.

She pushed Kate away and pulled Katherine around her like a shield. 'Yes, as a matter of fact it did. I've actually got some material for you. We can go over it later if you like. I took the liberty of drawing up a few memos for you on the non-compete stuff as well. I just finished a case that has some corollary issues with yours.'

'Sounds good. We can talk after the sessions today. Legal is only needed in the morning and early afternoon.' He indicated with an arm that they should precede him into the conference room but she felt him at her back.

Throughout the morning session Katherine listened to the company president drone on. There wasn't much to say at that point so she frowned in the appropriate places. Allied had some problems that might very well end up in court. They'd come up with several innovations in both packaging and shipping but their contracts were open to interpretation in some cases with regard to their non-compete and confidentiality clauses. Meaning some of the people who knew the freaking secret box formula, or whatever the hell it was, could take it to another packaging company without problem.

Dix had taken over the in-house legal counsel position for Allied Packaging and Shipping eighteen months prior and the horrific problem had slowly come to light. Leah had suggested Katherine as someone to consult on the issue and that's how she'd first come in contact with Charles Dixon.

He'd called and something about his voice and his manner had made her respond. Made her let him push her buttons. She secretly liked it because it was something just between them. He flirted but nothing too outrageous. He didn't waste her professional time, which meant a lot to her. Something about the slight accent, the dark masculine bass of his voice always made her want to melt into a puddle of female goo.

After her past experience with office romance, she'd kept co-workers strictly off the sex menu. That would fall under the utterly wrong choice category. Until him. Why was she even thinking about fucking? They were not paying her $375 an hour to have fantasies about Charles Dixon shoving her against a wall, ripping her panties off and fucking her until she wept.

But he wasn't precisely a co-worker. She was of counsel, he wasn't her boss. Technically, there wasn't really an issue.

She dug her fingernails into her palm to make herself stop thinking about Dix driving himself into her cunt over and over, his pants pooled around his ankles, the scratch of the wall at her back, his fingers digging into the flesh of her bare ass, her skirt bunched up around her waist. The delicious tang of his sweat tickling her senses as she held on and let him take her.

Jeez-a-lou, she did not just have a 'Dear *Penthouse*' letter fantasy while sitting in a conference room! Flushed, she shifted in her chair and met green eyes that knew exactly what she'd been daydreaming about.

Dix pushed his very sexy glasses up the bridge of his nose and the whisper of a smile touched the corner of his mouth before he shifted his attention back to the endless Charlie Brown-like drone of the president again.

'We'll break for two hours and meet back here. Katherine will give us an overview at that time,' Dix finally broke in.

'Wanna grab a bite?' Kate leaned in and asked Leah. She needed a recap from last night and a bit of a reality check about Dix too.

'I wish. I have to deal with these guys and then the conference-services person. We can hang out afterwards.'

'Good. You clearly have a story to tell.' Kate laughed softly.

'And don't think I'm not going to ask about the Dix thing.' One of Leah's eyebrows rose and Kate blushed.

'Katherine?'

Kate turned to answer Dix. 'Hmm?'

'Those memos? And did you want to get some lunch?'

Lunch? Hell no. Him, naked? Yes.

'Oh sure. They're upstairs.' They started towards the elevator and he kept his distance. 'Do you want to meet me in the restaurant? I'll be right back down.' He might want to keep his professional hat on until the evening. In her hormone-laden rush to get him alone, she'd totally forgotten to think about that.

'No.' He guided her into the elevator with a hand at her elbow. Totally professional, and yet . . .

They were silent in the hall as they walked to her room. She slid her keycard into the slot, opened the door and turned to tell him these oh-so-professional things when he closed the door, locked it and used his body to press hers against the wall.

'Kate?'

No words came. He made a sound in the back of his throat and, before she could breathe, his lips were on hers. Hot. Insistent. Urgent like he couldn't have waited another single moment before he kissed her.

So very wrong. It was so dirty, so bad, so wrong and she couldn't remember if anything had felt better than his hands on her. One hand cupped her throat as he plundered her mouth, the other nimbly unbuttoned her blouse and pinched her nipple through the fabric of her camisole and bra.

Heat swallowed her, washed away all common sense and she gave in. Reaching between them, she shoved off the suit jacket and, foregoing the shirt, headed straight for his belt and the button and zipper of his pants.

Silk. First the silk of his boxers and then the hot silk of his cock as it spilled into her hands. He arched, gasping into her mouth. She swallowed the sound and made an answering one when he sucked her tongue.

Her thumb spread the wetness at the head of his cock in circles around the crown. She reached down and held his balls before shoving his pants down.

'Fuck, fuck, wait. Kate,' he murmured against her mouth, 'I want to taste you.' He fell to his knees and she nearly lost hers as he looked up her body into her face.

As if she planned to stop him.

He grabbed her ankles and drew his hands up her calves, pushing her skirt up and up, stopping when he saw the band of her stockings.

'I've been thinking about this for the last month. Since I took you standing in that deserted parking lot in San Francisco.' He leaned in and circled his tongue over the lace of her panties. Her hips jumped forwards.

'Thinking of my panties?'

'Imagining sinking to my knees and pressing my face to your pussy, Kate. Look at you so pretty beneath your clothes, so sexy. I like that it's just down one layer. So aloof but scratch the surface and, well, here we are.' Hooking his fingers at the sides of her underwear, he yanked them down and she stepped out of them.

From her vantage point, she saw the flecks of grey in his hair and it only made him sexier. She gave in and ran her fingers through it.

'Spread your feet.'

She did and he took one of her legs, put it on his shoulder and, without further preamble, pressed his mouth against her, holding her labia open with his thumbs.

A shock of raw pleasure rode up her spine and her head fell back against the wall.

'Hold yourself open, Kate, I need my hands free.' Each word vibrated off her pussy and she jerked involuntarily as she reached to hold herself open to his mouth.

Licking, flicking, his tongue teased, tasted, tempted, seduced her. His fingers traced her gate and slowly pushed up into her, first one, then another.

She closed her eyes against the pleasure, trying to keep control, trying not to grind her cunt against his face. It was so good between them, so raw and hard edged she didn't know how to process it. So she just let it happen. Let him devour her pussy, rode his hand as he fucked into her, let him bring her off so hard she had to bite her lip to keep from yelling as she climaxed.

He stood and kissed her hard. She tasted herself and him,

tasted what was to come in just moments. Her legs quivered as she heard the plastic of a condom wrapper being ripped open. Disappointment whispered through her, she'd wanted to taste him too. But before she could be too upset about it, he'd spun her to face the wall, her hands pressed against it as he nudged her ankles wide.

Her back arched, offering herself to his cock without any words. None was needed as the wide head of him pressed against her and then inexorably into her body, bit by bit, until he sheathed balls deep within her.

The hair stirred at the back of her neck as he drew a shaky breath.

'Fuck me. I need it,' she whispered. And she did. Needed him buried in her.

He groaned and began to thrust. His grip at her hip was so tight that she knew she'd bear a few fingerprint bruises there. Her body stretched to take him and then shrank as he pulled back out. Over and over, he stroked the nerves deep inside her.

'Harder.'

In answer, she thrust back against him, meeting his stroke. With a groan, he increased his speed and intensity until he fucked into her so deep and hard that her breasts came out of the top of her bra, stroking against the pebbled grain in the wall.

He traced his fingers along her lips until she sucked them into her mouth, reluctant to let him go and lose that sensory pleasure. Until he found her clit and stroked it with just the right amount of pressure.

Before long, another orgasm began to settle into her cells, building and building as he fucked her, as her nipples abraded the wall, as his fingers played against her clit and the other hand gripped her so tight.

When it hit her, her pussy clamped down on him, spasmed around the delicious invasion of his cock and flowed through her body. A strangled moan in her ear and one more hard press deep into her cunt and he came too, breathing hard, his head resting on her shoulder.

8

Dix struggled to catch his breath and get himself together as her pussy continued to flutter and clutch around his cock. Her honey, hot and silky, slid down the stalk of him, down to his balls and the need to fuck her again pounded in his head. Disbelief that they'd only taken five steps into her room before he'd shoved his face into her pussy and eaten her until she'd come with a strangled cry swamped him.

Before that first phone call, he'd been happily single. Content with playing the field and finding female companionship when it suited him. But Katherine Edwards changed that in ways he wasn't even sure he wanted to contemplate.

When he'd seen her downstairs, looked into those big blue eyes of hers, he'd known they would end up having sex the first moment they were alone. He had no patience where she was concerned. Showing up in Chicago to the CLE she'd been attending four months ago on sort of a whim, he'd just wanted to exorcise the jones he had for her. He hadn't expected the power of it. He'd been reeling ever since.

Her reserve, thet outer layer that screamed all business, did something to him. Made him want to draw down to her basest level and revel in every step he took her.

'It's wonderful to see you again, Kate.' He pressed a kiss to the nape of her neck and pulled out carefully. He went to dispose of the condom and, when he returned, she'd put herself to rights but the image of the tops of her stockings seemed to be burned into his retinas.

She looked at him, clearly unsure of the situation. He'd never seen her flustered before and it charmed him on some level.

'Why don't we order up some lunch and look at those files?'

'Good idea. The files are right there.' She indicated a neat stack of blue folders marked 'Allied'. 'Any preferences?'

'Oh, I have many of them.' He grinned, unable to resist teasing her, ruffling those feathers of hers. She blushed and rolled her eyes.

'Fine,' she said. She ordered lunch for them both and hung up. 'I seem to remember you like turkey. I hope so since that's what you're getting. Oh and fries. Maybe you'll get fat.'

He laughed and brought the folders with him to sit down. Her scent still clung to his face and hands, and his cock stirred in response.

They worked for the next hour as she explained the cases she'd rounded up. Damn, the woman was sharp.

He sat back, impressed with her work. 'You may have just saved us a huge amount of money. I want to present the new employment contracts tomorrow if that works for you.'

'I do it all for the thrill of employment law.'

'You shouldn't hide your sense of humour under a bushel so often.' He sat back and stole a French fry from her plate.

'I don't hide it. I just showed it to you, didn't I?'

'All that and more.'

She sent him a smug smile and he leaned in to kiss her temple.

'But I mean, not behind closed doors. I understand what's between us is private, Kate. I promise you that. I respect your job and I'd never do anything to endanger it.'

'This shouldn't ... it's not something I normally do.' She waved her hand back and forth between them. 'I work really hard to be taken seriously, if it got out ...'

He took her hand and kissed it. 'We've gone over this, Kate. I know that. Believe it or not, me too. I try to keep a strict line between business and pleasure. But we don't work for one another and we're professionals. I'm sure we can manage a few days of fun with our work schedule. So did you tell Leah?'

'I did last night. Rest assured all your advance reviews were quite good.' She relaxed a bit.

He laughed. 'That's good to hear. Even right now I want to fuck you again. This every few months thing isn't enough to sate me.' He hadn't wanted something this badly for a very long time. The girls were out of town with their mother up at the lake house for another week. He had the time to spend on the buttoned-up Katherine and he planned to do so every minute he could.

He brought her hand to his mouth again and drew one of her fingers in between his lips slowly, licking and sucking as he kept his gaze locked with hers. Her pupils expanded and her breath puffed out. If he had to be her Pied Piper, he would. In fact, he loved the idea.

'I won't encroach on your professional space. You're here to do a job for Allied and I respect that. But we are going to fuck again. And again. You know that.'

'You're awfully sure of yourself.'

He certainly was when he heard the breathy note in her voice. He hadn't worked his way up from public housing blocks in Boston to give up when he wanted something. And he wanted Kate.

'Can you have dinner tonight?'

'Most likely I'll hang out with Leah after the conference. It's been even longer since I've seen her than the last time I saw you. But afterwards? We could get a nightcap or something. Or do the girls need you at home?'

'They're off with Eve for the rest of the week so I'm all yours. Call me when you're free and we'll get together then.'

'Oh, OK.' She checked her watch. 'We need to get back soon.' She gathered the files, then stood and put them into her case. 'I'll have Leah get these to the conference-services person to get copies made then, shall I?'

'Good idea. Can you fit this into your presentation tomorrow?'

He straightened his tie and put his jacket back on as he watched her smooth her hair and reapply lipstick.

'I can, yes. I made up some PowerPoint stuff to fit into the presentation while I was at the office yesterday.'

By the time they approached the elevators, all anyone would have seen were two colleagues discussing business.

9

'Damn it.' Brandon laced his hands behind his head and pushed back in his chair to stare at the ceiling.

Heather had left him a mess.

It wasn't a mess he couldn't take care of, but it wasn't exactly the way he wanted to deal with his first week in charge. Brandon always kept detailed notes and files, records of emails and phone conversations. Heather had liked to scribble on scraps of paper and sticky notes and, though she claimed to have forwarded and copied him on all her correspondence, Brandon couldn't find a damn thing.

So far, the only plus to this job was the bigger office and the nicer desk. He sighed, tilted his chair back on to all four legs and stared at the computer screen. Nothing helpful there. The Allied Packaging conference had already started but, though he'd been able to set up the rooms for the morning sessions, he couldn't find any of the details about how they were supposed to be set up for after lunch.

No use whining about it. He'd have to bite the bullet and get down there, deal with the person in charge.

She was waiting for him in the Susquehanna conference room, and she didn't look happy.

'Leah?'

At the sound of her name she turned, her brow furrowed, and Brandon knew immediately he should have used a more formal address. Which, well, crap, he would have if he'd known it, but, since Heather hadn't left him any notes, he didn't.

Damn.

The air in the room had been set to a moderate temperature but her look dropped it by about twenty degrees. 'Why is this room not set up according to my instructions?'

Because my boss is an idiot, Brandon thought. 'I'm sorry. Tell me what you need and I'll do it right away.'

'It was my understanding all of this would be taken care of,' Leah said.

'I'm sorry,' he repeated and pulled his pen from his shirt pocket. 'Just give me a list and I'll get right on it.'

She blinked at that. Her chin came up the tiniest bit. 'A list?'

He'd just clicked the pen and put the tip to the pad of paper, but at her tone he skidded a sudden line of ink. Brandon looked at her, and all at once all he could remember was how good she'd smelled, how the fringe of her skirt had brushed his cheek and how she'd sounded when she told him to get out. She sort of sounded like that now.

She sort of sounded scared, and his stomach twisted. What had he done to make her sound that way? His notepad curled in his hand when he clutched it tighter.

'A list.' The words snagged in his throat and he cleared it. 'Of what you want me to do?'

Today she wore a severe black skirt that came to just above her knee and a tailored white shirt. She'd left the top three buttons undone. His gaze went to her feet. Black heels, pointed toes.

His throat got drier.

When she closed the distance between them, he didn't back up. Even in her heels she had to tilt her head to look up at him. Looking down into her face it was impossible for him not to think of how she'd looked from another angle. From at her feet.

Despite the differences in their heights, she didn't seem to have any trouble staring him down. Brandon drew in a breath and held it as she took another step closer. When he let it out, slowly, deliberately, trying hard not to make sound, the fabric of his shirt brushed hers. Leah stared at him in silence, without blinking.

This was not the right time for him to get hard, but his dick had a mind of its own. It didn't help that he could smell her perfume and feel the heat of her body even through his clothes, or that she cocked one leg to bring it up alongside his. Or that her skirt rode up when she did it and he swore he glimpsed a flash of bare thigh. Or that she was the sexiest woman he'd ever met.

'Each of these tables is to be set with four pitchers of water and eight glasses. Each place gets a legal pad and pen.' Her voice was pitched so low he'd have had to strain to hear it if she hadn't still been so close. There was no room between them for him to lift his pad and take notes, and when he shifted slightly she gave her head a tiny shake. 'You don't need to write this down. You will remember it.'

He absolutely would. From outside the room he heard the sound of voices. Leah blinked, but she didn't move away or take her gaze from his. There was no way this could look good if someone saw them, he thought as he stared into her deep-blue eyes, but she didn't seem to care.

'At three p.m. we'll be breaking for refreshments. I've ordered bagels and fruit with cream cheese. Three dozen. Exactly. Coffee, tea and bottled water.'

He nodded and breathed in her scent. This was his job. He was good at it. But this ... this was something that had nothing to do with work. She would probably slap his face if he tried to kiss her now. Or slap him with a sexual harassment charge. But, holy crap, did he want to kiss her. He wished he'd done it last night, in her room, when they were on the couch and it would have taken only a second to lean over and take her in his arms.

'Brandon.'

He jumped a little inside his skin when she murmured his name. His hard-on throbbed, almost painful, trapped inside his briefs. The knot of arousal in his gut tightened and heat flooded him from his chest to the edge of his hair. He felt it and blushed harder at knowing she could tell.

And ... crap ... she moved just the smallest bit closer ... Could she feel how hard he was? She had to know it. His dick had grown to the size of the Empire State Building, a tower in his pants. There was no way she couldn't feel it between them.

'Yes?' he managed to say without sounding like too much of a jerk.

'Can you do all this for me?'

'Yes.'

She tilted her head just slightly. She didn't look scared now, though her smile still wasn't anything like it had been last night when she was with her friend.

'Exactly like I said?'

He hadn't studied for this test, whatever it was. 'Of course.'

'Good.'

She moved away from him and he let out a breath. His heart pounded so hard he heard it thunder in his ears. He could've cut diamonds with his hard-on.

Her smile got broader when he put the legal pad in front of his crotch. More heat burned the tips of his ears. He wore everything on his damn face, an ex-girlfriend had told him, and now he wished he didn't. Leah was looking right through him, she knew exactly what she'd done. He just didn't know why.

'I expect this all to be done precisely the way I want it,' she said.

This might be a test he hadn't studied for, but Brandon had always been a very, very good student.

'And if it's not?'

Leah smiled a little. 'Then I will meet you in your office to discuss how you can improve your performance.'

Once again he recalled the chill of ice cubes in his hands and the way she'd looked staring down at him. There was an awful lot a man on his knees could do for a woman. 'And if it is? Will we still need to meet?'

'Oh, yes, Brandon,' she said over her shoulder as she moved towards the door, 'we'll still meet. But we'll do it in my room.'

10

Shit shit shit. What the hell? Kate cursed herself. She'd just had sex during the business day. At work essentially. Christ. That was not in 'right decision' territory at all.

And what a smug sexy bastard Charles Dixon was. Good Lord. He'd been right of course, they would have sex again. But it would have been possible to avoid it if he'd applied himself. God knew she was unable to when he was around. And she hadn't told him about her transfer yet. He may just change his mind when she did.

A very unprofessional snort threatened to escape so she turned her attention back to the discussion and the president's whining about feeling attacked. Nothing worse than a man who always made excuses. She had to ride them on this issue with Dix. The president had to deal with the situation or the outcome could be disastrous.

Now who was making excuses? She had to do the very same thing. Tell Dix about her new job and deal with the outcome.

Leah looked flushed and a bit mussed up at the edges. The meeting with the conference-services people must have annoyed her. Good thing the Allied offices were local so they could just go through them should the people here at the hotel be unable to take care of things.

When they finally broke for the day, Dix gave her a professional nod and left, speaking to his personal assistant, Carlina Southam, who'd shown up. Kate needed to grab Leah to get an update on Band Boy and fill her in on her little interlude with Dix that afternoon too.

Whatever she did, she shouldn't think about Dix's ex-wife Eve and the fact that the personal assistant was blonde and petite too. Was it on purpose? Did he notice? Ew.

She caught up to her friend near the elevators. 'Leah, you and I have a date with some dinner, drinks and gossip.'

'We really do. I've got to change and then we'll get out of here. I have lots to tell you.'

Oh, that sounded promising.

'Come by my room when you're ready to go.'

Once they got to a table and drinks were in front of them, Kate spilled the whole Dix story from that afternoon and Leah just looked at her shaking her head.

'I don't know why you're so tense. No one can tell and I know you better than anyone. People can have relationships. You'll be two hours away so it's not like you'll be in the same office.'

'It all remains to be seen if he's into me anyway. And truthfully, Leah, I don't know how I feel either. He's got two teenaged daughters and an ex-wife. An ex-wife who is one of those helpless women who calls him to fix crap at her house like they're still married.' She took several bracing gulps of her drink. 'I can handle being second to his children, that's only right and I expect his priorities to be straight. But I won't be second to a woman he divorced but who won't cut the apron strings. It's one thing to share a dude for an afternoon, but I'm not going to share full time.'

Leah watched her silently, waiting for her to finish.

'And yes, OK? How can I compete with that anyway? With a history? With kids together and memories of summer vacation and a honeymoon and stuff. I'm not ... shit, this is all way premature anyway. I haven't told him yet and it's not like he's said he wants a relationship more than what we have. Enough about me.' She waved an impatient hand. 'Tell me about Band Boy and last night after I left.'

Leah didn't say anything for a long, long minute. 'There were some issues this afternoon, but then he did everything I told him to do. Perfectly. Exactly.'

Well, there was something else clearly. Kate settled in to get the rest of the story. 'So? I'm missing a problem. Wait a minute. Are you telling me Band Boy from the bar last night is the conference-services person?'

Leah dropped her face into her hands briefly, then looked up, nodding. 'I told him if he did everything I said that . . .'

No way was Kate going to derail whatever was coming next so she just waited, silent, for Leah to finish.

Leah let out a small, embarrassed groan, but when she looked up her eyes were shining. 'I told him he had to meet me tonight. In my room. In –' she looked at her watch '– an hour.'

'Mrs Robinson! You're going to show Band Boy what he's been missing with all those back-seat gropes after the sock hop.' Kate laughed but sobered when she caught Leah's struggle between horror and amusement. 'OK, I'll lay off but I must hear every detail. That's my price.'

'There won't be any details,' Leah said. 'I don't think.'

Kate snickered, but didn't push it, and they moved on to gossip about how horrible the comb-over of one of Leah's co-worker's was. Because that's what friends did. Let each other off the hook when they didn't want to talk.

11

He did everything just as she'd said to. Pitchers, glasses.
Bagels. For some reason, the bagels had seemed particularly
important. And, cripes, it wasn't like he'd had any doubt
about his ability to make everything just right – it was his
job, after all, and he was good at it. But standing there with
his cock threatening to bust out of his pants and her
murmuring 'You don't need to write that down, do you?'
had made him all the more nervous that he'd forget.

He hadn't seen her after that, other than a quick glimpse
through the doorway. She hadn't seen him. At least he
didn't think she had. If she had, she hadn't acknowledged
him and, cripes, he was obsessing.

He grabbed a bottle of water from the small fridge in his
office and drank it back in a few gulps, then wiped his
mouth. Every muscle in his body wanted to leap out of his
skin, like his nerves were on fire and all he could think
about was the soft scent of her.

Would he really go to her room again? Should he? What
if she'd been playing with him? Girls did that, he'd discovered. Then again, he'd already decided she wasn't a girl.

He wasn't stupid. Telling him to come to her room had
been a blatant but surprising invitation. The way she'd
looked when he was picking up the ice, he'd been sure he'd
crossed some line, done something wrong. Pushed some
button. That had been it, he thought, tidying his desk to give
his hand a mindless task to complete. He'd pushed a button.

But what kind?

'You think too much,' his last girlfriend had said. She'd been the same one to tell him he wore everything he felt on his face. Maybe that had made it easier for her to cheat on him and lie to him about it for six months.

Screw it. He wasn't going to think about it any more. He'd done what she told him. He'd earned his 'reward'. He was going to her room.

There was no reason for anyone to think anything about him going up in the elevator, but nevertheless his palms were sweating when he pushed the UP button. Inside, the mirrored walls showed his rumpled hair, which he smoothed quickly, and his work clothes. He couldn't do anything about them. Dark pants, white shirt, plain black tie with a tiny pattern of dots. He'd left his suit jacket downstairs in his office. Shoot, he should've left his tie, too ... The elevator door opened on Leah's floor.

He was absolutely going to get laid.

His hand raised to knock on the door, but he didn't do it. Instead, Brandon let his knuckles just rest on the door. His head bent. He looked at his feet and neatly polished shoes. The carpet beneath them had been new just a year ago, but the geometric pattern already looked scuffed along the baseboards. He laid his palm flat on the door, pressing.

He was absolutely just going to walk away.

He'd been led by his dick before and he knew he would be again. That was a fact about being a guy. Sometimes the little head took over from the big one. He knew it, the way he knew girls liked him because he had good hair and a nice body, and because he had straight teeth. Big hands. Whatever. He'd been put together all right, thanks to the best of both his mom and dad, and he wasn't going to complain about it. He just wished, sometimes, that the girls who hit on him because he was 'hot' gave him credit for being something else too.

He couldn't stop thinking about the way Leah's voice had sounded when she gave him her list. She hadn't sounded at all the way she had when she'd told him to get out. She'd looked him in the eye, too, without looking away.

His dick throbbed a little, getting stiffer. He pressed harder on the door, his head still bent. His hair fell forwards, over his eyes, but he didn't brush it away.

If he knocked, this was going to happen. If he didn't, he could walk away from this. The conference would be over in a couple of days and he wouldn't really even have to deal with her much, if he made sure to set up the rooms the way she wanted. He hadn't needed to write it all down after all.

Before he could change his mind, Brandon knocked firmly on the door. Three times. Then he didn't know what to do with his hands. Pockets, at his sides, on his hips, nothing felt right. It wasn't as though he should be carrying flowers or candy, but he wished he was holding something.

Long minutes passed while he waited for her to open the door. He'd just convinced himself she wasn't going to when he heard the faint scritch-scratch of the chain being drawn back. The knob turned and the door eased open.

Leah didn't bother shielding herself with the door as though she hadn't been expecting him. She opened it all the way at once. She hadn't changed her clothes from earlier and the top buttons on her white blouse were still undone, but her hair had loosened a little, small hanging tendrils around her face.

He could smell her, a subtle whiff of perfume. The scent of roses and something else he couldn't identify. He wanted to press his face to the base of her throat and draw in breath after breath of it until he could figure out what it was.

'Well, hello.'

She didn't step aside to let him in and Brandon stayed on the doorstep. He started to speak, paused to clear his throat, tried again. 'I'm here.'

'So you are.' Still, she didn't step aside.

Leah looked him up and down without hiding her assessment. He wished again he'd changed his clothes, or shaved, combed his hair. Something. He was utterly convinced she was going to turn him away and completely uncertain of what he'd do if she told him, again, to go.

'You did everything I requested, and very nicely,' Leah said in a low voice. Her tongue slid along her mouth like she was tasting her words before she said them.

'I'm good at my job, Leah.'

She blinked when he said her name. It had come out a little harder than he'd intended. Brandon braced himself for her frown.

Instead, she smiled. 'Well, then. I guess you'd better come in.'

And because he wanted that too, he did.

He'd done everything exactly the way she'd told him to and now he was here. She could have pretended not to hear the knock on the door. She supposed she could even have made up a reason not to let him in.

But she didn't want to.

She was going to do this. Her heartbeat pounded in her wrists and the base of her throat and in strange places like behind her knees. Places she wanted to feel his mouth.

She stepped back, one, two, three. He moved inside the room. 'Close the door, Brandon.'

He turned to do it and Leah admired not only his swift obedience but also the curve of his ass. She took another two steps back and waited for him to turn around. It took only moments, but felt like for ever.

He didn't ruin it by talking. Other men would have stood there as if in challenge, but he stood with his hands open at his sides. His expression was open, too, those dark eyes searching hers and his full mouth slightly parted as though he had words to speak if only she'd grant him the permission.

She had to stop letting her imagination run away with her. Just because he looked so pretty at her feet didn't mean that was where he thought he belonged. It didn't mean she had the right to put him there, even if the thought of it weakened her knees and made her hands shake with desire.

'You did very well today.' Her voice didn't shake. Good. Leah busied herself fixing a glass of iced water so she had an excuse not to look at him for a few minutes.

'Thank you.'

The ice clinked in the glass as she raised it to her lips and sipped. Cool liquid chilled the inside of her throat but did nothing for the heat blossoming all through her. She set the glass down carefully on the table and looked at him again.

'Take off your tie.'

She knew the sound of a command and the hidden, secret thrill of obedience. She knew how free it felt to have the illusion of having no choice, of not having to think. Of only having to do. But what would he do?

His left hand went to his throat and pulled loose the knot of his tie in a slow, see-sawing motion. With the other he pulled the tie's loose end until it came free of the knot and trailed through his fingers. He pulled it slowly through his shirt collar and held it in one hand.

She wasn't going to do something silly and clichéd, such as tie his hands with it. There were rules to this, but that didn't make this a game. Leah looked into Brandon's eyes, still so seriously staring at hers.

Tension, as thick and sweet as honey, filled the space

between them. Now was when he'd break it by reaching for her, she thought. But he didn't.

'Did you come here to fuck me?'

His mouth opened wider. Incredibly, he laughed. It was a self-conscious laugh and utterly sweet. It swept over her from head to toe and set her every nerve on fire.

Brandon ran a hand over his hair and looked away from her. He shifted, first on one foot, then the other, before finally meeting her gaze again. 'Yes.'

She'd held her breath without realising, waiting for him to make up some story, or a lie, but at his honest answer she let out the breath in a slow, easy hiss. She didn't know what she was going to say until she said it and, when she did, she felt as surprised as he looked.

'No.'

'No?' The hand holding the tie tightened on it. His eyes searched hers as his tongue came out to trail along his lower lip.

He didn't take a step towards her and nor did she move towards him. Yet the distance between them got infinitely smaller all at once. Downstairs, before, she'd been so close she'd been able to feel the press of his cock against her thigh. Now Leah imagined how hot his skin would feel against her hand if she gripped it.

She shook her head and backed up until her ass just nudged the edge of the table. She inched her skirt up fraction by fraction until the hem just brushed the tops of her thigh-high stockings. The lace of her panties would be showing by now, easily glimpsed if he angled his head just the right way.

Inside Leah's head, everything had gone white noise.

She'd felt this before, a handful of times. The first time she'd bound a man's hands had been in a barn on a summer night with her best friend at her side, and her mind had filled with this same nothing sound. The first time she'd allowed herself to be tied, wrist to wrist, to the bedpost and taken from behind with her eyes blindfolded she'd heard it too.

But now ... now she sipped in air one small breath at a time as she looked at the man in front of her. White noise. White light. She blinked, but her focus had gone soft and fuzzy around everything but Brandon.

She was slipping into something and she thought she might be frightened if she didn't want it so very, very much.

'Use your mouth on me.' Her voice was thorn-snagged satin, smooth but rough at the same time.

He didn't move. Leah shifted the hem of her skirt infinitesimally higher. She parted her legs. Her fingers curled into the dark fabric of her skirt, so pale against her bare thighs. She could hear him breathing and that sound, too, filled her mind.

'Now,' Leah said, and Brandon dropped his tie to the ground and got on his knees in front of her.

12

He didn't go for her panties right away. Instead, Brandon brushed his lips over the elastic edge of her stockings. He hooked his fingers into the edge and pulled it down. The elastic had left a red mark and he kissed it, slowly. Then he licked the line it had left behind.

Leah shuddered and wound her fingers into his thick dark hair as Brandon nuzzled the inside of her thigh. His big hands slid up over her ankles and her calves and stopped at her knees. His fingers were so long they reached all the way around to the ticklish spot behind her knees.

The table creaked when her ass pushed back against it. It was a flimsy thing, not meant for hard-core fucking atop it. Leah let the hand not holding Brandon's hair grip the table's edge. She wasn't going to move. Not now. Not even if they broke it.

He kissed her cunt, then looked up at her with his lips still pressed to the lace. His hot breath covered her clit in a tangible caress. Even on his knees he was so tall he had to bend his head to get his mouth between her legs. Leah opened her thighs a little wider, eased back a little on to the table to make it easier for him.

Nothing about him had ever seemed shuttered, but shadows flickered in his eyes now when he kissed her again. He moved his mouth back to her inner thigh, his eyes on hers. He bared his teeth, the nip on her sensitive flesh so unexpected Leah let out a strangled moan. At the sound he stopped. Licked the small spot on her flesh he'd just abused. When he looked up at her again, the tiniest hint of a smile curved his mouth.

Without thinking twice, Leah twined her fingers tighter in Brandon's hair. She'd been right about him. The sound he made when she tugged sent a bolt of pure pleasure slamming through her. For a second his eyes closed and that fine mouth went a little lax. He looked up at her again, all trace of a smile gone, his eyes ablaze. She relaxed her grip, took her hand away.

She didn't wonder if he was going to pull away. She knew he wasn't. Again his hot breath eased over her bare flesh and over the lace at her crotch. His hands slid to just above her knees, then higher. Up her thighs, up and up, until his fingers curled into the waistband of her panties.

She drew in a breath, but, before she could let it out, he'd yanked her panties down her thighs to her knees. In sharp contrast to the slow sensuality of his initial exploration, Brandon pulled the scrap of lace down her legs until her wide-spread thighs wouldn't allow them to go any further, then used one hand to push her legs closer so he could get the material over her calves and past her ankles. His head bent, eyes following the progress. His hair brushed her thighs, tickling.

He hadn't hesitated to put himself between her legs, but now he looked up at her again without moving further. 'Tell me again what you want me to do.'

Leah didn't care if he needed confirmation because she'd almost scared him off with the hair-pulling or because it got his dick hard. All that mattered was he was asking her for it.

'Use your mouth on me.'

Brandon kissed her thigh. 'Here?'

She saw no trace of a smile on his face or heard one in his voice, but she wasn't able to forget the sound of his laughter when she'd asked him if he'd come there to fuck her. He was teasing her, a little ... and she liked it. Blind obedience wasn't attractive; she'd never known how anyone could find it so. The bottom line was, she wanted Brandon on his knees in front of her, feasting on her pussy, because he wanted to be there and not because he wasn't man enough to say no.

'Higher.'

His lips trailed upwards along her skin but he angled his head to keep his mouth from reaching where she wanted it most. He kissed her thigh again, so lightly it would have tickled had she not been so attuned to every brush of his skin on hers. Then he kissed her other thigh, too, and nuzzled against it. His shoulders rose and fell as he breathed her in. He was smelling her.

This realisation weakened Leah's knees and she gripped at the wobbling table to keep herself from buckling. 'Higher, Brandon.'

A small but unignorable noise leaked from his throat at the sound of his name, and Leah let one hand drift up to release her hair from the anchor of its clip. It fell down around her shoulders, over her face, and she tipped her head back, eyes closed, lost in the sensations his mouth and hands were giving her. He liked it when she said his name. He liked it when she pulled his hair. Knowing these two small facts led her to another. He liked it on his knees for her, too.

His lips hovered over her clit, so close that when he spoke the air moved over her even though his mouth didn't. 'Tell me what you want me to do.'

She'd never much liked dirty talk for the sake of it. Most often men wanted her to say things such as 'I can't wait to suck your huge, stiff prick,' or 'Stuff my pussy full of your cock, baby.' She'd never really had one ask her to tell him what, exactly, she wanted him to do to her.

'I want you to lick me.' She spoke around a groan. His mouth was so, so close to doing just that.

She couldn't look down at him. Her back had arched and she'd kept her eyes closed. The edge of the table cut into both her palms as she gripped it. She felt his hand move up her thighs and she parted them wider at once. Now her ass shifted against the table, rocking it. She waited, tense, for him to comply.

Long seconds passed. Her stomach muscles and calves had begun to protest from holding the awkward position. She opened her eyes.

'Brandon,' she murmured, and her cunt pulsed at the way his entire body twitched when she said it. 'Lick my clit.'

His mouth opened and a deep breath escaped him as his hands moved on her thighs. He made that noise again, not quite the one he'd made when she'd pulled his hair, but a fucking sexy one just the same. All at once she was desperate to know what he'd sound like when he came.

Later. That was for later. Now she had his face between her legs and she was going to take advantage of it.

'Now,' she repeated gently, and threaded her fingers through his hair again, not yet pulling but reminding him she'd have no trouble doing it if he didn't get started.

His mouth fastened on her cunt. He sucked her clit gently, then set to work with a steady, slow pattern of tongue strokes that had her arching her back in moments to thrust herself closer to his mouth. When his hands slid behind her to hold her ass in place, Leah realised she'd been wriggling.

Leah had been with men who minced around her cunt like it was an appetiser, some small bite to whet their appetites. Others had regarded her cunt and their tongues as long-distance lovers or, worse, some x-marked treasure for which they'd lost the map. Brandon ate her pussy like he'd been born for just that reason.

He took his time. Moved slow. But he paid attention, too, shifting when she shifted and moving faster when her body tensed against him and she murmured instructions. Leah paid attention, too, as best she could with ecstasy shooting through her with every swipe of his tongue and stroke of his fingers. When she praised him with a simple, 'That's so good, just like that,' she heard the intake of his breath and the immediate muffled moan that came after. The sound of him taking such pleasure in pleasing her urged her to keep going when passion might otherwise have forced her silence. The more she said, the more he reacted, the more she found to say and the less she worried about sounding stupid.

Her voice had gone low and ragged and she sipped at the air to keep it steady. She gave herself up to the white noise in her head, the low, hidden thrum of erotic power she'd craved for so long but which had eluded her for nearly as long. Back tipped her head as her body arched towards him. Her grip flexed in the thickness of his hair and she tensed, listening for the shift in his breathing to tell her he was getting off on this as much as she was.

Orgasm welled within her, and Leah didn't fight it. She focused on the pleasure of his lips and tongue, the occasional scrape of his teeth on her tender flesh as he licked and sucked and nibbled. She drew close to the edge and he slowed the pace without her having to say a word.

He shifted again. She heard the pop of his joints as he moved but, if the position was hurting him, Brandon didn't complain. He only fixed his hands more firmly beneath her rear and held her closer to him so he could use the tip of his tongue to drill the super-sensitive place just above her clit.

'Right there.' The words purred out of her like the sound of paper tearing. Her cunt pulsed in the first wave of climax, but it held off.

Brandon, breathing hard, backed off a little. He kissed her thighs again as one hand slid from under her to stroke lightly along her labia and clit. Leah opened her eyes. She looked down at him.

He was looking at her. 'I want to make you come.'

He said he wanted, but it sounded as though he were asking permission. Another ripple of climax fluttered through her. She let go of his hair and put both hands back on the table, holding tight as she moved to keep the edge from digging into her.

'Use your fingers,' she said, watching the way his pulse beat at the base of this throat, where the shirt lay open to show his skin. 'Put them inside me. I want you to fuck me with your hand ... oh ... God, Brandon!'

She'd used his name deliberately before, but it slipped out of her without warning when he did as she said and slid one long finger inside her. Then another. When her mouth shaped it, when her tongue pressed it out from behind her teeth, it sounded like an endearment. She watched his face, the way he blinked, fast, when she said it.

So she said it again. 'Make me come, Brandon,' Leah whispered.

He moved his fingers, her pussy so slick he had no trouble sliding all the way in and out again. 'Now?' he asked, and again there was that slight smile, the tip of lips that was so damned fucking sexy.

'Now ...' The one-syllable word broke in half as he put his mouth back to her clit.

He fucked her smoothly with his fingers as his tongue kept up a steady, circling stroke on her swollen clit. They were going to break the table, and she didn't care. There was no stopping any of this now. She couldn't have stopped it if she tried. Her body rode wave after wave of exquisite pleasure, not sharp or jagged, not rough and tumble, but smooth and sweet and oh so fucking delicious.

Leah had never been a screamer. Coming took too much of her breath to waste it on a shout. She did, however, say his name again in a random, rambling stream of praise. The buzz and hum in her mind eased. She blinked as she came down. The muscles in her belly and thighs leaped as her clit twitched in the aftermath of her orgasm, and she murmured a soft command for him to ease off.

He did, then sat back to rest his ass on his heels. His knees must have been killing him, she thought, when she could think. Leah licked her lips, aware of how suddenly dry her throat had become and how her ass had gone mostly numb except for the stinging line of fire from where the table edge had dug into her flesh.

She eased herself to standing. Her skirt fell down to just above her knees again. She reached for the glass of iced water she'd poured earlier and drank it back, before replacing the glass on the dresser with slightly shaking hands.

When she turned back to him, she'd managed to get herself under some semblance of control. She thought he'd have gotten to his feet already, if he wasn't reaching for her arm to spin her around to try to kiss her, but Brandon still sat back on his heels. Watching her.

When she turned he got up, moving slowly and a little stiffly, maybe, but she thought that was from the tent pole in his pants and not necessarily from pain. Now he would try to kiss her, she thought, and tensed, waiting for it. Brandon didn't try to kiss her.

He had come up her to fuck her. She knew, too, that he'd liked what she had him do. That his dick was hard and that probably he expected her to suck him in return for the favour he'd granted between her thighs, if he didn't expect her to let him put his cock where his fingers and tongue had been just moments before.

He was so big, too, she thought with another delicious

shiver. Big, strong hands. Long legs. He'd have a cock to match and, if he fucked the way he'd gone down on her, she was in for a treat.

Leah turned. 'You're very good at that.'

He laughed again and, even though he'd made her come hard enough to see stars just a few minutes ago, her body responded.

'Thanks.'

He took a step towards her. She took a step back. When he gave her a curious look, she shook her head a tiny bit. She looked pointedly at the front of his black dress trousers, where there was no mistaking the bulge, then into his eyes.

'Do you still want to fuck me?'

'Yes.' His laugh was hoarser this time, but he didn't move towards her.

'Do you think making me come deserves a reward?' The question slipped from her mouth in a tone cooler than she'd intended.

She'd caught him off guard. 'No, I –'

'You have a lovely mouth, Brandon, and you use it exceptionally well.' She crossed her arms and tilted her head, then walked slowly around him while he stood still.

The hum was back, dimmed a bit by being sated with orgasm but still tantalising. Leah came back around to the front of him, close enough for him to reach out and grab her if he wanted. Or dared.

He didn't.

She looked him over. His hair, mussed from her grip, begged to be smoothed. She didn't touch him. 'I am not in the habit of fucking people I work with,' she said at last, matter-of-factly. 'I'm sure you can imagine how that would complicate my job.'

'Yeah.' He cleared his throat. 'Believe me, it's not some-thing I do all the time, either.'

'I believe you.' She did, though he could have been lying. With looks like that he could be screwing his way through every housekeeper and waitress and desk clerk in this place.

'Leah ...' Brandon's voice dipped low for a moment. 'Did I do something wrong?'

'No, baby, you did everything just right.' The endearment slipped out before she could stop it.

He looked startled, then pleased; then a shadow of confusion passed over those perfect features. 'I thought you wanted –'

She stepped into his arms, their bodies pressed together, and he shut up immediately. His erection pressed her belly and Leah slid her hands around to hold on to Brandon's very tight, very fine ass. She pulled him a little closer and was glad she'd kept her heels on so she didn't have to tilt her head back quite so far to look at him.

'You pleased me. Today,' she said softly, 'and just now.'

He put his arms around her. 'Good.'

When he bent to kiss her, though, she turned her face so his lips ended up on her cheek instead of her mouth. Already she was getting wetter, thinking of what she would say. What he would do. He was so much bigger ... she already knew he was acquiescent ... but how far could she push him before he pushed back?

'No?' He murmured into her ear.

'No,' she said.

If he was angry, he didn't show it. They stayed just that way, bodies aligned and his mouth close to her ear. She put her hand on his chest. Even through his shirt she could feel the heavy thump of his heart, beating too fast. She put her mouth to that spot, her breath heating the fabric.

He drew in a ragged breath. Through his pants, she felt his cock leap. She slid her other hand to cup him, stroked him through the cloth until he groaned into her ear. He was so big and yet such a small thing could bring him low. This was power, beneath her hand. The power to bend a man to her desire.

The static of her arousal flared in her head and for a moment all she could do was rub his cock and press her face to his shirt. When he slid a hand beneath her skirt to find her bare skin, she moved away. She left him blinking, reaching for her. His face had flushed and sweat had dampened the hair along his brow.

She didn't want to fuck him. Not so soon. Not because she thought it wouldn't be good, or that she had some misguided notion that it would be a mistake, but for the simple, plain reason that letting him fuck her would give him some measure of control, and she wasn't giving any up. Not now. Maybe not ever again.

And wouldn't that make her just like Mike had been? Always taking, never giving? The thought shocked heat into her face and she turned away, unable to meet Brandon's eyes.

Was she as bad as Mike?

13

When Dix knocked on her door, Kate opened it quickly, looking soft and feminine. Her hair was down instead of the sleek bun she'd confined it in earlier.

'Hi, come in.' She stepped aside and he went into the room.

He dropped the stuff he had in his hands and pulled her into his arms. 'Hi. You look pretty.' Leaning down, he dipped his mouth to hers, brushing it across her lips, capturing her sigh.

His fingers sifted through her hair and he gripped it, wrapping it around his fist to angle her the way he wanted. A needy sound escaped her throat and his cock clenched in response.

She opened to him, the warmth of her mouth inviting him inside. Their tongues slid against each other as her taste seemed to drag him into a spell.

Her fingers kneaded his biceps as she swayed slightly, as if dancing to music they made with their contact.

'Now, that's a much better hello,' he murmured as he broke the kiss. 'I brought some files in case anyone saw me. I also brought some fruit and cheese to go with the bottle of white wine.'

'Before we get started, I have something to tell you.'

His heart stuttered a moment. Would she tell him she was seeing someone else? Was she breaking things off?

He led her to the couch and sat her down with him. 'Go on.'

'I accepted a job in Philadelphia and I bought a condo.' Her words were quick, so quick he didn't understand them at first. Then he understood and the tightness in his chest loosened.

'Wow. Well, good. Congratulations, Kate. That's great news.' He kissed her and pushed her to the sofa with his body, loving the way she felt beneath him. 'Now I won't have to wait months and months to see you. When are you moving?'

'Let's go into the bedroom, this is a sleeper sofa and the bar is in the middle of my back.'

He laughed and helped her up. 'Fine, but get naked.'

She looked at him over her shoulder as she left the room, took off her T-shirt and tossed it at him. Mmm, braless. Her breasts swayed as she moved to the bed. He grabbed the soft-sided cooler with the cheese and fruit and put it on the table nearby.

Never taking her eyes from his, she shucked her pants, the tiny panties followed and she soon stood there totally naked.

'I'm the only naked one. Why is that?'

'I have to open the wine. Lie back so I can look at you. I just want to eat you up, you're so fucking beautiful.'

She settled on the bed, leaving her thighs open enough for him to catch the glisten of her pussy.

He poured her a glass of wine and laid out the food. 'I think you should undress me.'

She got to her knees. 'Oh good. I like this part.'

He was so masculine and sexy as she pushed the shirt up and over his head to expose the hard hot skin of his upper body. She drew her palms over his belly, through the hair on his chest. Unable to resist, she flicked her tongue over his left nipple, delighting in the way he groaned. In so many ways she felt she knew him from all their conversations but they hadn't spent more than a week together face to face. So much of his physical body was still something to learn.

His hands slid down her back, down the curve of her spine, as she snuggled up to him and nuzzled his neck, breathing in his scent. While she nibbled his ear lobe, she lazily undid his jeans and shoved them down.

And then she slowly kissed down his chest. Over his pecs, down the hard stomach, pausing to scrape her teeth over his belly button until she got off the bed to kneel at his feet, eye to, er, eye with the part she wanted most.

So soft and yet hard. She breathed in the musk of his sex, the heady mix of pheromones that marked him in her senses. His skin was hot as she rubbed her cheek across the line of his cock, dipping down to his balls.

Her heart, which had been pounding as each new inch of him was revealed while she undressed him, slowed as the narcotic effect of his body came into play.

'Suck me, Kate,' he said quietly.

Grabbing the root of him, just at the manicured patch of dark-brown hair, she angled his cock and took him into her mouth with a moan of delight. His cock came alive under her tongue as she tasted, teased, licked, laved and flicked him from root to crown. His balls lay heavy in her palm, drawing closer to his body when she gently scored them with her nails.

So much power there, with a cock in her mouth. A cock in your mouth can't lie. It's not about anything other than wanting, and he wanted her as much as she wanted him.

Incrementally, she relaxed enough to take him deeper and deeper each time she moved. His hands on her shoulders urged her but didn't press or force. Instead he locked his knees and let her set her dreamy pace of in and out. He hardened, the texture of his cock changing the closer he came to climax. It occurred to her in the back of her mind that she actually knew him well enough to tell that. It wasn't something she could say about many men.

'Wait, fuck, I'm going to come,' he gasped, but she continued to work his cock, wanting to bring his release, wanting that intimacy between them, craving the power of drawing him to climax.

He growled incoherently and flexed his hips forwards, his fingers digging into the muscles of her shoulders when he came, flooding her with his essence and his taste, sharp and unmistakably his, filled her.

'Mmm.' She kissed the head of his cock and looked up at him. His green eyes lazily took her in and the pirate smile was back.

'I see your game, darling Kate. I like it.' He pulled her up to him, into his arms, bringing them skin to skin from head to toe as he kissed her greedily.

She laughed as he tossed her on the bed and followed. 'I'm shaking with anticip-p-pation.'

His eyes widened a moment before he laughed. 'Now lookie here, a *Rocky Horror* fan. I think a midnight show is in our future. I can definitely see you dressed up in a short black French maid costume. Yes. For now, drink your wine, you'll need the fortification.'

They drank the wine and ate in companionable silence. As relieved as she felt at finally telling him she'd moved and at his response of being glad he'd see her more, she couldn't help feeling the stuff that hadn't been said.

It was . . . odd. She wasn't the type to tiptoe around things, which she supposed is what lay at the root of her discomfort. Despite her hesitation at pursuing more than the occasional afternoon in bed with him, she did want more. It was that she didn't know if she wanted all that came with more. Or even if he wanted more. A muddle. God, suddenly her life was a muddle! Wishy-washy even. Still, naked, slightly drunk, with a hot naked man next to her in bed wasn't the time or place to have the do-you-like-me-or-not-like-me discussion.

Next to her, he sighed, a purely male sound of satisfaction and sex. It sent her skin into gooseflesh and her body reacted, tightening, hardening, heating.

'Now that I've had some wine and some food, I need something sweet.' Rolling, he got to his hands and knees, then pushed everything but her off the bed.

Her bottom lip caught between her teeth, she watched, waiting to see what he had in store for her next. Not one to disappoint, he grabbed her ankle and pulled her towards him, kneeling between her legs.

His palms, slightly callused and large, caressed her from toe to neck, over and over, until she was totally and completely relaxed. Through her half-lowered lashes, she took in the way he dipped his head to drop kisses over her shoulders and chest. She arched her neck to allow him access and hummed her pleasure as he dragged his teeth over the sensitive spot just below her ear.

The heated wet of his mouth trailed downwards. First to one nipple and then the other. Each cooling as he abandoned it to nip and lave the other one. Her legs moved restlessly on the bed, her thighs seeking to close to squeeze, easing the pressure in her pussy, but his body held her spread.

Finally, he moved down again, kissing her belly, over her mound and then tonguing the crease between thigh and body.

A sound of impatience gusted from her and he chuckled darkly. 'Kate. Sweet Kate, be patient. This pussy is all mine and I plan to taste you on *my* schedule. You can't deny me for a month and expect me to rush through a blow job like some teenaged boy.'

She watched in stunned awe as he took a long lick, his eyes still locked with hers. Settling on his belly, he cupped her ass, served himself of her body and got down to the business of eating her pussy like a starving man.

Her hands found his head, the cool silk of his hair sliding through her fingers. Her eyes fell shut as her head dropped back to the pillows and she let go and gave in to everything he gave her.

So wet. Her pussy was so wet and he made it that way. It wasn't that he'd ever not liked giving a woman head but this woman's cunt drove him insane. Her taste, the way her clit hardened, begging him for more, each dip and fold of her made him crave her even more.

He wanted to wallow in her for days. The news that she'd be moving just two hours away took him by surprise, but a pleasant one. He liked the idea of having her in his life regularly. He'd dwell on that later.

Her thighs trembled on his shoulders, the flesh of her ass fitted in his hands perfectly as he moved his mouth from side to side through slick folds.

'Please,' she sighed.

'Such pretty manners,' he said, his lips against her clit. Her body vibrated with the words as he'd intended. Sucking her clit between his lips, he plunged two fingers into her body. Her back bowed and she cried out. Not. Quite. There. Yet.

Twisting his wrist, he hooked his fingers and found her sweet spot. Her body tensed as he began to stroke it in time with the gentle sucking of her clit. Her honey rained hot on his palm, her scent flooded his system, blinding him to anything else but her.

There.

The fingers gently sifting through his hair tightened as she gasped a breath and came so prettily. On and on she went as he continued, his mouth on her, her body clutching the fingers buried in her.

Finally, the tension fell from her and she relaxed on to the mattress, boneless.

'You're so fucking gorgeous when you come, Kate.' He kissed his way back up her body, then leaned over her to fish in his pants for a condom.

'You're pretty hot when you're eating my pussy,' she mumbled from beneath him.

He hadn't laughed in bed, not like he did with her, in a very long time. Since the early years with Eve and it had always been one-sided with her anyway.

Wrong image. He pushed that one out of his head and got on his knees where she followed, scrambling up to take the condom from him and roll it on his cock herself.

She shoved him back and scrambled atop him, a smug smile on her lips.

'Bossy. I like that.'

'I know.' Reaching around her body, she guided his cock true and sank down quickly, her pussy swallowing him in one hard, fiery rush. The breath punched from him, the sensation of being surrounded by her grabbing him low in the gut, settling there as she rose up, the muscles in her thighs flexing, her breasts, those lovely full breasts, swaying.

'Fuck. That's so good.'

'Mmmm.' Her nails dug into his ribs where her hands rested to keep her balance.

The light in her eyes, the sweet smile, the way she swivelled on him taking her pleasure while bringing his at the same time, all parts of her he couldn't let go of. Haunted, he might have said even a month ago, but it had shifted to something more pleasant and he couldn't identify just when it had happened.

He cupped her breasts, thumbs sliding back and forth over her nipples as they drew tighter, darkened. Her lips were slightly parted, her breath soft as she laboured over him; strands of her hair slid back and forth across her shoulder as he looked up at her.

His cock wanted to explode. His brain urged him to wait, to not leave the heated embrace of her pussy. He tried to think about the memo he had to write, tried to think of the latch on the back window he needed to fix, but the soft wet sounds of their bodies meeting over and over drew him away from any thoughts but the way she felt clasped around him.

The scent of sex hung between them, of clean sweat, wine, strawberries and her pussy. Heady, tangy, spicy and he realised he'd been imprinted in some sense. Fuck. Like a lovesick boy. Only not so much.

He tipped to one side, taking over, increasing the speed and pressure of his thrusts. Taking it in her stride, she drew her knees up high, opening up, and it grabbed him by the balls.

'Make yourself come, Kate.' He was close, he wanted her there with him.

Her hand burrowed between them and she gasped softly as her fingers made contact with her clit. She held them there, letting the movement of his thrusts provide friction. Dix admired her restraint, the way she drew the pleasure out in tiny, incremental bits. She made him greedy, he wanted more, wanted to gorge himself of her.

Her eyelashes fluttered, her cunt tightened and she came with a soft exhalation of breath. It was too much to resist then and he pressed hard and deep as climax rushed up his spine and emptied endorphins into his system.

He rolled to the side and kissed her shoulder before he got up to dispose of the condom. Each time they were together she felt drawn closer to him emotionally. The last time it hadn't mattered so very much or seemed so big. She lived in Seattle and he in Harrisburg. She'd come home and accepted the offer and began to deal with the move within days of their last visit.

'So when are you moving? You never said.' He settled back beside her in bed.

'Now actually. I closed on a condo yesterday.'

'Why didn't you say anything, Kate?'

'I didn't know what to say. I didn't tell anyone actually. Well, I did tell my parents when I made the offer on the condo; I had to get some financial info from my dad. But I only told Leah yesterday. I needed to do it alone.'

'What do you mean you didn't know what to say?' He sat up.

'Do you want to do this right now? It's nearly midnight. We have early meetings.'

His mouth hardened into a flat line and he sighed. 'Let's get to sleep. We can talk about this tomorrow.'

'You can't sleep here! Oh my God, what if someone saw you leaving my room, or even coming in and then you never went home?'

'We're adults, Kate. This is stupid. I live fifteen minutes away. Why don't you sleep over there instead?'

'We can't be seen together like this. It's not professional. I have to be here early to deal with some faxes I'm expecting anyway. And I can't just stroll in five minutes before you and pretend we didn't spend the night together.'

'You did just fine after this afternoon's romp. Fuck professional. I think you're being unreasonable. No one cares.' He got up and began to put his clothes on.

'Easy for you to say.'

'What does that mean? Who are you, Kate?' He looked at her, his hands on his hips.

'It means men can make all sorts of decisions, do all sorts of things women can't do and be seen the same way. If we got caught by anyone at Allied you'd be fine. Hell, they'd wink-wink you and pat you on the back. I'd be the piece of ass.'

'That's the dumbest thing I ever heard. Who cares if someone knows we're having sex? It's not like a state secret. This isn't the dark ages. You're a woman in the twenty-first century.'

'Get out. You don't know what you're talking about. Get out.' Rage made the warmth of their evening wear off. He didn't know anything. She'd learned the hard lessons about the difference between how men and women were perceived early on. She couldn't pay for his wilful blindness about the situation. She wouldn't.

'What are you pissed about? We're having a fight and I don't even know why.' He put his shoes on and she shoved his stuff into his hands as she moved him to the door.

'That's why we're fighting, Dix. Now go.'

'What is it with women? You all seem to expect us to read minds. I can't read minds. Just tell me what the issue is.'

'Well, now it's also that you actually had the audacity to compare me to all women.'

'I was married, it's not like I never dealt with a woman before.' Frustration was clear on his face and she wanted to whack him with a pillow.

'Did you just compare me to a woman who calls her ex-husband to open a jar of pickles because she's too inept to hit the bottom of the jar to displace the air in the seal?'

Recognition of his error crossed his face and then what must have been confusion about whether or not he should be mad or defensive replaced it.

'Just. Go. Go before you make it worse. Please.'

He shook his head and let out a long exhale. 'I don't even know why we're fighting. I want to wake up next to you and suddenly you're shoving me out of the door insulting my ex-wife. Help me understand.'

'Dix.' She paused, counting to ten. This wasn't a man who could be managed. She wouldn't have been attracted if he was. She appreciated he wanted to deal with their issues right then, but she wasn't sure of everything herself. It certainly wasn't something she wanted to try to parse out at midnight with another day and a half of the meeting left.

'Are you breaking things off? If so, you owe it to me to tell me why. We're good together.' Dix grabbed her hand and kissed it.

'No. I'm not. I don't even know what we have anyway. But I need some space to think and so do you. About what this is and how and if it can work. I'm tired and really annoyed with you and I need to sleep. Please.'

He dropped his stuff and took her into his arms. 'I know what this is. Damn it.' He kissed her hard and fast. 'But OK. I'll go and we will talk soon.'

After he left, she slid down the door at her back and sat on the floor for some time.

14

Brandon's gut churned. His dick had gone down but his balls still ached from unspent arousal. He took one hand from the steering wheel to tug at the crotch of his pants, but that gave no relief.

He could still smell her and taste her, and he doubted he'd ever forget the way she'd sounded when she came. It wasn't the first time he'd ever gone down on a woman, but it had never been like that before. The way she'd moved, the way she'd said his name ... the sheer speed at which she'd had an orgasm. He'd never minded spending a while with his mouth between a woman's thighs, but he'd come to expect the necessity of taking his time. He'd been with Leah for ten, maybe twenty minutes from the time he walked into the room to the time she told him to leave.

His knees hurt too, and he grimaced when he down-shifted into the turn on to his street. He'd blown one out playing soccer in high school and the other had been messed up skiing. They didn't usually bother him unless he tried to do too much, but even in church he'd never spent that much time on his knees.

Now, thinking of it, he groaned aloud and punched the radio volume to turn it higher. Normally he listened to the radio or used his tuner to play his iPod, but his fingers fumbled on the controls. When the CD started it was like a jolt back in time.

Karen had made this CD for him, just before he'd discovered she'd been cheating on him. She'd surprised him with it, putting it in his car and leaving a note on the dashboard for him to play it. He didn't know exactly when she'd done it, because the sticky note had fallen off the dash and he hadn't found it until a week or so after they'd broken up. It was a CD of love songs and sex songs, as Karen had called them, and he'd never been able to convince himself she hadn't made it for her other boyfriend but only accidentally left it for him.

The song that came on first made him groan again. 'Lick'. A woman singing about the joys of cunnilingus. Fate was too cruel.

He pulled into an open spot in front of his building and turned off the ignition, but the music kept playing. His dick throbbed and his balls ached. He swiped his tongue over his lips, tasting her. He put his hand to his face, smelling her.

'Did you come here to fuck me?' She'd asked a question. He'd given her an answer. He'd made her come crying out his name, but when it was over she'd acted like it was all just part of the service, like using his tongue to make her come was the same as bringing her bagels and making sure there were enough water pitchers filled.

He should've been pissed. Instead, he was more turned on than he'd ever been in his life. Brandon shifted in his seat again, looking out on to the dark and empty street as he listened to the music Karen had chosen for him and thought about another woman's taste.

'I could let you fuck me,' Leah had said with her back turned to him. 'I'm sure you'd be very good at it.'

He hadn't said anything, not sure what she wanted him to say. She looked over her shoulder at him as she poured herself some more water and as she sipped. He'd had the feeling she was testing him again, maybe waiting to see if he were going to be an asshole and demand she let him have sex with her.

He didn't like it when women assumed they knew what he was like just because they'd met a few jerkwads along the way. Karen had assumed he was cheating on her, so she said, because that's what good-looking guys did. She'd used it as an excuse for lying to him. The fact he'd never even looked at another girl the entire time they'd been together hadn't meant anything.

'Tell me something,' Leah had said when he didn't answer. 'Did you like that? What I asked you to do?'

'Yes.'

Her dark-blue eyes had left him feeling she could see right through him. 'I want you to go home now, Brandon.'

He couldn't help the way he reacted when she said his name like that. Soft and low and full of promise. She'd lifted her chin as though she expected him to protest.

But, even though his dick was so hard he thought it might tear a hole in his pants, and even though he wanted to pin her back against that table and slide inside, to lose himself in her slick heat, Brandon had only nodded. He didn't speak, not trusting his voice.

'I want you to think about me tonight when you're jerking that fine thick cock in those big strong hands.'

He'd been ashamed by his groan, but she only looked pleased and a little startled. He thought now it was because of what she'd told him about that asshole, Mike, and how he always wanted to be in charge, but, at the time, all he'd been able to do was focus on not making a fool of himself by spilling in his pants like a kid.

'You'll do that for me, won't you?'

Say it, he'd thought, holding back a breath.

'Brandon?'

'Yes!'

'And tomorrow,' Leah had said quietly, pinning him in place with nothing but her gaze and the sound of her voice, 'you'll tell me exactly what you did. Exactly how it felt. I want to know every detail of it.'

'And ... then?'

'Then,' she'd said, 'if I like what I hear, and you've pleased me again, then maybe I'll let you fuck me.'

With that, she'd dismissed him.

And he'd gone, like a lapdog.

No matter how often he had to do it for his job, Brandon detested being made to jump through hoops. He thought about calling her a bitch, but the word wouldn't come. It didn't fit. There was a difference in someone making demands just to watch him squirm and what Leah had done. He couldn't have said what it was. He just felt it.

It was the look in her eyes, something vulnerable. And surprise, like she never really expected him to do what she asked. And lust, unmistakable, when he did.

What bothered him more than anything wasn't that she seemed to be playing some sort of game that only she knew the rules to, but that she assumed he didn't want to play too.

'Bad Touch' by the Bloodhound Gang came on next and Brandon stabbed the radio silent. He took a few deep breaths and swiped his hands through his hair. He pressed the front of his bulging crotch until he could get out of the car.

He felt feverish. Sweaty. The dull ache in the pit of his stomach reminded him of the time he'd been hit full-on in the nuts by a soccer ball. He'd gone down on the field clutching his junk without even the breath to scream and that had been bad enough, but it was the dull throb that had persisted for hours after that had really messed him up.

His knees creaked in protest as he got out and shut the car door. He lived on the top floor of an old brownstone, converted to apartments. Three in all, his the smallest.

Two guys he thought might be a couple lived in the middle apartment, but he hardly ever saw them. The ground-floor pad housed a trio of girls just out of college who all worked downtown: Chris, Kris and Crissy. It was like a bad 70s jiggle sitcom sometimes and tonight was no exception.

'Brandon!' Their door opened and Crissy looked out as he paused to check his mailbox.

Mail in hand, Brandon climbed the three steps to the first landing. 'Hi, Crissy.'

'We're having a party to celebrate. Chris got a new job. Come in!'

It was already late, and only a Tuesday. He had to work in the morning. His crotch twinged as he moved and he thought of Leah.

'Sure. OK. I could use a beer.'

'Goody!' She clapped and stepped aside, but not too much, to let him in.

His arm brushed her full breasts as he passed. His dick, already at half-mast, responded. He thought of junior high, when all the boys had taken to carrying a notebook with them at all times so they'd have something to hold in front of them if they got an unexpected hard-on.

Not that this one was unexpected. Heck, a breeze could blow on him the right way tonight and he'd get hard. Brandon tried not to look down Crissy's blouse as she took him by the elbow to lead him further into the apartment.

'Look, guys! It's Brandon!'

He knew Chris and Kris by sight, and some of the other faces turning to greet him looked familiar too, but thankfully Crissy was already pulling him into the kitchen for a beer so he didn't have to actually say anything to anyone.

Two beers later, the buzz in his head was finally managing to put a bit of a damper on the buzz between his legs. He was on the couch with Chris on one side and Kris on the other, while a giggling Crissy settled on his lap with an arm around his neck to serve him a shot of tequila he didn't want.

Brandon had a double handful of taut thighs, soft breasts, firm buttocks. He was drowning in tits and ass. Under Crissy's elliptically trained butt, his cock was as stiff as it could get, trapped against his thigh.

'C'mon, it's a party,' Crissy said as she put the shot glass to his mouth.

'I have to work tomorrow!' He didn't mean to let his hand wander up and down her bare thigh, but it was there and so was his hand and, God, she felt so good.

On either side of him, the couch dipped as more people piled on or got off. The tang of pot tickled his nose and he fought a sneeze. Crissy wriggled on his erection and there was no way she couldn't notice he was sporting a steel rod in his pants.

'How come you never party with us?' Crissy asked into his ear. 'You're a party pooper.'

'I have to ... work ...' He couldn't finish when she shifted on his lap, her tight ass settling just right on his hard dick.

'All work and no play makes Brandon a dull boy, you know.' Crissy looked into his eyes.

His mouth was already open when she kissed him. She tasted like tequila and corn chips and smoke, and she kissed without much finesse but with a whole lot of enthusiasm. She was warm and willing in his arms but, when she broke the kiss to whisper an invitation into his ear, all Brandon could do was sit and stare at her.

What the hell was he doing? Twenty minutes of Crissy on his cock wouldn't be worth the hassle of dealing with her after that. Twenty? Hell. He'd be lucky if he could make it to five. And it wouldn't be fair to screw her knowing he'd be thinking of another woman the entire time.

'I have to go,' he told her.

'No . . . stay . . .' She kissed his cheek, his jaw, his neck. Her hand wiggled inside his shirt and found bare skin, but Brandon was already clutching her wrist to keep her from exploring more.

He didn't want to screw Crissy. The woman he wanted had told him to go home and think about her and, no matter what else he did tonight, that's what he'd be doing. Crissy tried to kiss him again but stopped when he didn't respond.

She rocked her ass on his erection. 'What's wrong?'

'Nothing. But I really do have to work in the morning. I'm sorry.'

She leaned in to speak in his ear again. 'What I'm sitting on says otherwise.'

What she was sitting on wouldn't mind, but he did. 'Thanks for the beer.'

She got off his lap when he pushed her gently and stood. Her pretty face grew lines when she frowned, a fact Brandon doubted she'd appreciate. She put her hands on her hips.

'Are you queer?'

'No.'

'Huh.' She eyed his crotch. 'I just had to ask.'

'No, I'm not queer.' He smiled at her, though she didn't smile back. 'I'm just –'

'Bad break-up, yeah, yeah.' She waved her hand in dismissal. 'We know all about it.'

'What do you know about it?'

'Oh, Kris works with Jeremy Bench, who used to go out with Deb Houser, whose brother is room-mates with Ben Miller.'

'Who's dating my ex-girlfriend.'

'Right.' She gave him a drunken smile. 'Poor baby, she rocked your world, huh?'

Leah had called him baby, too, but from her it had sounded like sweet, dripping sin and on Crissy's lips it only made him scowl. 'I gotta go.'

'Bye.' Her mission failed, Crissy was already looking for her next target.

Brandon let himself out. By the time he got up the stairs to his apartment, the ache in his groin was enough to make him walk with a limp. There was only one solution for it. Again he wanted to curse Leah, call her a bitch, but he couldn't pretend that, for someone who didn't know him at all, she'd managed to get right inside him.

By the time the pipes stopped whining and the water was hot enough in the shower to fill the air with steam, he'd stripped out of his work clothes. He didn't even try to stop the sigh of relief when he shucked out of his briefs and finally freed his erection.

He stepped into the shower with a hand already on his prick. Stroking. Groaning.

He stopped. She'd said she wanted to know all the details and he didn't intend to disappoint.

He was close already, but too close. Stroking himself hurt almost more than it felt good. He needed to go slow. He wondered if Leah had known that.

He wondered if she were thinking of him now too.

Brandon bent his head into the water and let it pound down on his neck and shoulders. They ached too. His entire body did, actually, with the tension of hours.

His shower was small, but the building had a communal water heater, so there was always plenty of hot water. Still bent beneath the spray, he put a hand on the wall at shoulder height for support. He leaned, taking the pressure off his knees one at a time.

Steaming water sluiced over his shoulders and down his back. He breathed in, slowly, and let the breath out. Water slid over his chest, down over his cock, tickling.

When at last some of the ache had eased from a few of his muscles, Brandon put his hand on his cock again. He stroked easily but slowly. His eyes closed.

There was no way to count the thousands of times he'd done this, jerked himself to coming, but he'd never done it on command before. Now, thinking about her thinking of him doing it, thinking of how he'd tell her tomorrow how it had felt, what he'd done, the sensations building in his shaft and balls seemed extra heightened.

Her cunt had spasmed on his tongue. He'd been able to feel her coming around his fingers as her clit leaped and jumped under his lips. He'd done that to her, made her feel that way. He'd made her come.

He groaned out loud, Leah's face in his mind. The water was washing her taste from him. He opened his mouth to let the hot water swirl around his teeth. He spit, a fierce jet that splattered the wall.

His hand was a poor substitute for the heat and wetness of her body. He wanted to feel her around him. He wanted her mouth under his. Damn ... He groaned again ... He wanted her nails raking his back as he drove into her again and again and she screamed his name.

His hand stroked harder. His hips pumped forwards. His fingers clutched and slid on the shower's plastic interior, finding no purchase.

He wanted her hands in his hair, pulling hard when he found her secret places with his mouth and fingers.

He said her name and let the water fill his mouth again.

His balls tightened, so heavy already. He pushed harder into his fist. Faster. His knees bent a little, hurting. The water was so hot it had begun making him feel a little faint. Or maybe it was his impending orgasm, which felt like a freight train barrelling up from his groin to his head.

She had blue eyes. Dark hair. She smelled of roses. She tasted sweet. She turned him inside out and upside down.

He shouted when he came, a garbled string of words that might have been mistaken for a prayer. Or a plea. His cock throbbed as he spurted. Hot come splattered the shower wall, each burst wringing another low cry from him until at last, spent, Brandon hung his head and let the water roll over him.

'Leah.' He mouthed it, then laughed.

What the hell exactly was he going to say tomorrow?

15

Oh fuck. Why did she agree to talk to him at all? Why did she give in and act as if what was happening between her and Dix was anything but an affair?

Ruthlessly, Kate twisted her hair back and chose a darker lipstick. She had to play ball-buster in the meetings and she needed to look the part. So what if she wore her sexiest panties and bra? No one knew but her and it wasn't because she wanted to appeal to Dix.

But first she was having breakfast with Leah. Leah who'd see through any bullshit.

'Why am I doing this?' she asked the mirror. The woman had the audacity to shrug back at her. She cocked her head. She did have that glow. The look of a woman who'd had a man shove his cock deep into her wet, hot cunt and ride her like a pony. Twice in one day. She wanted to laugh out loud but instead the woman in the mirror raised a brow and smirked.

Great, now she was going crazy and talking to herself. She didn't use to talk to herself before Dix. Damned man, all delicious and smart and, gah, irresistible.

Shaking her head, she dabbed on a bit of perfume, checked herself out in the mirror and headed towards the door.

But then her cell phone rang and a quick peek at the display showed it was her mother. Sighing, she steeled herself and answered.

'Where are you? Your dad and I stopped by your new place yesterday and you didn't answer when we tried to buzz up. One of your neighbours let us in, Katherine. You know how dangerous that is? We could have been axe murderers or stalkers.' Her mother took a deep breath and Kate readied herself for another volley of mother guilt. 'Your father and I drove all the way out to your new place from Bala Cynwyd! You know how your father has to stop a lot and go to the bathroom and you weren't even there.'

Kate shuddered. Not axe murderers, but her mother was an emotional vampire. A tiny bully of a woman obsessed with appearances and tags on the inside of clothing. A woman who'd been on a diet since 1965 and who, Kate was convinced, had never had an orgasm. Shirley Edwards was entirely devoid of carnality on any level. She enjoyed nothing but tearing other people down to make herself feel better.

Her father loved to tell everyone how good he was. How kind. How very moral and upstanding while he checked out and left Kate and her siblings to the mercies of his wife. The kind of man who never came out and said anything specifically bigoted but it poured off him in the way he looked at other people, in his catchphrases and innuendos.

Kate had been glad to go to college and then after the fiasco, where she'd learned exactly how different men and women were expected to act in the workplace, she'd headed for the west coast. That had been the major plus to living in Seattle. But, as her sister Diandra told her, she was a big girl. She was back and Kate refused to allow them to ruin it with their presence. Moving back to Pennsylvania was a good thing, damn it. She busted the asses of people in court all the time so why did she cry like a girl instead of kneecapping her parents like they needed?

Di and her girlfriend lived in Boston. Once at Christmas

dinner, Di told their mother why she'd gotten her tongue pierced. Best. Holiday. Dinner. Ever.

Kate realised her mother had been talking and decided to interrupt. 'I said in my email that I'd be away at a conference for a few days. I'm in Harrisburg. I'm on my way to a meeting just now so I have to go. I'll speak to you when I get back home.'

'What are you doing in Harrisburg? Your neighbourhood is nice enough except for the junkie who let us in. Did I tell you about that? Well, your father says he hopes you got a raise coming out here. You know *they* can afford it. When are you due back? Why don't you live in a suburb instead of in town? You can afford a nice house for what you paid for that place.'

Kate hung her head. Her bones wanted to turn to rubber as the life was sapped from her. 'A conference, as I said. Lawyers go to those a lot. Glad you like my neighbourhood.' She wouldn't ask how they inferred that the person who let the upscale-looking older couple into the building was a junkie instead of a helpful citizen, and she really wasn't going to touch the salary comment. She had to go to breakfast and she couldn't eat if her head blew off. 'Anyway, I need to go. I'll speak to you later.' She snapped the phone shut with a satisfying flick of her wrist and made a mental note to call Di later on.

Hanging up on her mother made her feel much better, even if it was petty. Kate left the room with a smile on her face and her hunger renewed.

Leah was already seated in the restaurant when Kate arrived. She shot an amused look at her friend, who totally had something to tell her.

Kate turned to the server who'd appeared at the table. 'I think I need the spinach and feta omelette with some nine-grain toast, coffee and a tomato juice, please.'

Leah ordered plain oatmeal and dry toast and then studied her fork. Very carefully.

'How about the weather, huh? Whooo, hot today, I heard on the news. My new place has a great view, by the way. The building has a pool. You need to come up to visit and we can gape at boys way too young for us and make up stories about them. You can order them around and they'll stutter. It'll be a hoot.'

'Bitch.'

Kate snorted and sipped her coffee. 'Tell me something I don't know. Like, say, why you are so fascinated in the silverware and have a blush creeping up your neck. Spare me anything but the naked, sweaty details because I won't believe them.'

'You tell me something first,' Leah challenged.

'What, are we in third grade? OK, I just hung up on my mother. How's that?'

Leah jerked her head back, surprised. 'You hung up on Shirley? Wow. Did she ask if you were a lesbian again and start wailing about Diandra and how she'd perverted you to her ways?'

'No. I only heard veiled comments about the Jews and some junkie who let them into my building. I need to hang up on her more often. It was better than a nice run.'

'What isn't better than running? Freak.' Leah poked at her oatmeal and Kate wrinkled her nose.

'While you're working on your cholesterol over there, why don't you spit out the fucking details already. I'm going grey.'

'Oh God, oh God, oh God.' Leah buried her face in her hands so she wouldn't have to look at Kate.

'That good, huh?' Kate didn't sound very sympathetic.

In fact, Leah thought as she braved a glance at her friend,

Kate shone with what they'd always fondly called the 'freshly fucked glow'.

'Nice F.F.G., Kate.'

'I could say the same for you.'

'I didn't fuck him.' Leah's throat closed on the words and she looked around the hotel restaurant to make sure they couldn't possibly be overheard.

'Why not?'

'I . . . didn't want to.'

'What a lame excuse.' Kate stabbed her fork into her omelette and ate a few bites.

'I just didn't want to,' Leah repeated.

'So what did happen? Because I know something did.'

Leah told her everything, how he'd shown up at her door, how she'd told him to go down on her. How he had done it. What she'd told him to do when he got home.

'Do you think he did?'

'I don't know. Oh God, what the hell was I thinking?' Leah wished she'd ordered pancakes so she could drown herself in syrup. 'I have to work with this guy, Kate!'

'I know what you mean. I really do.' Kate sipped her coffee. 'But not forever, at least. And he's not your co-worker.'

'This is just absolutely not the right time for me to be getting involved with someone new,' Leah said.

'Relax. It's not like you have to marry him.' Kate slathered jelly on her toast and bit into it. 'And besides, it sounds like he got off on it. I mean, really got off on it.'

'Yeah, well.' Leah made a sour face. 'I got off on Mike tossing dollar bills on the floor and making me crawl around and pick them up too. The first time.'

'Mike saw *Nine and a Half Weeks* too many times, it sounds like.'

Leah laughed. 'Yeah. Well, I guess I did too. But it's not what I want.'

'Is that what you're afraid of, sweetie?' Kate put down her toast and gave Leah a sympathetic look.

'I won't be like Mike.' The fierceness of her reply startled Leah.

Kate frowned. 'You're not like Mike.'

'But it's like . . . when I told him to get on his knees for me and he did it . . . I felt . . . It felt like . . .'

Kate waited, just listening, not trying to fill the space Leah couldn't fill with the words she couldn't say.

'I felt powerful. But it was more than that.'

Kate smiled. 'There's nothing wrong with that.'

'I'm powerful all day long,' Leah pointed out. 'I don't need to be some uber-bitch in the bedroom, too.'

'Were you being a bitch?'

'I'm sure he thought so.'

'Do you really think he thought that? Did he seem angry?'

'No.' Leah sighed and studied her bowl of unappetising oatmeal. 'But how do I know? I made him go down on me, then I told him to leave. I didn't even give him a handjob.'

'Some guys, believe it or not, get off on that. You told him to go home and jerk off thinking of you, Leah. I bet he did it. And later he's going to tell you all about it. And you're going to love it.'

Leah groaned. They were right back where they'd started. 'Oh God!'

Kate laughed. 'This is good.'

Leah fixed her friend with a mock-glare. 'It's so not good. Dammit, I need pancakes.'

She waved at the server to take the order, then shoved the oatmeal aside. Then she fixed Kate with a steady look. 'And what about you? What's going on with you?'

Kate couldn't say she was shocked at what her friend had told her. Not really. Band Boy got his thing on and Leah finally grabbed hold of what flipped her switch.

Why shouldn't a woman be able to like what she liked without apologising for it? So Leah liked to top Band Boy and make him lick her pussy. Contrary to what Leah thought, or felt she should think, it didn't make a woman a bitch because she liked to take the damned reins in bed. It wasn't Kate's cup of tea but it was clearly Leah's and more power to her. If she'd just accept it and stop fighting it.

Ha! Look who was muttering to herself mentally like a loon. Leah had cornered her about Dix twice already and, from the look in her eye, Kate wasn't going to be able to dodge again.

'What do you want this thing with Dix to be? I mean, if you had your choice.' Leah ate the pancakes she'd exchanged for the oatmeal.

Kate took a deep breath. 'I like him. He's different. He's got the bad-boy thing working but he has a job. He has a life and he's not a loser. I can talk to him. He listens to me, makes me laugh. The sex is phenomenal. If he didn't have an ex-wife who was the biggest, fucking helpless twat ever, if he didn't have kids, if things were different I'd want to be with him. Or at least to explore that direction. But he does have an ex-wife who can't change her own light bulbs and he doesn't seem troubled by that. And I just don't want to talk about it or think about it right now. I can't.'

Leah sighed and nodded, letting it go.

When they dropped some money on the table and headed towards the elevators, Leah touched Kate's arm.

'You know I'm only giving you a temporary pass on this whole thing with Dix. I want to hear everything about the talk you two have.'

'Yeah, yeah. I know. I have another hour and some change before I need to get in and bust some corporate balls so I'll be on my way. Try to save time for me later.' She leaned in close to Leah. 'But if you get a chance to have Band Boy trim your hedges, we can catch up another time.'

17

The rooms were already set up with everything the group needed. Brandon had made sure of everything himself. He'd even called the bagel place to confirm the delivery. He'd never had a problem with their service, but he didn't want today to be the first time.

'You OK?' Melinda, the front-desk clerk, asked. 'You look a little flushed.'

'No, I'm fine.' His tie felt a little too snug around his neck though.

'You sure?' She leaned on the counter to stare at him. Melinda liked to joke that she was Brandon's surrogate mother, since his real mom lived so far away. She brought him hot soup in a Thermos on cold days and had invited him home for dinners more times than he could count. 'You don't look fine. You look like you're going to jump out of your skin if someone hollers boo.'

'Nah.' He took a deep breath but made sure not to be too obvious about it. There was no way he was going to tell his self-appointed surrogate mom that he was a horny bastard just waiting until he could be alone with a woman who probably was only going to tease him again ... or that he half-hoped she would.

'OK, if you say so.' Melinda didn't look convinced. 'I have some Prevent-A-Flu back in the office. Maybe you should take some.'

'I'll drink some orange juice, OK?' He smiled, hoping to

ease her fears that he was about to topple over with some grave disease. With the imminent erection he knew was ready to spring up the moment he saw Leah, there was no chance of toppling.

'You do that. You want to come over for dinner Saturday night or do you have a big date?' Melinda laughed. She knew he hadn't been doing much dating. 'Or do you have to work?'

'I probably have to work.'

'They work you too hard,' she protested. She was more protective than his own mother.

'I need the money,' Brandon said simply.

Melinda tutted but, before she could say more, she had to turn to the man who'd walked up to the desk. 'Hi. Can I help you?'

'I want to talk to him.' The guy jerked his chin towards Brandon.

It was that guy from the bar the night he'd met Leah: Mike, the ex-boyfriend. Brandon stood taller, consciously straightening his shoulders, making himself bigger.

'What can I help you with?' He kept the question carefully neutral, not pretending he didn't know the guy, just not acknowledging him as anything other than a hotel guest.

'You really want to do this here, buddy?'

At the tone of the guy's voice Melinda looked like she might leap over the desk and get between Mike and Brandon and, as much as Brandon appreciated her sentiment, he didn't need a babysitter.

'We can go into my office.'

Mike nodded, hard. Brandon didn't nod and he didn't hurry, and he didn't look over his shoulder to make sure Mike was following. He pushed open his office door and left it open, still without looking, and took a seat at his desk. He tilted back in his chair and gestured at the rickety chair with the bad leg in front of his desk. 'Have a seat.'

Mike stayed standing. 'I want to know how long you've been fucking my girlfriend.'

Brandon didn't blink. 'From what I hear, buddy, she's not your girlfriend any more.'

'She tell you that?'

'It was pretty obvious the other night.'

Mike scowled. He looked like a lawyer but acted like a bully. Brandon didn't like being bullied. He smiled, not to take the sting out of his words but to give them extra.

'How long? Since that night? Or before then? You'd better tell me.'

'Or what?' Brandon set all four legs on the floor with a thump. 'What are you going to do? She doesn't want to be with you any more, man. Have some pride.'

Mike growled. Literally. The sound rose from deep in his chest and surged out from behind clenched teeth. His fists clenched.

It took everything in him, but Brandon didn't rise to the blatant challenge. He smiled instead.

Mike sneered. 'Fucking pussy,' he said.

'Apparently I am,' Brandon said. 'And you're not.'

Mike bared his teeth. 'She can't possibly like you better than me. You don't know what she likes.'

Brandon said nothing.

'Did you get her on her knees yet? Did she suck your cock? That's what she likes, man, can you handle it?' Mike jerked his chin again, his jaw set. 'She likes it when you tie her up and spank her, did she tell you that? Can you give it to her like that? I don't think so.'

Heat flooded him at this rant and Brandon gritted his teeth. 'I think you'd better leave.'

'Or what?' Mike mimicked in a falsetto voice. 'What are you going to do?'

'I can call security and have you escorted out of here, for one thing.' Brandon got to his feet, slowly, immensely satisfied by the way Mike had to tilt his head to look up when he was done.

'Big man.' Mike gave a silent 'Ooh'. 'I'm impressed.'

'She doesn't want to be with you any more,' Brandon said. 'Respect that.'

Mike sneered again, his laugh derisive. 'Respect? That little bitch doesn't need respect. She needs my hand on her ass –'

Mike found himself backed up against the closed office door with a fistful of his shirt in Brandon's hand before he could finish speaking. His words died off with a squeak. Brandon gripped just a little tighter, not quite hard enough to shake him but there was no doubt in either of their minds that he could.

'You'd better leave,' Brandon said. 'Now.'

Mike sputtered and wriggled out of Brandon's grip, but had no place to go. The office was tiny, the door was still closed and Brandon blocked his way. He straightened his shirt and jerked his shoulders back and forth a couple of times.

'Too much of a pussy to even punch me, huh?'

'I'm at work, man.' It seemed like a simple enough reason to Brandon, who had no intention of getting fired over this asshole.

'So?' Mike, as though sensing he could keep pushing, got up in Brandon's face as far as he could, which, considering the height difference, wasn't as much as he probably wanted.

'You're not worth it.'

Mike's eyes narrowed. 'You think you're hot shit, don't you?'

Brandon sighed, bored. 'No. I don't. But I think you are a piece of shit and, if you don't get out of my office, I really will call security to have you removed.'

'You can't give it to her the way I can. Just remember that.' Mike shoved past Brandon, who stepped aside, to yank open the door.

'I'll keep that in mind.'

Mike turned, still not ready to let it go. 'You really are a smart ass, aren't you?'

'No, man. I just can't be bothered with you.' Brandon backed up, hands lifted. 'You've got some sort of agenda and I don't have time for it. I'm at work. She doesn't want you. You should get over it.'

'She doesn't want you, either.' Now Mike sounded sort of desperate and Brandon would have felt bad for him if the guy hadn't already acted like such an asshole.

He wasn't going to play peacemaker with him, either. Brandon knew how it felt to be walked out on, but he'd never gone after Ben Miller, the guy Karen had cheated on him with. He'd wanted to smash the guy's face in, sure, but he hadn't done it. He'd never even confronted Karen about her infidelity.

'That's not any of your business.'

'Anything Leah does is my business. She's mine.'

'Not any more.'

Mike shrunk a little, shoulders sagging. 'I'll get her back.'

'You can try, I guess.' Brandon shrugged, then went back to his desk and sat down. He clicked open a file on the computer, not really paying attention to it but not wanting to give Mike any more of his time either.

'How long? That's all I want to know.'

Brandon sighed and looked at him. 'What difference does it make, really?'

'A huge fucking difference.'

'You want to know if she left you for me, is that it? Will it make you feel better? Or worse. God, man.' Brandon shook his head. 'And you called me a pussy. Grow some balls.'

Mike glowered. 'If I see you with her –'

'Give it a rest,' Brandon said sharply. 'I'll kick your ass and you know it.'

Understanding flooded the room between them, and Brandon groaned inwardly at the alpha-dog posturing crap. Mike's fists clenched, but he made no move towards the desk or out of the door. He opened his mouth as though to speak, then closed it. Opened it again.

'You don't know what she needs.'

'I think I know exactly what she needs,' Brandon said as he thought of the way she moaned his name and how she'd come on his tongue.

Something must have shown on his face because Mike growled again, but kept his distance. Then he slammed open the office door so hard the handle dented the wall, and he stormed out. Brandon waited a minute, thinking Mike might come back, but he didn't.

He stared at his computer, the tension over the confrontation stiff in his neck and shoulders. Nothing about this situation could be good. Leah had broken up with the guy only a couple of days ago and, Mike still had a thing for her. Who was to say she wasn't going to go back to him and was only using Brandon as a convenient way to get off in the meantime? Why should he expect this to be anything else, really, but sex?

Except they hadn't even had sex, really.

He passed a hand over his hair and then tugged at his too-tight tie as he remembered her hand on his crotch, her scent in his nose and her taste in his mouth. She wanted the details. He'd give them to her.

And after that? Well, he'd just have to see what happened.

17

Dix had driven home the night before far too fast and just a little bit recklessly. What the hell had happened between them? One minute she'd been sweet and hot and the next she'd been enraged and shoving him out of the door.

Of course he'd gotten next to no sleep. His skin smelled of her, her taste lay on his fingers, on his lips and he liked it there.

When she'd told him she had taken a job in Philadelphia and had moved, he'd expected to feel panic but instead a sense of warmth had settled over him. It was two hours, but two hours wasn't a seven-hour plane trip. It was drivable on a Friday after work. It was drivable if she met him halfway to have dinner during the week. They could have something real. Build it into something more.

A relationship. Something he'd been sure he'd never have again after his divorce. Something he'd been sure he never wanted again after Eve had wrung him out.

After seven years in the wake of his divorce he'd never once yearned for anyone. It had been Kate who'd appealed to him so strongly. Kate who was the total opposite of his ex. At one time he'd thought he needed a feminine woman who needed to be taken care of. It'd made him feel manly. For a while. Until he realised he was a parent to his kids and his wife. A wife who patently refused to be a full partner in their relationship and what could he say? After seven years and two kids he had no right to demand she be a different person. He'd tried, she hadn't, and in the end he'd walked away. From Eve, not his kids. Never that. Charles Dixon knew his priorities and he was proud of that.

He knew what he was. What he wanted and what he needed.

How could Kate say she didn't know what they had? She was full of shit. That's what it was. The woman was one of the sharpest legal minds he'd ever come across and she was a scared dumbass if she thought he'd just let her keep him at a distance and call the shots.

He wanted her. He would have her. Because she wanted him too. There had to be a story behind her reaction to his wanting to stay over with her. He saw the panic on her face, heard the vehemence in her voice when she'd spoken about the differences between how men and women were allowed to act.

He pulled his car into a spot at the hotel. He had to admit, after a night of going over every moment of the evening before like the obsessive compulsive he was, she was right. To a point.

He could live without sleeping over until the conference ended the next afternoon. Then they'd sleep over. No fucking question about it.

Once inside the hotel he was on a mission. After a brief look around, he came around the corner to catch a glimpse of her standing outside the hotel restaurant. She and Leah stood close, heads bent towards one another, laughing. The two had an easy rapport, a connection easily perceived even from across the room.

He found that interesting. Leah was such a cool, accomplished woman but, when the two of them were together, they both warmed, gave a deeper glimpse of the women behind the business façade. That was the Kate he wanted to know, although the other woman, Katherine, in her business suits and tight but chic chignon, fascinated him as well.

He admired Kate's dedication to her career. Understood keeping walls up between the personal and the professional. He did the same thing, never mixing business with pleasure despite the steady flow of offers from the women he worked with. Hell, Carlina tossed her tits in his face several times a week. But dipping his cock into a hot blonde who worked for him wouldn't be worth the potential complication and he knew it.

Smiling, he leaned against the wall and continued to watch them talk and laugh. It was silly in a way, but he'd been glad he hadn't broken his work rules because now he had Kate and nothing stood in his way but her silly defensiveness.

Finally, Leah headed one way and Kate the other, back towards the business centre. Quietly and single-mindedly, he moved to intercept her.

Not before admiring the way she looked from behind. It wasn't as if her skirt was very short or her clothing tight. No, she wore her tailored navy-blue suit just right. It was her attitude that intrigued him more than just her physical package. Her back held ramrod straight, her steps precise and yet graceful. Whatever it was worked on him in an elemental sense.

As if she'd sensed him, she turned and looked over her shoulder, her eyes widening just a bit as she saw him.

'Katherine, I've got some files for the presentation but I realise I've left them in my car. Would you like them now or shall I bring them in later? Are you on your way to a meeting?'

She hesitated a moment before answering. 'No. I was just on my way to check for some faxes. But it can wait a few minutes.'

He led the way out the side of the hotel and into the parking garage. It wasn't quite eight but the heat already shimmered from the pavement just beyond. It was what his gut felt like suddenly as she walked beside him.

He looked around but the lot was empty. He'd parked his Mustang at the back to avoid any dings and other cars. Come to think of it, what a wise choice. All alone with her out there.

Once he opened the passenger door, they stood behind it, partially screened.

'You look beautiful today.' He stepped close. So close her body heat buffeted him. She didn't move away at all, in fact, she leaned towards him slightly.

She smiled. 'You're full of shit. I'd return the compliment but you know you look handsome. Only a man like you could work the purple shirt with the grey suit and make it look totally suave instead of totally eighties.'

'Well, sure, I know I look handsome. But I'd never complain about a sexy young woman telling me so.' Not complain at all. Hearing her compliments made him want to preen like an idiot. He stepped a bit closer to her, his resolve slipping.

She looked around but realised, as he had, how secluded it was. 'I thought you wanted to talk.'

'I do and we damned well will. Tonight after the meetings are over. Alone in your hotel room. Naked so it's not nearly as easy for you to get mad or run off.'

She raised a single brow at him. 'So this is? What?'

'This? Katherine, darling, I left the files in the car. Look, there on the seat. Terribly unprofessional of me but I had this woman on my mind. The scent of her cunt still in my nose. Mouth watering for a taste again. I forgot everything once I pulled in and knew you were inside.' Not a line at all, but the truth. She made him forget himself.

Her pupils nearly swallowed her irises in the low light of the garage. He was close enough to her that her scent, the sweet spice of her perfume, the simple clean smell of her shampoo and soap blocked out the acrid stench of heated asphalt and melting rubber.

Nothing happened as time stretched between them. They stood, swaying to the music their chemistry made, not touching, as desire hung in the air like sweet smoke.

At last he broke the moment when he couldn't resist touching her any longer. He brought one of his hands up to her waist, then tucked it in between her jacket and her body. Her blouse was cool and smooth as he slid his palm over the curve of her hip, up and across her breast, cupping it through her bra. Her nipple beaded instantly against his palm.

'This is such a bad idea.' Her voice was the merest whisper and held no conviction at all.

It *was* a bad idea. Stupid. Foolhardy even. But he wasn't going to stop. Need for her beat at his senses. The rational part of him knew they were in public but it wasn't being heard by the rest of him who wanted to cover her body with his and fuck her.

'Are you wet?' He kept his voice very low but she heard him.

She nodded without speaking, looking entranced.

'Are you wearing any panties?'

She nodded again. He caught sight of the flutter of her pulse at the base of her neck. Her lips parted and she arched into his hand.

With his other hand, he inched the material of her skirt upwards. He groaned when his fingertips brushed the top of her stocking. The difference between the lace and then the silk of her bare thigh shot to his cock. Under her clothes she wore stockings and expensive lingerie. He loved the seeming contradiction of her, naughty and proper all mixed together like the dirtiest college professor fantasy ever.

That would be a fun game to play sometime. He smiled

inwardly. They would have time for all sorts of games now that she was so close.

'Do you want me to touch your cunt? Put my fingers in it? Play with your clit? Fuck you right out here? Is that what you want?'

Her breath came quickly until she swallowed hard and licked her lips. 'Yes. Yes to all that.'

It was as if Kate watched herself on a movie screen. Standing out in a public parking lot, a man pinching and twisting her nipple through her bra while the other hand, oh Christ, burrowed under her panties and fingered her. Unreal. Wrong and stupid and so ridiculously hot she burned for it.

The breath shot from her lungs over and over and she widened her thighs. He hummed his satisfaction and thrust two fingers deep into her cunt while his thumb played across her slippery, swollen clit.

Good. So fucking good. His hands on her, playing her in a way no other man ever had. Had ever dared to. Charles Dixon knew what she wanted, even if she was afraid to admit it to herself. Which terrified and titillated all at the same time.

She'd grabbed his waistband to keep her feet but realised how close the bounty of his cock was. Making quick work of his zipper, she wrapped her palm around his cock and gave it a pump.

He groaned, flexing his hips. 'Yes. Grip me tighter.' His voice was taut and it made her dizzy as his breath stirred the strand of hair near her ear.

She caught the scent of her body, of her honey, heard the wet sound of his fingers inside her pussy. Higher and higher she went as his thumb worked her clit. She rolled her hips, grinding herself into his hand.

Taking what she wanted from him. What she needed. She smeared the slickness across the head of his cock as he began to seep pre-come. She'd entertained the idea of coming at the same time but quickly rejected it as she teetered on the edge of climax and then fell over.

Her gaze never left his as her cunt convulsed around his fingers, as her breath caught and she tamped down a moan.

A moan that escaped when he brought the hand he'd used on her pussy to his cock, making himself wet with her lube. She watched the stalk of him, glistening with her. Watched and held her breath as a tremor worked through her thighs.

Dix smiled as her mouth made an appetising little 'O' when he wetted himself with her scalding hot juices. He was so close he fished a handkerchief from his pocket.

He wanted her to suck him off. To get on her knees in that parking lot and surround him with her mouth, his hand gripping her hair as he fucked her that way. To know the asphalt dug into her skin but she wouldn't care. All she'd want was his cock in her mouth.

Not today. It was pushing it too far as it was to be doing what they were. But he couldn't stop and he'd never forget the way she looked as her panic and resistance had melted into submission to the pleasure he delivered.

'I wish I was inside you now, your cunt wrapped around me as I drove into you over and over,' he murmured as he fucked her fist.

She licked her lips and he only barely resisted kissing her. If someone saw them it might look suspicious but his back was to the open part of the garage. But if he kissed her, that would be in view of anyone who walked by.

'I wish you were inside me too,' she whispered back.

In retrospect, he dimly registered external sounds but had ignored them as he'd hurtled towards orgasm.

'Mr Dixon?'

Kate jumped back and he quickly tucked himself back in but it was too late. When he turned he faced Carlina, and there was no doubt she knew exactly what was going on.

Shit. Shit and shit again.

Kate moved away from him and he reached out, cuffing her wrist. He didn't want her to leave.

'What is it, Carlina?' he asked like he hadn't been doing anything more than talking. He wished the surprise had deflated his cock. He knew he'd be in serious pain in a few minutes. He'd been about two seconds from coming.

'What the hell is going on here?' Carlina crossed her arms over her chest and glared. 'Who is that?'

Kate shook herself free and moved to grab the files on his seat.

'All this time I make myself available to you and you tell me you don't mix business and personal. You're un-fucking-believable!'

'Carlina, is there a business reason you're here? You're out of line just now.' Dix moved within grabbing distance in case Kate tried to bolt.

'I said, "Who is that?"' Carlina was looking kind of nuts.

'Miss, I suggest you take a deep breath and get hold of yourself.' Kate's voice was cool, detached, professional.

'Oh, you can go to hell! He's only using you to fuck, you know. It's what he does. God knows I've watched it enough over the years.'

This was going bad in a hurry.

'I'm going to leave you to handle this situation. I'll see you inside.' Kate moved to walk away but Carlina stepped in her way.

'I suggest you take yourself over a few steps and let me pass.' Kate had no idea what was going on but she got the gist of it. This little bimbo had it bad for Charles Dixon. Had he been fucking her on the side? There was a lot she didn't know about Dix. She didn't think he'd be involved with a subordinate but he was a highly sexual man. Who knew for sure?

'You think you can just come into town and snag him?'

Ignoring her totally, Kate turned to Dix and raised an eyebrow. 'Charles, you need to handle this.'

Dix exhaled violently. 'Carlina, let Ms Edwards pass and get yourself under control.'

'*This* is Katherine Edwards?' Carlina looked her up and down with a sneer. 'You've got to be kidding me. Dix, what does she have that I don't? Certainly not tits.'

Class perhaps? Self-control? Kate pulled herself short on the last one. Hell, if she had self-control she wouldn't have been standing in a public parking garage with a man's dick in her hand. In any case, just because Kate didn't put them on display and carry them around on a serving tray didn't mean she didn't have any breasts.

She reined herself in. This wasn't high school and she wasn't going to get into some hair-pulling match over some guy.

'You're making a scene,' Kate said calmly. 'What I'm doing here and who I am is none of your concern. Your behaviour, however, when it involves me, is mine. Now you get yourself under control and stop this tantrum immediately or I'll call the police.'

'There's no need for that, right, Carlina? Come on now, this is a silly misunderstanding,' Dix intervened.

Kate sent him a look designed to singe his eyelashes off and stalked straight at the bimbo, who did move aside once it was clear Kate wasn't going to stop.

She went into the building, head swimming with vicious little I-told-you-sos. This was what happened when you made the wrong choices.

If it got out that she ... oh God. Kate inhaled sharply and headed towards the business centre to pick up the faxes. Then she'd look at the files and deal with doing her job. It was all she could do at the moment and it would keep her from obsessing on all the 'what if' scenarios her brain would want to cook up.

18

'Looks like your girlfriend is pissed off. What do you think the bigwigs in town would think if they knew you were fucking a co-worker?' Carlina taunted.

Christ, had she always been so petty?

He ground his teeth to cut off the scathing remark he'd wanted to make. One of them needed to be in control. 'You're being wildly unprofessional and inappropriate. I don't know what your problem is, but I suggest you get it under control immediately. A written notice will be going into your file that you've been reprimanded for unprofessional behaviour. My private activities are none of your business. This is something I've been quite clear to you about over the time you've worked for me. And lastly, but most importantly, don't threaten me.'

'You think I'm just some dumb blonde to be shoved aside at the first sign of pussy?'

Dix wanted to laugh. Yes, he was thinking she was a bimbo but if she had any idea just how much pussy he got she'd probably be even more unhappy than she was at that moment.

Still, what wasn't a laughing matter was her behaviour. It was one thing to be upset and to feel shoved aside, but he'd never acted in anything other than a professional, detached manner with Carlina. Sure he checked out her tits, God knew she shoved them in his face often enough. But he'd been a man long enough to know how to be discreet about that sort of thing.

He certainly couldn't have her working for him after this display. At the same time, he now had to think very carefully about his next steps because of the risks to Kate and his job. Carlina could do damage even though she had no real leg to stand on. And Kate was spooked enough as it was.

'I think you should leave now. Go to work or, better yet, take the day off for some mental health time.' He'd talk with Leah about this situation later on. In the meantime, he'd check up on Carlina's office behaviour and figure out how he'd deal with Kate.

'If you think you can just shove me to the side you're out of your mind, Charles Dixon! If you can't see what you're missing, others sure can. Fuck off.' She turned and stomped to her car, got in and drove away, leaving the stench of burned rubber in her wake.

With a muttered curse, he headed back towards the hotel. And Kate.

'Katherine, may I speak with you for a moment?'

Kate halted, holding the files and faxes against her chest like a shield.

'We've got a session later this morning. I really do need to go over these files and the faxes that've just arrived.' She kept her voice even, despite wanting to kick herself at what she'd allowed in the parking garage.

'That's a good idea. Let's do that. Let's go somewhere quiet then, shall we?' He took her arm and began to steer her towards the elevator.

'There's a small room in the business centre we can use.' She was so not going to let him in her hotel room. They'd end up fucking and she didn't know if she was angry with him or not. She knew she was angry at herself though.

'We're dealing with issues of confidentiality, Katherine. Let's use your room.' He used that 'reasonable man' voice, the legal one. What the hell could she say?

She wanted to growl her annoyance but instead she sighed and shook her arm free discreetly before heading into the elevator.

Once they got inside the room, she held a hand out to ward him off. 'We aren't having sex so don't even think about it.'

'Kate, darling, I'll think about it all I want. I like to think about it. In fact, I think about it all the time. Even when I'm actually having sex with you I think about having sex with you. What can I say? You inspire me.' The arrogant prick tossed himself effortlessly into one of the chairs and smirked at her. 'For the time being though, I think we need to discuss what just happened in the garage.'

'I thought it was women who always wanted to talk things out.' She frowned and sat way out of his reach.

'You're such a smart woman but really, so fucking defensive. You're angry, just say so.'

Her blood pressure shot up ten points. 'Don't. Don't you fucking take that smug male tone with me. You're the one who has some crazy secretary ready to boil my damned bunny.' Not to mention the woman totally needed to do her roots. Kate wanted to ask how much he paid Carlina because she needed a raise to go to the salon more often.

A snicker boiled up but she dug her nails into her palm to keep it inside. She'd share it later with Leah. God, Leah was going to shit her pants when she got wind of that scene downstairs.

Obviously caught off guard, he laughed. 'My apologies for any tone taken. I would really like to discuss why you're angry and what happened down there. Because I care about your perception and feelings.'

'All right, your secretary is unstable and if my intuition is correct – my intuition as an attorney – she's going to be trouble. For both of us most likely. Are you involved with her?'

He grinned. 'Would it bother you if I was?'

She narrowed her eyes and bared her teeth at him.

He put his hands up in surrender, laughing. 'I'm sorry about that. I was teasing. And can you blame me? Kate, you're great fun to tease. No, I'm not involved with her. I don't get personally involved with the people I work with. Never a subordinate.' He paused and looked up at her in a rather fetching manner. The gleam in his eye told her he had something of a sexual manner to say next. 'Although, can I say I have had this rather filthy fantasy about you playing my secretary? I bend you over my desk and fuck you so hard all the stuff falls off the top. Yeah, I've had that one more than a few times. Makes it hard to stand up after I've been at my desk for a while.'

A flush bloomed outwards from her gut. 'Can we please get back on topic?' She wanted to laugh but if she did it would only encourage him. Not that the idea of being bent over his desk while he fucked her from behind wasn't alluring but they had to deal with psycho assistant first.

'Yes. I'd say I was sorry but I'm not. I like you, Kate. I'm attracted to you. I enjoy being with you but I also respect you.'

She crossed her legs, pretending to be prim but really she wanted to squeeze her thighs together to ease the ache. 'Thank you for that. Now, back to your assistant. Have you had problems with her before? You're going to need to note today's incident in her personnel file. Talk to Leah about it. You have to document this accurately and carefully for future reference. If you have problems in the future you want to be able to terminate her without any problems.

Is she vindictive? Has she had problems with other employees in the past? Does she have access to key files and information?'

Dix had been about to tease her again when it hit him. He stood up. 'Fuck, I'm an idiot. She made a comment about ... I need to get to a computer and a phone. I need to see if she's accessing any files she's not supposed to.'

'My laptop is here but you'd be better off in the business centre with faster computers and non-spotty wireless.' They headed for the door. 'Did you at least have her sign the new confidentiality and non-compete stuff I sent over last month?' This could be an even bigger nightmare if he hadn't. Thank God she'd sent them when she had.

'Yes. Everyone in legal did.'

They got off the elevator and headed down the hall to the business centre. 'Excellent. That's one problem down anyway. I'm going to look over all this.' She indicated the files and other papers. 'I'll just be in the next room. Let me know if you need my help.'

19

Leah held her breath when she entered the conference room, but, although there were many people mingling around in it, not one of them was six foot four and still growing with dark silky hair that begged for her fingers to fist inside it. The room itself had been impeccably prepared with a dozen small touches nobody else would have noticed but her: the extra stack of legal pads and container of pens with the hotel logo on the table near the front, the already pulled down screen for the presenters, the extra bowls of hard candies on the tables. Details she hadn't requested yet appreciated.

But no Brandon to thank for them.

Maybe she'd gone overboard last night, she thought as she nodded and greeted men and women whose names she knew, most of whom she'd hired, but had never met in person. Maybe she'd scared him off. Or, more likely, freaked him out.

She knew Kate was right. There were plenty of men who got off on the games she'd played with him the night before. She'd met a few of them. Sissy boys, Mike had always called them, derisive. Mike had never been that good at seeing much beyond the bare black-and-white skeleton of dominance and submission. For him D/S had come straight out of a series of pulpy porn novels and cheesy movies. He'd been very good with the physical aspects of it: the clothing, the equipment, the scenes. But he'd never quite grasped the emotional depths of power exchange that had always so appealed to Leah.

Brandon wasn't a sissy.

Leah busied herself with tidying the already perfectly straight pile of notepads while everyone else got settled. She had to introduce the corporate bigwigs giving this morning's talks and then she was free to go. She needed to check in with the office, make sure nothing had caught fire while she was gone. She'd do that from her room, using the hotel's complimentary wireless connection. She'd have a few hours, uninterrupted, while the morning session went on.

She realised, of course, that she was already plotting how to spend those hours and it wasn't alone.

Her ears burned and she swallowed hard, focusing on her hands performing the useless tasks. He might not even be working today. Or she might not see him. She wasn't going to go looking for him, that was for sure. And he wouldn't know to come to her room unless he came looking for her . . .

He was there when she turned, as she'd known somehow he'd be, like her wishing for him had brought him to her side. 'Leah? Is everything all right for you?'

She didn't dare say his name. It would have come out sounding like a caress and she couldn't have that here and now. Instead, she nodded. 'Yes, thank you.'

Nobody watching them could have guessed what had happened. Not by the distance he kept so carefully between them, or the way she stood, not even leaning towards him. Not even by his smile, which was nothing but professional.

'Maybe I could talk with you about what you want for the afternoon session. In the hall.'

All her fears about him vanished in the thirty seconds it took for him to say that. Leah's insides went straight away to liquid, to heat. To the promise of what was coming.

'Of course.' She turned to Walt Devries, who'd come looking for a pen. 'Walt, could you do me a favour? I have to talk with Mr Long about some arrangements for this afternoon.'

Walt, as usual, looked slightly startled to be spoken to, but nodded. 'Sure thing, dingaling.'

Leah looked at Brandon, who did an admirable job of not laughing. 'Thank you, Walt.'

Walt tipped an imaginary hat and went back to perusing the pens, knocking over the container. Pens rolled across the table and some scattered on to the floor. Leah didn't dare catch Brandon's eye again, just led the way out of the conference room and into the hall.

'Here,' he said, holding open a swinging door that led to a staff corridor.

She could hear the steady thump of machinery and saw a few housekeeping carts lined up along the hall. All the doors were closed. She caught the scent of chlorine. This must be the back route to the gym and pool.

She turned as he let the door swing shut behind them. It had a window in it so anyone could look through. A door down the hall opened and closed as a housekeeper came out with an armful of towels and dumped them on her cart. She then pushed it down the hall away from them without even looking in their direction.

They weren't alone, and somehow that made it all that much better.

She did not ask him to tell her. Asking him would defeat the purpose of having told him to do it in the first place. She waited, silent, her eyes on his face, watching his lips part.

'I was in the shower.' He pitched his voice low. Discreet, which she appreciated. But not ashamed, or nervous, or embarrassed. He didn't lean in to whisper in her ear to force intimacy. He simply spoke. 'The water was really hot. I could still taste you.'

Leah's breath caught in the back of her throat.

'I stopped at the apartment downstairs before I went home.' Brandon moved slightly closer, though not crowding. His dark eyes locked on hers. 'There's a girl there. She wanted me to go to bed with her.'

For an instant, surprise kept her silent, but then she found her voice. 'But you didn't.'

He shook his head slowly. They both leaned against the wall. Perhaps six inches separated their shoulders. If she spread her fingers and he spread his, their hands would touch. Neither of them moved.

'No. I went upstairs instead, and I got in the shower and I made myself come thinking about how you tasted and how much I wanted to be inside you.'

His voice got impossibly lower as he spoke, and stuttered a little at the end, but his eyes never left hers.

'And now?'

'I want it even more,' Brandon said.

'Are you sure about that?' Leah tried not to whisper but it came out that way.

He nodded, solemn and unsmiling. Their fingers inched towards each other but, before they could touch, the door swung open. The woman who burst through it focused immediately on Leah.

'Leah!'

Leah turned, putting on a cool exterior that belied her inner turmoil. 'Carlina.'

Dix's personal assistant, as usual, wore her skirt just a little too short and tight for a professional appearance, but not quite enough to be reprimanded for it. Her blonde hair had been teased high on the crown and left to fall around her shoulders in perfect, smooth strands. Today her usual thick eye make-up looked smudged, and her lipstick had smeared.

'I need to talk to you.'

'All right.' Leah looked at Brandon. 'I'm just finishing here. Can it wait?'

Carlina shook her head so that her hair swung. Leah couldn't help thinking the other woman did it on purpose because she knew exactly how she looked. There was no mistaking the assessing look she gave Brandon. With a sigh she kept locked behind her teeth, Leah gestured to the door. 'I'll be right there.'

Carlina nodded. She shifted her gaze around the hall as though expecting to see someone who wasn't there. She gripped her briefcase with one hand, then shifted it to the other. 'OK.'

She didn't move, and Leah realised the woman wasn't going to. Leah gave Brandon a glance and he smiled a bit, moving away from her without making it seem like he'd been standing too close in the first place.

'I need to talk to you privately,' Carlina broke in. Her voice had gone higher pitched than normal and was more than a little shaky. 'Can we go someplace?'

'Carlina, I don't have a place to talk to you that's more private than here.' Leah wasn't about to take Dix's assistant to her hotel room.

'I'll see you later,' Brandon said quietly, edging away, and caught her gaze again.

She didn't miss the flare in his gaze. Didn't have to guess at what it meant. Leah's stomach hit a place somewhere around her toes before bouncing back up.

Carlina, on the other hand, wasn't satisfied with only a quarter of Leah's attention. 'I'm quitting!'

Leah's gaze snapped away from Brandon to look at the other woman. 'What?'

'I'm quitting.' Carlina looked stubborn and ready to burst into tears at the same time.

'OK, this really isn't a conversation we can have in a hallway.'

Before she could even turn to ask him, Brandon held open the swinging door. 'You can use my office. It's private and I don't need it right now.'

'Thank you,' Leah said. 'Come on, Carlina.'

They followed him down a set of back steps. With Carlina following behind her, Leah admired the view of Brandon's long, long legs and lean hips. He glanced over his shoulder with a smile and caught her looking.

He was already inside her, she thought with a sudden hitch-thump-patter of her heart.

His tiny office made Leah feel very privileged to have the space she had at Allied's corporate headquarters. Brandon's desk had seen better days, his chair needed new upholstery and his computer looked as though it would creak with protest if anyone actually tried to use it. But it was private and, by the way Carlina looked, Leah was going to be glad of the space.

'Thank you,' she told him when he pulled out the chair for her, then the other for Carlina.

'No problem. Can I get you anything? Coffee? Hot tea? Water?'

'Nothing for me.' She actually did crave a cup of hot tea but didn't want to bother with sugar and lemon and all of that with a potential crisis on her hands.

'Nothing,' Carlina said. She hadn't put down the briefcase, which seemed strange. She clutched it to her side, though it had to be an awkward position.

Brandon nodded. 'If you do, I'll be around.'

He ducked out of the office. Leah watched him go. No matter what else was going on, he really was good at his job. Above and beyond the call of duty, even. He knew how to take care of business.

Maybe later, he could take care of her too. But for now, Leah turned with a sigh to face a red-eyed Carlina. 'What's going on?'

20

Dix eased into a chair in the business centre with a heavy sigh. One-handed, he logged in to the Allied network while he held his cell to his ear with the other. Christ on a crutch, what a mess.

'Yes. Carlina Southam. I want to know what she's been accessing on the network,' he said to the IT guy once he'd answered.

As his assistant, Carlina had the ability to view and print virtually anything. He hoped she wouldn't be stupid. But now that he'd thought on her last comment a while longer, he really wondered just what she'd meant by someone who appreciated her.

When the network tech came back online and told him what Carlina had been into just minutes before and what she'd sent to the printer, Dix cursed violently. Exhaling sharply, he ordered her locked out of the network immediately.

He scrubbed his hands over his face. He needed to find Leah and he needed to find her right away.

'What?' Kate looked up when he tapped on the door to the adjoining room where she'd been working.

'Carlina's been in the system recently. Just minutes ago she accessed and printed out our new distribution plan and the contracts with Nationwide and Point Place.'

Kate's eyes widened. 'Interesting. Let's walk and talk.' She gathered her things and they moved towards their cluster of conference rooms. 'She must have run right to the office after she left here. You know this means she's already had someone in mind. I mean, the woman can't be stupid if she survived being your personal assistant, not if you weren't enjoying her company in other ways. So she's not stupid and she's clearly a woman who feels scorned. That equals big problems.'

He winced and she snorted.

'So it's time to circle the wagons. Do you have a copy of her employment contract with the addendum? Get that and also you need to see just what else she's been printing. Check her emails. Freeze her out of the system immediately. At least you've got the non-compete and the confidentiality agreement.'

He held up a stack of papers. 'I had them fax over the addendum with the non-compete and her basic contract. I've printed out the printer logs as well so I have back-up of what Carlina's been up to.'

'Smart. Now to find Leah. I don't want to scare you, but she's going to be hot about this.' She sighed. 'Too bad it's not just you. Then I could be amused at your expense when she knocked your head off and ate it with some salsa on the side.' She indicated a tall dark-haired man he'd seen around the conference. 'Oh there's Band ... er ... Brandon. He's the conference-services manager. He'll probably know where Leah is.'

He'd been about to get her to spill what she'd started to call the conference guy when she caught his attention.

'Brandon, have you seen Leah?' she asked.

'Yes, she's using my office to meet with someone. It looked pretty intense.'

'Let me guess. Blonde? Female?'

Brandon nodded, admirably not showing any lurid interest in the issue. 'Just down that back hall.'

Just then, Kate's cell rang and she looked at the display with a frown. 'That's my office. I need to take this. Come find me if you need my assistance. I think for now it's best I stay out of the immediate situation.'

He agreed. Smart call.

'I'm quitting,' Carlina announced again with a quiver of her lip that didn't seem entirely put on. 'I just thought you should know.'

Considering Leah was the Head of Human Resources for the entire company, that seemed like a smart decision. 'You know you'll need to give two weeks' notice, Carlina.'

'No! No, I don't.' Carlina opened her briefcase and pulled out a sheaf of papers that looked too pristine to be anything other than newly printed. She waved the papers at Leah. 'I have a right of early termination.'

'Let me see that.' Leah took the papers and looked them over. 'You realise you'll forfeit your termination package, including all accumulated vacation hours and bonuses? And that you can't contest this later should you decide to? That means you can't come back and apply for unemployment citing extenuating circumstances or something.'

'Of course I know it! I work for the legal department!' Carlina sniffed.

Leah studied her, wondering what the hell was going on. 'It's very unprofessional to leave without notice. You can't expect to get a good recommendation from me or from Mr Dixon.'

'Oh.' Carlina laughed harshly. 'He'll give me a good recommendation. Not that I need one.'

'You're leaving for another company?'

'I got a new job, yeah.'

Leah sat in silence for a minute, puzzling this through. 'Carlina, I have to ask you. Did something happen?'

Carlina didn't answer at first. Her eyes shifted from side to side and she sniffled loudly. 'Can't a person just quit for no reason?'

Leah didn't have the other woman's file in front of her and couldn't be expected to remember all the details of her employment, but, from what she could remember, Carlina had garnered decent if not exemplary progress reports. Dix had certainly seemed satisfied with her, though Leah had wondered if that had as much to do with Carlina's big chest and blonde hair as her proficiency at her job.

'You've had good progress reports and even got a bonus this last quarter. If something happened to change how you feel about working for Allied, Carlina, it's my job to find out what it is. We don't like to lose valuable employees.' It was a standard mouthful of words Leah didn't really mean, but she had to cover all the bases. If Carlina had a complaint that could come back to haunt them later, Leah needed to document it. It was too bad the world had gotten so litigious, but that was the way things worked.

'Let's just say I got tired of not being valued.' The emphasis on the last word twisted Carlina's mouth into ugliness. 'I'm going to work for a company that values me. That's all. I don't have to explain myself to you. Or anyone!'

'But you do have a non-compete agreement in your contract.' Leah was glad the woman had brought a copy, though Carlina didn't seem pleased Leah had brought up that point.

'Fifty-mile radius from Allied.'

'Any of Allied's offices, I think.' That was their standard contract.

'I'm fine.'

'Can you tell me who –'

'No.' Carlina shook her head. 'And you shouldn't even ask me that. I'm sure it's not legal.'

It wasn't illegal, but Leah conceded. 'Well, if there's nothing I can do to convince you to stay and you won't share with me your specific issues, I guess all I can do is say good luck.'

Relief washed over Carlina's face the way Technicolor washed over Dorothy when she stepped out of her house and into Oz. Leah didn't understand it, but at least the woman wasn't crying or snivelling, or, thank God, threatening some sort of discrimination or harassment lawsuit. Leah had had a few of those over the past couple of years and they were a nightmare, all around.

She stood to stretch her hand across the desk. 'I'll have to prepare the appropriate paperwork, of course, which I won't be able to get to until I'm back in the office, but I'll call Jeanette to make sure she gets the process started. Should we consider this your exit interview?'

'Yes.' Carlina's palm was unpleasantly sweaty in Leah's. 'Sure.'

'You realise once I make the call you won't be allowed back in Allied's building without a security officer, right?'

Carlina's expression closed and her eyes went shifty again. 'I already got all my stuff.'

That wasn't necessarily good. When employees quit or were fired, Leah usually made sure to supervise them cleaning out their offices and had security escort them from the building, a fact Carlina, as a member of the legal department, certainly would have known. Yet there she stood with only a briefcase, not a file box full of purloined sticky notes and extra rolls of tape.

'OK, then.' Leah's smile had nothing to do with her wishing Carlina well and everything to do with the fact this interview was over and she could turn her attention, hopefully, back to Brandon. She glanced at the clock. She wasn't needed for the afternoon session with the bigwigs for another couple of hours.

Pleeeeenty of time.

Without another word, Carlina got up. Her briefcase banged the arm of the chair, then the desk. Before she had time to turn to the door, it opened and banged the chair, which she'd shoved aside. Brandon apologised, stepping out of her way, but the only place for him to go was around the desk next to Leah and even then the space was tight.

Not that she minded, but it was distracting.

Carlina hadn't taken but one step towards the doorway when Dix showed up, leaning against the frame as casually as a man waiting for a bus.

She froze like a deer in the headlights and Dix barely held back a sneer.

'Going somewhere, Ms Southam?' He wanted to laugh at the look of surprise on her face. 'For someone who doesn't want to be thought of as a dumb blonde you're sure working hard to act like one.'

Leah's eyes flew wide for a moment but she hid her confusion quickly.

He stood in the doorway barring Carlina's exit.

'Dix?' Leah asked.

'You can't stop me from leaving. I just quit.' It was actually pretty ballsy of Carlina to stand there and pretend she wasn't holding a case filled with stolen documents.

'Why, I can actually. When you're in possession of stolen property. That is what's in the briefcase, am I right? If I'm not, you'd better produce those papers and right away or I will call the cops.' Dix couldn't believe her nerve.

Leah moved to intervene. 'Cops? What's going on here?'

'Oh, she didn't tell you she'd printed out copies of our new distribution plan and the contracts with Nationwide and Point Place?'

Carlina's heavily lined eyes narrowed on him but he didn't care if she was angry. He'd paid her well, treated her with respect and she'd just tried to fuck him over and for what? Clearly this had been her plan for a while if she had a place to run to when she left. It wasn't just about Kate and what she'd seen in the parking garage.

'It's not very clever to use your own log-in code when you're stealing from a corporation's legal department. It's so easily verified.'

Carlina spewed a very undignified curse as her mouth spread into a flat line of frustrated rage.

'Oh now, sweetheart, don't get all flummoxed. Just admit defeat. Give me the documents and anything you've removed from Allied not belonging to you. That way we can avoid any more drama.' He probably shouldn't have said 'sweetheart' but he'd fallen back to sarcasm to keep from calling her a crazy bitch.

Carlina began to squawk about his not being able to search her without a warrant, as if he were bound by the need for one. Christ. Leah looked pale and the conference guy watched through observant eyes.

Dix's smirk broke and he shifted to stand closer to Carlina. 'Well then, shall we call the police, Ms Southam? I'm sure they'd love to hear all about what you've been up to. They might even care that I'm holding you here until they arrive. Do you like to gamble?'

21

A big part of Brandon's job was knowing when to stay the hell out of the way. Right now was one of those times. Leah and Mr Dixon had confronted that blonde woman in his office and, from then on, everything had started going downhill.

It wasn't the first time he'd been asked to call the police, but, even though he'd started dialling, Dixon had told him to hold off. Apparently they needed to deal with this on their own. That was Brandon's cue to leave.

He checked on the conference space and found nothing out of place. The food had all been delivered and set up without problem and the Allied employees were taking full advantage of it. He made sure there were enough beverages and glasses and that the coffee carafes were full.

Nobody had to point out the importance of the two men and one woman who'd just arrived. He could tell by the low-pitched hum of conversation that preceded them as well as their expensive suits, shoes and accessories. They all carried iPhones and leather cases he guessed cost more than his month's salary.

These must be the big bosses he'd heard Leah say were on their way. He stepped up to them. 'Excuse me? Are you here for the Allied Packaging and Shipping conference?'

The men both turned but it was the woman who answered. 'Yes, we are.'

'Brandon Long.' He offered his hand and she shook it. 'I'm the conference-services manager here. The room for the next session is being prepped right now, but we've got some food and beverages set up for the break.'

'Thank you, Brandon.' The woman squeezed his fingers and gave him an up-and-down glance he didn't miss. 'Bob, Roger, I'm starving. I'm going to grab a bite.'

'I ate on the plane.' Roger patted his ample stomach. 'We need to meet with Leah Griffin and Charles Dixon, son. Any idea where they are?'

'Yes, sir. They're meeting in my office. How about you all help yourselves to something to eat or drink and I'll go get them?'

Roger looked at the spread of cheese, crackers and small pastries. 'Well, OK, maybe just a bite.'

The business centre had a small kitchenette area in a corner where the two halls met to make it easier to set up and break down food and drink service. Brandon filled a spare carafe from the cabinet with hot water from the dispenser and grabbed a mug along with a few Earl Grey tea bags and some packets of sugar. He didn't know how Leah would take her tea, but she didn't impress him as the artificial-sweetener sort.

He knocked on his office door and waited for an answer before he went in. Inside, Dixon was sitting on the edge of the desk glaring at Carlina, while Leah stood with crossed arms in the corner. The silence in the room was enough to deafen him.

'The people you need to see are here,' Brandon said.

Dixon looked up. 'Thanks.' He went back to staring at Carlina, who wasn't saying anything.

Brandon eased past Leah to put the carafe and the mug on the desk. He put the tea bag in the mug and poured the water over it, then handed it to her. She looked at him with an expression of faint surprise.

'I thought you could use this.'

Her expression turned steady and assessing. 'Thank you.'

He smiled at her. 'You're welcome.'

It took her a few seconds, but she smiled back.

'Should I send them down here or tell them you'll be up?' Brandon had no idea what, exactly, was going on, just that none of the three looked happy about it. At least the cops hadn't shown up yet.

'Don't tell them to come here. We need to get this squared away first,' Dixon said sharply.

'Brandon, I need to print some documents from my laptop. Can I use your printer?' Leah's gaze had gone cool and professional again.

'Of course. Absolutely.'

She reached into the pocket of her suit jacket and pulled out a keycard. 'My laptop is in my room on the desk.'

'I'll get it for you.' He took the keycard. Their fingers brushed. It was the wrong time to be thinking about being in her room and what he'd rather be doing there than fetching a computer, but he thought it anyway.

The small flash of interest in her eyes led him to believe she was thinking it too, but Brandon simply took the keycard and left the room. Once in her room, he found the computer, including the case with all the necessary cords that had been shoved on to the floor by the chair, without a problem and returned to his office in less than fifteen minutes.

Now Leah sat at his desk while Carlina remained in the other chair and Dixon had taken a place in the corner. Their conversation hadn't even paused when he came in. Dixon was outlining some sort of list of actions and Carlina was agreeing, sullenly. Leah had an occasional comment.

Brandon didn't need to get in the way. He set up Leah's laptop for her on his desk and plugged in all the cords, making sure the USB cable reached to his ancient printer. It only took a few minutes, but, by the time he'd finished, all three of them were staring at him.

'Let's get on with it,' Carlina said irritably.

'For someone who's in possession of stolen documents with a threat of police involvement hanging over her head, you're pretty demanding,' Dixon said.

Carlina launched into a litany of complaints to which Dixon only laughed and that meant nothing to Brandon. He paid attention only to Leah, who looked over her computer set-up, then at him.

'Thank you,' she said.

There was a wealth of meaning in that simple phrase.

'You're welcome,' he answered.

She met his gaze. From behind them, Carlina let out another string of muttered accusations, each met squarely by Dixon. Leah looked over at them, then back at Brandon.

'We'll need some more time here. Fifteen minutes, at least.'

'I'll come back then.'

She nodded and bent her head over the keyboard, her fingers tap-tapping away. Brandon made himself scarce again, heading upstairs to check once more on the conference facilities. The food had been devoured like a scourge of locusts had gone through it, and he used his walkie-talkie to call down to housekeeping to come and clean up the mess. He looked for the three big bosses and spotted them sitting together in the cluster of armchairs at the far end of the conference area.

Fifteen minutes hadn't yet passed. He didn't know exactly what was happening in his office, only that she'd asked for some time before facing the trio of bosses now sipping coffee and talking so seriously about stuff Brandon knew had to be so boring he'd poke out his eardrums if he had to deal with it for longer than a few minutes.

'Can I bring you anything else? More coffee?' He'd been a waiter during college and the skills had come in unexpectedly handy in conference-services management. 'Hot tea?'

'No thanks.' Bob, the oldest of the three, looked at his watch. 'Listen, what's taking them so long? We need to get this show on the road.'

'Just take us to the office,' Roger said. 'This is ridiculous.'

Brandon glanced at his watch. It was cutting it close, and he didn't owe these people anything. However, he wasn't about to let them into his office if Leah wasn't prepared to handle them.

He didn't have to worry about figuring out a way to keep them there, though, because Leah and Dixon showed up, both looking ready to do battle. Not for the first time, Brandon was glad he'd chosen a career far, far away from the hassles of the corporate battlefield. His job might not have a lot of prestige or a big salary, and he might have to do a bit more bowing and scraping than he liked, but at the end of the day he went home and didn't have to think very much about anything.

'Thank you, Brandon,' Leah said. 'For everything.'

'Anything you need,' Brandon told her and, after a second, she nodded.

It was a promise.

22

Kate took the call with a frown as Dix stalked away with Band Boy.

'Katherine? It's Chandra Pulliam.'

The senior partner who'd been her liaison through the transfer.

'Hi, Chandra. What can I do for you?'

'I received a rather interesting phone call a while ago. A woman told me she'd come upon you and Charles Dixon having sex in a public place this morning.'

Ice slid down Kate's spine. *That fucking bitch.*

'I'm sorry? Did you just say sex in a public place?' All those years as an attorney and she found it wasn't that hard to sound stunned. She was stunned.

'That's what she said.'

'I saw Charles Dixon this morning. I've worked with him rather closely on this issue. He's their legal counsel. I didn't have sex with him this morning.' Which, well, OK was a slight lie depending on your definition of 'sex' and 'with'.

She had no words to express just how pissed off she was at Dix's psycho assistant. She wasn't in trouble. Not per se. But having a senior partner receive a call, even from someone with an obvious angle like that stupid cow Carlina, wasn't a good thing.

'Let me hazard a guess here. Was your caller Carlina Southam by any chance?'

'Yes. You're familiar with her, then I take it?'

'She's Dix's assistant. He and I were in the parking lot earlier today. I'd gone out to retrieve a file he'd left in his car. She approached and went off. She didn't want to let me pass when I tried to leave. Made odd threats. I suppose now I know what she meant. Chandra, I am friendly with Dix, you should know that.'

'Being in a parking garage isn't a crime. And unless you meant retrieving a file as a reference for public sex, I'm not worried.'

Walking a thin line here, she was playing a silly game of words, but Kate wasn't going down for what Carlina thought she saw or, hell, for what happened. Not without a fight. What she'd done was stupid, yes. But the call to her boss by that bimbo was ridiculous.

'No, Chandra, it wasn't a reference. He did have a file in his car and I did retrieve it from him and left him out there with her.' All true.

'Fine then. As for you being friendly, well, look, there's no problem with you having, um, relations with Charles Dixon. You're both adults and you're not technically employed by the same people. But this sort of thing, public sexual activity, you could be arrested, lose your licence to practise here before you even start working. It's not good for the firm.' Chandra paused. 'Now, all the stuff needed to be said has been said. What is going on with this woman anyway? She didn't sound particularly together when she called.'

Kate let go of a bit of her internal tension. Chandra was a good person and had the potential to be a friend. She'd been given a reprieve and there was no way she'd find herself in a compromising situation like that again. She had to keep her head around Charles Dixon and her panties in place.

'I don't think she is. Apparently she made some sort of threat so it's no surprise she called you, I suppose. I've spoken with Dix about this particular employee. I understand she may have attempted to remove documents from Allied's system. There's a meeting right now between Dix, Allied's HR manager and Southam.'

Chandra blew out an obviously disgusted breath. 'An unreliable witness then, isn't she? Damned loosey-goosey system they've got at Allied,' Chandra grumbled into the phone. 'I've got faith in you. But if you're in a room with her, just know where the nearest exit is.'

Sad but true. Contracts attorneys didn't deal with as many insane people as some others did, but Kate agreed Carlina was a potential threat. 'Well, that's why they hired us. They did use the non-compete and confidentiality documents I drew up for them. The woman signed them as well as the whole legal department. I don't know about the rest of the company. This is on the agenda for today. Their out-of-town big power is coming in this morning.' Kate kept her voice low but she did notice when the bigwigs came into the room.

Kate made her goodbyes and quickly finished reading over the papers she'd been sent. She had a feeling she'd be needed soon enough.

Nausea roiled through her as she tried not to think about how stupid she'd been downstairs. She never should have let him touch her much less shove his hand in her panties. And what possessed her to jerk him off out there afterwards? It could have waited but, no, she had to do it out there. In public and look what happened!

It was her own fault and an error in judgement she couldn't afford to repeat. That road meant the loss of her career. She loved what she did and was damned if she'd let her pussy take control because, unless she radically changed her work conditions, her pussy couldn't pay her mortgage.

Kate had managed to get through the papers and to get

herself together by the time Leah came out some moments later, Dix at her side. Leah motioned her over.

'I know you've met via phone and through correspondence but let me do the official introductions here. Katherine Edwards, this is Bob Adams, CEO of Allied, Roger Santiago, CFO, and Lara Conrad, Senior Vice President. Katherine is our of counsel on the matter of the confidentiality and non-compete employment contract issues.' Leah's voice was cool but Kate knew her friend enough to see the strain around her eyes.

She shook hands and demurred a bit when Roger gave her a few compliments. Kate noticed the gaze at her breasts and was glad she wore a suit jacket. It was time to get hard on these people.

'On that topic, we've got a problem.' Dix straightened his tie.

'I'll get Walt started working on the other sessions while we discuss the Carlina situation,' Leah said. She excused herself as Brandon showed them down a long hallway to one of the breakout rooms.

'You can meet in here. It's private. I'll have some beverages sent in momentarily.' Brandon was gone quickly.

Kate moved to the table and pulled her laptop out, readying herself.

'What in the hell is going on, Dix?' Bob asked.

'My assistant resigned this morning.' Dix paused. 'She also helped herself to several confidential production and distribution plans and other related information.'

'She what?' Roger pounded the desk and Kate held in a sigh. The man was a bag of hot air.

'It's handled now. She's returned what she printed and two memory sticks of data. She signed the confidentiality and non-compete clauses three weeks ago. She can go elsewhere, but they can't use whatever she may bring them.

I've made that very clear to her. If anyone uses that data, I'll make it my life's work to make them sorry.' Dix's posture was relaxed but the feral gleam in his eye convinced Kate he was quite serious.

Well now, that was very sexy. An intelligent man who used his strength the way Dix just had made Kate want to fan herself right there at the table.

Leah came back and Brandon was right behind her with carafes of hot coffee and tea and some pastries. He left again after making sure there was nothing else they needed.

Dix had been going back and forth with the bigwigs who continued to dither and not make any real decisions.

At the end of her rope, Kate interrupted. 'Frankly, this conference couldn't have come at a better time. This issue is a time bomb. As I've said multiple times, Bob.' Yes, yes, it was sort of petty to rub it in but he'd given her so much grief over something so simple she couldn't just let it go. For months they'd been stonewalling her at the top, arguing over what were relatively small sums of money for the new contract addendums while paying her hourly fee and wasting her time.

'I take full responsibility for what happened,' Leah said.

Kate turned to her friend. 'Leah, it's not your fault there weren't any protocols in place. She worked the system because she knew she could, and she had an agenda –'

'That's enough, Ms Edwards.' Roger looked stern. 'The fact that an employee almost walked out of here with half a million dollars' worth of packaging secrets is disturbing.'

Oh no, he did not just shush her when she'd been telling this gasbag the same fucking thing for months and months. She turned to him and levelled her best lawyer stare – the one she learned from the federal judge she clerked for – his way. She pushed her glasses up her nose and narrowed her eyes just a bit.

'And I'm saying Leah couldn't have stopped her. Why? Because you had no protocol. If Dix hadn't figured out she'd taken the files in the first place –'

'I should've had her fill out the paperwork anyway,' Leah said.

'None of that paperwork's been approved yet. You can't use something you haven't approved. You can't use a process you haven't approved. That's the whole purpose of this meeting.' Kate stabbed at the file with a finger. 'And that –' she only barely held off calling Blondie bitchface '– employee knew it. She used it to manipulate the system. She signed the confidentiality agreement and attempted to remove material covered under that addendum anyway. A basic sweep of the network when employees separate from the company would be wise as well.'

Dix took a deep breath and held his hands up. 'We'll get the paperwork approved and all these protocols set into place so this doesn't happen again. Thank you, Kate. Your input has been invaluable.'

Did he just dismiss her? He did not, could not be. That would undermine her and toss Leah to the wolves when the three people from corporate were far more to blame for not wanting to spend the time and money to get the new contract addendums in place.

Kate didn't speak to him for long moments, not wanting to say something she'd regret. Instead she stared into Dix's eyes and dared him to dismiss her again.

In the background, the three corporate folks began to discuss the new policy options she'd presented them with. Leah was silent and Kate knew she'd need to talk to her friend about this whole thing later on after they'd quit for the day. If Kate knew her best friend, Leah was busily making herself culpable for Blondie's actions and probably global warming too.

She just kept thinking over all the things on her 'to do' list without breaking her stare at Dix. A great skill she'd learned back as a second-year law student. Didn't look like Dix's skill was as honed as hers. Hah! He shrugged very slightly and broke her gaze.

'Let's get this session going,' Dix said firmly and stood. 'Brandon, is the room ready?'

Band Boy nodded and went into action. The rest of the Allied people got up, still talking. They opened the door and Kate heard people begin to come their way. But Leah remained seated, looking pale and upset. She hadn't finished her tea.

'Leah,' Kate said, so low no one else but Leah could hear, 'are you coming?' She wanted to ask more but she knew Leah would hate to have attention brought to her like that.

She looked into Kate's face with a smile so fake Kate's mother would have been envious. 'Actually, if you'll excuse me, I'm going to go back to my room and check in with the office to make sure everything's under way.' She paused and looked past Kate to Dix. 'I don't need to be here for this session, right?'

'No,' Dixon said.

'No.' Kate moved in close to pick up her things, turning her back to the group near the door. 'Are you OK?'

'I'm fine.' Leave me alone, she added with her eyes. Kate bit her lip and shook her head.

'You and I are going to talk later,' Kate said before standing again and moving back.

Leah felt well enough to roll her eyes at Kate before she gathered her things and left by the door at the other end of the room.

23

Kate snagged Brandon's elbow as he made for the door. 'You are going after her, aren't you?'

Brandon looked at her, remembering how she and Leah had laughed together the night he'd met them. He had guy friends who were close, but he knew he'd never understand what it was like for women to be best girlfriends. 'Should I?'

She nodded and let go of his sleeve. 'I think so.'

He smiled. 'I was going to anyway.'

'Good boy.' Her mouth tilted into a grin. 'Don't let her shut the door in your face.'

'I won't.'

When he reached Leah's floor a few minutes later, he found her standing in front of her door holding a bottle of Coke. Her shoulders had slumped and her brow creased as she rubbed it. When she looked up at him, her expression pained, he hoped she'd smile. She didn't.

'You have my key,' she said.

'I do. Sorry. Let me get that for you.' He pulled the keycard from his pocket and slid it into the lock, then opened the door for her.

She pushed past him without a word and set her computer case on the desk. After a moment, Brandon followed. Gone was the earlier sweet tension and anticipation. He let the door close anyway, less concerned with getting in her pants than making sure she was OK. She didn't look OK.

'Looks like everything's going to work out all right.' He stood in the middle of the room while she stared at him, her arms crossed, without expression.

'I hope so. She could have caused a lot of trouble for the company. Firing trouble,' Leah said in a voice devoid of emotion. 'It could have meant my job. I really screwed up.'

He didn't know what to say to that, or how to make her feel better, or if he should even try.

'This wasn't how you imagined it, huh?' Her laugh twisted her mouth. 'Sorry to disappoint you.'

'It's all right, Leah. I didn't come up here just for that.'

She laughed again, the sound mocking. 'Right. Sure. Then I guess you can just leave now, right? Go on.'

She didn't know him, he reminded himself. An orgasm didn't mean she did. He shook his head. 'Not until I know you're OK.'

'Aren't you a goddamned Boy Scout?' she said and gave him her back.

'Eagle Scout,' he told her to make her laugh, but it didn't work.

She looked over her shoulder at him. He couldn't read her eyes. She twisted the cap off her pop bottle and drank from it, tipping her head back and not looking away from him. He watched her throat work, watched her swipe her tongue along her lips. She acted like she was pissed off.

'Look. If you want me to go, I'll go. I just thought –'

'What?' She put the bottle down and took a couple of steps towards him. 'You'd get to fuck me now? Is that it? You came up here hoping I'd lift my skirt for you again, right?'

He took a step back at the vehemence of her tone, but she'd whipped out a hand to grab his wrist and pull his hand close to her hip.

'Touch me like this, right?' She laughed, low and throaty. 'Like that would fix anything.'

'I'm not trying to fix you,' he said in a low voice, not pulling his hand away because that would be too much like giving her what she seemed to want.

'You're just being nice, right?'

'You make that sound like a bad thing, Leah.'

She dropped his hand from her hip but didn't move away from him. Her throat and cheeks had flushed and her breasts rose and fell rapidly with her breathing. Her eyes were a little glassy, with lust or tears he couldn't be sure and refused to take a chance on figuring the wrong one.

'Your job is to make things work out around here, right? Well, you did that, Brandon. Very well too.'

'Thank you.' Why were they fighting? And she'd said his name, which made him remember once again the taste and smell and feel of her. He didn't back up.

'So now you think you need a reward, is that it?'

At last, annoyed, he advanced a step to stare down in her face. 'It's not about that!'

'No?' she challenged, not retreating. She had to tilt her head to look into his face, but she was right up in it.

'What's so wrong about just being nice to you? Making sure you're all right? Where's the crime in that?' he asked, angry, his own breath coming faster as his hands itched to yank her towards him and bury themselves in her hair.

'I don't need you!' Leah shouted as both of her hands came up to shove his chest.

On instinct, Brandon captured her wrists as she pushed him. Her pulse beat fast there, against his palms. He held her tight so she couldn't get away. She didn't try. Slowly, carefully, he lifted first one of her hands to his mouth, then the other, to kiss each of her fists.

'But you want me,' he said.

* * *

Dix tried not to look at Kate too often during that next session. The set of her mouth spelled trouble. For him most likely.

They'd managed to get Carlina to hand over everything she'd printed and copied from their system. It was over. And it highlighted the need to institute company-wide protocol. Not just exit interviews but better employment contracts.

'This isn't just a plus for the employer, although it certainly is that,' Kate said in her smooth, cool Katherine voice. 'It's also good for the employee because you need to offer them something as an incentive to sign this contract. If you offer them something long term in exchange for their loyalty to Allied and you show them that loyalty, you'll keep your employees longer and you'll lose the ones who are integral to Allied's system far less often.'

By the time they'd finished, she'd bullied and coaxed even the most reticent of the Allied old-timers into finally approving the protocol he and Leah had been pushing for months.

'Let's break for lunch then. The next session will begin in ninety minutes.' Dix tried not to look immediately her way as the meeting ended but failed.

She was already involved in an intense conversation with Roger, who'd tried several times to silence and bully her to absolutely no benefit. She'd just blinked at him for long moments and then moved on to her next point.

Dix moved in close and joined them.

'No thank you. I appreciate the offer, I do. But I've just transferred to the Philadelphia office of the firm. I'll continue on as you need me. Charles here is more than able.' She waved in Dix's direction without looking at him. 'Too many lawyers at Allied would end in murder.' She did look at him and he tried not to wince at the vicious gleam in her eyes. 'You don't need two attorneys on staff anyway. This was a specialised situation and now it's taken care of. Now if you two will excuse me, I have several things I need to attend to.'

Without another look at either one of them, Kate left the room, back ramrod straight.

Kate didn't let go of her emotions until she'd ordered room service. She slipped her iPod into the dock, found the correct playlist and hit PLAY. She probably shouldn't be listening to Peaches during the work day but she was really pissed off.

That scene in the garage wasn't Dix's fault. She was an adult. He hadn't forced her to act that way. No, Kate had wanted it, wanted the thrill of the illicit contact.

Even the crazy assistant wasn't his fault. Not most of it anyway. His reaction though? That was his fault and it really set her teeth on edge.

Mostly, she was mad at herself for allowing things to go as far as they did and they would have concluded with her making him come all over her hand no doubt. During business hours. While she was on the clock at a conference. That was simply not acceptable.

She could have lost her job. Worse, she could have lost the respect of the community of people she dealt with professionally. After all the years she'd spent carefully erecting the wall around her professional life she'd nearly tossed it all away and for what? It wasn't like she couldn't have sex with him in private at another time. She wasn't a thrill junkie. It'd just been flat out stupid and she only had herself to blame.

Kate wished like hell Leah was around to talk to but, from the look on Leah's face when she left the session, she had her own problems. Later Kate would check on her but it looked like Band Boy had that handled at least in the short term and hopefully Leah was riding him like a pony. *Heh.*

Sighing explosively, she went to the door for the food but found Dix out there with the room-service cart, actually making another order. The nerve of the man.

'Oh, Katherine, there you are. I thought we could go over some of the earlier session together. I've just placed a lunch order and I'm told it'll arrive shortly.' He smiled at her, a sparkle in his eye.

'Charles, I was actually taking a work break for a bit.'

He laughed and pushed in with the room-service cart. 'Sorry to make you work, Katherine. But you know what they say.' He sat and watched as the food was laid out on the low table and she signed for it.

Once the hotel guy left she rounded on Dix. 'What the fuck are you doing?'

'Sitting here, looking at a woman I can't wait to be inside of. I'm a bit hungry though. Those conference bagels are like rocks.' He rubbed his flat belly.

'Your humour is unsuccessful.'

'Look, you're pissed about the whole thing in the garage, let's just hash this out.'

He had no idea. He'd summed it all up as being about him. What a tool. 'I'm not interested in operating on your schedule, Charles Dixon!' God she was being pissy. 'And by the way, why the fuck do you call yourself Dix instead of Charles?'

He had the nerve to laugh. 'If your name was Charles and you wanted to be able to touch real live women and see them naked, would you call yourself Charles?'

She rolled her eyes. 'You think you're funny.'

'I am funny. Just admit it like you need to admit you want to fuck and we'll be aces.'

She sat and began to calmly unwrap her food. Calm on the outside anyway.

'For the record, Charles, even if my name was Charles I'd be able to get women naked.' She sniffed. 'I have actually, more than once.' She let that settle into his brain while she began to eat. 'Also? I'm not pissed at the whole thing in the garage. Not at you anyway. I wanted what we did. It brought me a great deal of pleasure. I'm not some fifteen year old who can't face her own desires, thank you very much.' She took a rather savage bite of her salad and levelled a glare his way.

'We'll be coming back to that first comment so don't think you can just toss off stuff like that. If you're not angry because I fingered you to climax out there, what is your problem?'

She took a deep breath. 'You're such a prick sometimes. My problem is manifold. Firstly, your fucked-up psycho secretary shows up and catches me with my hand in your boxers. While I'm supposed to be working. Then she flips out because she has wet panties for you and you haven't fulfilled her getting-fucked-by-the-boss fantasies. Then she calls *my* boss, yes, that's right, she called my boss here in Philadelphia and levelled accusations of unprofessional public conduct towards me. Thankfully, the fact that your fluff-brained psycho assistant stole from you actually puts me in a much better light.'

'Fuck. I'm sorry, Kate. I know how important it is to you to be professional. I can see why you're angry.'

She put her head in her hands a moment, striving for calm. 'As you put it so succinctly, it is important to me to be professional. And I wasn't.' Taking a risk, she looked up to find him narrowing his eyes at her suspiciously. 'Look, this thing between us has gone too far. I've broken rules and it's gotten me in a bad place. Something like this erodes respect for me, even from you.' She didn't want to eat, what she'd already eaten lay in her gut like lead. Her words fell from her mouth and even she didn't believe most of what she'd said.

He leaned forwards quickly and took her hands. 'Fuck that. I know what you're doing, Kate, and I'm not playing. We can keep our hands off each other while at work, I agree. I'm sorry. I really am. You know I never meant for you to suffer any negative consequences from our involvement. The thing in the garage was risky. Hot, but risky. I get that. We'll be careful from this point on. But this bit about me not respecting you? What the hell is that all about?'

'You dismissed me downstairs in front of the Allied people. You dismissed me with your bitch-faced skanky assistant. You can't fuck me and dismiss me. People don't dismiss me, Charles.'

Admittedly, it filled her with glee to watch him flinch when she called him Charles. Petty though it was.

'Well, well, well. There she is. The real woman beneath the polish.'

'Don't you fucking condescend to me. I'm a real woman all the time. Just because I don't shove my tits in my boss's face while at work doesn't mean I'm not a woman.'

'You're right. Of course you are. But you know what I meant, darling.' He slowly raised a brow at her.

Before he could dig himself in any deeper, room service knocked, announcing the arrival of his food.

24

God help him, Dix had never wanted to shove his cock into a woman as badly as he did right then. Katherine Edwards was magnificent in her fury and, when she got all remote and nasty, it only made her hotter. He probably needed therapy to uncover the roots of that particular attraction, but he preferred to revel in it.

Not that he'd ever compare her to his ex out loud or anything – he preferred his balls intact – but Eve had been so passive, so needy and without passion. Dix knew without a doubt why Katherine Edwards had interested him from day one. She was fiery, intelligent, independent and the total opposite of passive. She challenged him in a way he'd never been challenged by a woman before.

He settled in next to her instead of across from her like he'd been before. She was putting up a less than enthusiastic battle to push him away and he had no intention of letting her.

'So, revisiting the dismissal thing. When did I dismiss you exactly?'

'First in the garage with psycho blonde. I blew it off then as you needing to deal with how insane she was at the time. And then you did it again with the higher-ups. Oh, thank you for your valuable input.' She imitated his accent perfectly, right down to the mix of Boston and Central Pennsylvania.

He exhaled. Put that way, he had. 'I can see how you took it that way. It certainly sounds that way. But, Kate, I've told you before, I respect you. I was mediating, trying to keep things even because in the garage I knew you were upset and, frankly, I hadn't seen the crazy side to Carlina before and I was concerned at how quickly the situation was deteriorating. And with Roger and his idiot posse, it was about keeping things moving. Like we'd accepted the proposals you'd made and were moving on. If not, Bob wanders around and gets off task. I apologise if I made you feel dismissed.'

He turned to her and drew a fingertip down the line of her jaw.

'You're so full of shit. It's bad for me. I need a nice, uncomplicated man I can manage.' Her voice was quiet.

'Now who's full of shit? The last thing you need is a man you can manage, Kate. You need a man who's your equal. You'd be bored in ten minutes with a man you could push around. That's why you had no one regular until I came along and don't try to deny it. I'm going to stop playing anything other than sex games with you. Speaking the truth, Katherine, my love? I want you. You want me. You may wish you wanted some pushover, but you don't. You like it that I push back. I'm not going away. We're not over. In fact, I'm telling you right now, we're on. We're together and that's that.'

Her eyes widened even as he marvelled at the softness of her skin.

'You're insufferable.' But she didn't pull away from his touch. Her pulse beat steady against his thumb as he stroked over it.

'I'm good in bed, it helps you overlook my flaws.'

Ah, the corner of her mouth twitched. He loved that she didn't flip out and thrive on drama. She took responsibility for their little thing in the garage, didn't accuse him of being her seducer. She didn't cry or throw a tantrum either.

'Christ, I'm so fucking hot for you it's not funny.' He cupped her chin and brushed his lips across hers.

'Why?' she asked, frustration clear in her voice.

He moved to his knees in front of her. 'Because, Katherine, you're everything I never knew I'd want in a woman but find myself unable to live without.'

She blinked quickly, clearly befuddled by his declaration. For some reason, he found it endearing.

'We have to get back downstairs.' She slid the pad of her thumb over his bottom lip.

'There's still much left to be said. Namely we need to speak in detail about what's between us. About our relationship.' He smiled when she snorted softly. 'Tonight after the session is over. Right now I need to get to the office to be sure Carlina hasn't absconded with anything else. Don't run on me, Kate.'

'I'm not running. I'm just not convinced we have room for anything more than fun in bed every once in a while in our lives.'

He waved a hand dismissively. 'We are going to eat, I'm going to fill you in on the Carlina situation and then I'm heading out to the office. You want to come with me? Get a tour?'

'I need to check on Leah and then I have a session to run downstairs for the various department heads. I thought you had to be there as well.'

'You can give me a private session later. I'm sure the people downstairs will understand why I need to go put out this fire.' Sitting back on the couch next to her, he tore into his lunch and watched as she ate, making notes to herself.

'You have to be sure Leah doesn't take the fall for this bullshit with psycho girl. Got me? This is so not her fault it's not even funny and, if I hear she's being sacrificed because those bloated assholes at the top can't be caught out, I'll make everyone's life a living hell. With fire and brimstone and stuff. It won't be pretty.'

The prim way she'd levelled such a threat amused him. Still, he had no doubt she'd follow through if necessary. 'You and Leah go way back?'

'Since middle school. But it's more than that. Look, if she were culpable I'd be less concerned but she's not.'

'You want to give me background?'

She made a sour face. 'On what? Leah is the HR person. She's limited to whatever your internal processes are. Since you and I both have been arguing with corporate for months now to put one in place I don't think it's smart to make her liable for something she couldn't have prevented. Even with the processes in place it couldn't have stopped what happened today. Your assistant has wet panties for you and she's sort of nuts too. More than that, it's pretty clear she had an escape plan to run with the docs. A non-compete stops her from using the info but, hell, you can't stop access to all employees because she's crazy.'

'I get that and I agree. I've never done anything to lead Carlina on, Kate. I need you to know that. What's between you and me, that's different.'

She cocked her head at him. 'I don't think you're a predatory slimeball, Charles.'

'Stop it with the Charles.' He nearly growled.

She laughed and he realised she enjoyed needling him as much as he loved to do the same to her.

'I could call you Dick.'

'That's Richard. So clearly something is up with Leah to make you concerned. You want to share it with me?'

'No. There's nothing up with Leah. She's a friend and I'm protective of her, especially when I can see she feels bad for something that's not her fault. Just don't make me get medieval on your ass so to speak.'

'Fine, fine. Since we're together and all, why don't you tell me more about yourself?' He said it to needle her for his amusement but there was no denying he wanted to know more about her.

'Together as in the same room?'

'If you like. But we both know exactly what I meant.'

'We don't have time for this right now. I have to get moving soon and, if you go poking around, God knows what you might find.'

'Like what? Come on, Kate, shock me.'

'I don't want to play twenty personal questions with you. I already know you've got a line of broken-hearted secretaries in your wake.'

Dix snorted a laugh. 'Is that the best you've got? Oh I know! Do you want children?' He raised his eyebrows at her, proud of himself.

'In general or right now? And what about you? Do you want more kids? I mean you're still young. I imagine you'll find yourself another wife sometime. She'll be young and her skin will be firm and her breasts will be high and perky. Shame to mar them with breastfeeding.'

Kate needed to stop herself. This was heading into a place too raw for the both of them.

'I know your game, you know. You get nasty when you're backed into a corner. But what you don't know is how fucking hot I find it when you get nasty.'

'You find everything hot.' She crossed her arms across her chest.

'No I don't. But where you're concerned, probably ninety-eight per cent, yes. So, do you want to have children? My two are very good kids, I'm fortunate. Eve has done most of it. I've worked a lot.'

She didn't want to be charmed by the way he'd just lit up when he discussed his daughters but she was.

'In the future I imagine I will want children, yes.'

She did but she knew herself well enough by this point to

know she wasn't ready just yet. Apart from the basic you'll-never-be-ready stuff, she was old school about it. Anyway, she didn't even have a husband so kids were a ways off.

'In the future I can imagine marrying again and having more kids. I wouldn't want my girls to feel like I've moved on, I see a lot of that at work with the older kids from the first marriage feeling abandoned.' He looked her up and down slowly, his gaze like a physical thing.

She stood, annoyed with him but unfairly so. She didn't want to be that oversensitive woman who barked at her boyfriend over every little thing. Boyfriend? Lover. Yes, he was her lover. Women her age didn't have boyfriends and, if they did, she was pretty sure what they were didn't classify him as a boyfriend. Right?

'Why are you angry?' He moved to stand before her, leaning in to kiss her.

'I'm not angry. I don't want to talk about it now. I have to get downstairs.'

'I have meetings of my own in addition to the sessions here. Why don't you come to my house for dinner tonight? Seven? It's far enough away no one will notice. Take a cab over. I'll bring you back here or you can take a cab back, whatever you like. I won't expect you to stay over tonight. We need to talk and it's hard here.'

She wavered. Really she knew she'd already taken that step and admitted they were, well, something to each other. Just what remained to be seen. And what they could do and be to each other while she still maintained her professional distance. And stuff. Maybe.

'All right. I'll either borrow Leah's car or cab over.'

He grinned in a way that told her he'd never doubted she'd accept.

25

As Leah looked at Brandon, something broke open inside her.

She did want him. On his knees, on top of her, behind her, beneath her. Inside her. Leah's breath rasped as Brandon's mouth lingered on her fingertips. She was no longer clenching her fists.

He was bigger and stronger, and his hands locked on her wrists would have been difficult to break from had he intended to keep her prisoner. He let her break his grasp though, without flinching, though he couldn't have known if she meant to hit him again. She slid her hands up his broad, muscled chest and into the hair at the back of his neck.

He bent easily enough when she pulled him down, his hands going around her. Cradling, not caging. Leah brought Brandon's mouth to hers. She wanted to feel his mouth on her mouth. She wanted to taste him.

He stepped her back against the wall. The rough swirls of plaster poked her shoulder blades through her shirt, but Leah didn't care. Those big hands slid down to cup her ass. Then the left slid further, along the back of her thigh, to hook under her knee and raise her leg. Her skirt caught and Brandon used his other hand to push it higher.

His tongue stroked hers gently, but firmly. He was as skilled kissing her mouth as he'd been making her come with that tongue. He slanted his head to kiss her from a different angle, and the shift urged a small moan from her. He stopped at the sound and pulled back a little to look into her eyes.

'Take off my panties,' Leah whispered in a hoarse voice.

Without looking away from her, Brandon shifted his hands to slide beneath her skirt. His fingers hooked into the sides of the lace, but instead of pulling them down slowly, or even fast the way he'd done before, he yanked the flimsy material. Her entire body moved as the fabric held, then tore with a loud purr, drowned out by Leah's gasp.

The cool air on her hot skin urged out another breath from her. He was still staring down into her eyes, his expression dead serious. Lace fluttered against her legs as her panties fell to the floor in scraps she didn't look at. Now his bare palms skated up her bare thighs and around to her bare ass. At the feeling of his trousers against her bare cunt, Leah bit her lower lip.

'Touch me.'

His hand slid between them and she arched into the touch. Her hair snagged on the same rough plaster swirls and Leah reached up to yank it out of the twist she'd secured with hairpins. It tumbled down over her shoulders and face.

With her hair down, she always felt more sensual. The way the strands tickled her cheeks or the back of her neck or, if she was naked, her bare back, enhanced her desire. Pulling her hair down was a trigger for her, one she shamelessly used now though the way he was touching her meant she didn't need to trick her body into arousal.

His thumb unerringly found her clitoris and circled a moment before sliding lower. She was already slick, knew it without having to touch herself. Knew it by the way his eyes went a little wider when he touched her there, and how his mouth parted. Leah pushed herself against his hand, firm and urgent.

'Put your fingers inside me,' she told him. He did. 'Tell me how that feels.'

'Hot. Wet.'

She watched his throat work as he swallowed.

'Imagine it's your cock inside me.'

He groaned.

'Would you like that?' The question had only one right answer.

'Yes.' He leaned forwards but she turned her face so his mouth didn't reach hers, and he got it right away. He stopped his lips from touching her skin, just barely.

Power, sweet and heady, thrilled through her. He was picking up on all her cues. He could choose not to answer her. He could choose to walk away. He could even choose to ignore the unspoken rules she was laying out, but he wasn't, and knowing that whatever was happening between them was his choice, not something she was forcing on him, was so incredibly hot she was ready to come right then.

He shuddered against her. His hands moved under her ass and he lifted her, not so fast she couldn't react but without hesitation. He kissed her, hard, as she wrapped her legs around his waist.

'Bed,' she ordered between scorching kisses and tapped his shoulder to point him in the right direction.

She thought for sure he'd stumble or have to put her down before they got across the suite's living area and into the bedroom, but he was strong. His arms corded with effort and she had to do her share of clinging to him, but they made it. They had to stop kissing when he lowered her to the bed though.

'Sorry,' he murmured as the landing was a little harder than he probably assumed she wanted.

Leah grabbed the knot of his tie and held him in place until he looked into her eyes. He put a hand on either side of her to keep himself from crushing her. 'All I ask is your best effort,' she said, her voice rough but calm and straightforward. Honest. 'I'm asking you to fuck me, not choreograph a ballet. There are going to be missteps. I hope we get a little messy.'

His smile lit his face. 'Messy, I can do.'

This was going to be so much more fun than she'd even thought. Leah scooted back on to the bed, but when he made to follow, she put her foot, still in its black pump, on to his chest. His hand came up automatically to her ankle, but she didn't press her heel into his skin and he didn't try to knock her away.

'Stand up,' she said. 'Take off your tie. Then your shirt. I want to look at you.'

He looked a little sheepish, but he stood and loosened his tie. He tossed it on to the bed, then thumbed open the buttons of his shirt and let it hang open over a chest and abs that were as delicious as she'd hoped. He pulled the shirt off without turning the sleeves inside out and hung it neatly on the back of the chair.

'You take care of your things,' she noted.

Brandon paused, a hand on his belly, fingers splayed. 'Shouldn't I?'

'Some men don't.'

His hand moved in a small, hypnotising circle over the tight lines of his stomach. She watched the motion, thinking of how his skin would smell and taste, and of how he would sound if she buried her face in the patch of hair just below his belly button and leading to his crotch.

Something flickered in his gaze. 'I'm not some men.'

'You certainly aren't. Take off your pants.'

For an instant she thought he might balk at this step-by-step instruction, but Brandon only smiled. He went for his socks first, though, which wasn't what she'd told him to do but showed he was paying attention. A man in socks and underwear couldn't help looking ridiculous. In bare feet, he tugged his belt open, unzipped and stepped out of his dark trousers. He wore a pair of dark boxer briefs. And he did look fine.

'You fill those out very nicely,' Leah said, hoping to see him blush again.

He did, just a little, but didn't look away from her. 'Thanks.'

She got off the bed and walked around to him. She breathed in slow, languorous sips as she moved around him in a circle, one hand on his shoulder to act as her pivot point. When she let her fingers trail across his shoulder blades and down the other arm, his skin pricked into gooseflesh beneath her touch.

'You have a gorgeous body.' She wasn't trying to flatter him. It was the truth. 'You take care of yourself, too.'

His low laugh and the way he ducked his head endeared him to her. 'I try.'

What did she want? A smorgasbord of possibilities spread out in her mind, limited only by what she was willing to ask for. To demand, she thought with a secret smile, which he saw.

'Are you sure this is what you want?' He made a bracelet of his fingers for her wrist.

She didn't know how much she appreciated the question until she gave him the answer. 'Yes. I'm sure. Are you?'

He nodded, solemn.

'What do you want, baby?' The words slipped from her lips, slippery, like pulling beads on a string. She moved closer, very aware of how she was still dressed and he was mostly not. She reached to stroke her hand down the front of his briefs, the fabric soft but what lay beneath most definitely not. 'I want to hear you say it.'

'I want to be inside you.'

She shook her head slightly.

Brandon swallowed again. His gaze flared. The hint of a smile tugged that sweet mouth up, but he didn't give in. 'I want my dick inside you.'

'Dick is an ugly word,' she said and put his hand between her legs. 'Say, "I want my cock inside your cunt."'

He drew in a breath and let it out. She arched again into the magic his fingers were making between her legs. He bent his head to hers. Their cheeks touched, making heat. Maybe he was blushing. Maybe she was. His mouth found the curve of her ear.

'I want to put my cock in your cunt, Leah.' His voice snagged on the word, but not on her name. He nuzzled her lobe, then lower. She shivered. 'Please.'

She opened her mouth to speak but moaned, instead. Her arms wound tighter around his neck, holding him to her. 'God, yes. I want you to fuck me, Brandon,' she whispered, not believing the words spilling from her but unwilling to stop them.

This time when he pushed her on to the bed it was rougher but at the same time more graceful, one hand behind her head to keep her from falling. He moved over her, his mouth seeking hers. He captured her lips in a hard kiss, perfect, forcing her mouth to open for his tongue.

'Take off my shirt,' she whispered against his mouth, her fingers roaming his sides and over his ass.

Brandon sat up, straddling her. The bed dipped low on either side under his knees. His hands went to the buttons on her blouse and he opened the top two slowly. He bent his face to inhale her as he eased the buttons from the slots, then kissed each inch of exposed flesh as he pulled the fabric aside.

She wore a lacy bra that matched her panties, and with each breath her breasts threatened to surge free of the cups.

Brandon kissed each one, then sat up again to help her arms out of the sleeves. He was as careful with her shirt as he'd been with his, folding it and setting it to one side.

'My skirt.'

He slid a hand beneath her to tug at the zipper and she lifted her hips to help him. When he pulled the fabric over her hips, his hands were shaking. When she lay, naked but for her bra and her elastic-topped stockings, he looked over her body, then at her face.

'Touch me,' she urged, almost unbearably aroused that he was waiting for her to give him permission.

Leah spread her legs as much as she could with him on top of her. She thought he would go right for her pussy; she hadn't been specific, after all, and she already knew he understood how much she liked his mouth there. He surprised her.

Brandon moved off her to kneel on the bed at her feet. He put his hands on her ankles, cupping them loosely, then moving up over her calves. Her thighs. Her hips. His fingers spread, palm flat, he smoothed over her belly and up her sides, over her breasts, to the dip of her collarbone and across her shoulders, then down her arms to end with his hands in hers.

The action had put him in an awkward position, one knee between her thighs and the other to the side. He leaned over her. She tightened her fingers in his.

'Kiss me.'

He did, without letting go of her hands.

In a smooth motion, Leah reversed them. She pushed upwards against his hands as she rolled, careful not to catch him in a tender place with her knee. She ended up on top of him. His cock throbbed through the soft cloth of his briefs against her bare pussy. Her thighs gripped his hips. Her hair fell forwards, shielding them both from seeing anything but each other's face as she leaned to kiss him again.

They were still holding hands.

She was on the pill and had never missed one, but she was also not stupid. She'd picked up the package of condoms from the hotel gift shop earlier that day. It was better to have them and not need them than to need them and not have them . . . though no small part of her had known she would need them.

'I'm going to get up.' She looked into his eyes. 'I want you to be naked when I get back.'

His smile slayed her, utterly, so sweet and sexy and guileless and completely genuine. Band camp, her ass. This was the smile of a man who knew exactly what he was doing and how it affected her.

'Yes, ma'am.'

Her fingers squeezed his, hard, at his words.

'Do you like that?' he asked, his gaze searching hers. He tugged her a little closer so she had to let him support her weight with their linked hands or lurch forwards. She let him support her. 'You like me calling you that?'

She wasn't sure she wanted to like it, but there was no denying that she did.

Brandon's smile straightened a bit but didn't go away entirely. He lifted his face closer to hers, not quite kissing her but letting her kiss him if she wanted. His breath brushed her mouth. 'I like the way your skin flushes when you're turned on.'

'Do you?' She didn't kiss him, not quite.

The heat of his erection pressed between her legs. He pushed a little closer to her mouth but still didn't take the last fraction of an inch. 'Yes.'

She traced his upper lip with her tongue, then his lower, then sat up. He fell back, smiling. Leah got off him and went to the dresser where she'd stashed her make-up bag and the box inside. She pulled the package free. When she turned, he'd shucked his briefs and lay with his hands behind his head.

For an instant she envied him and that male comfort with his body, but then remembered she wore only a bra and stay-up stockings and hadn't even worried about the size of her ass or hips or tits. He had done that for her. Made her not think it mattered. Or maybe she'd done it for herself.

Now she let herself savour the sight of him. Long, long legs, long torso. He was smooth, with a few dark hairs on his chest around the nipples she wanted to suck and bite. He trimmed his pubic hair but didn't shave it, and she was glad. He was young enough. She didn't want to feel like she was fucking a schoolboy.

He watched her watching him and said nothing. His cock spoke for him, getting thicker as she watched. She'd like to put it in her mouth later. She'd like to hear him cry out her name.

'Should I be concerned you weren't going to ask about this?' She tapped the foil square in his palm.

'How do you know I wasn't going to?'

'Were you?'

He hesitated. 'I would have remembered.'

She laughed and shook a scolding finger. 'Don't tell me you're not a safe-sex kind of guy.'

'I've sort of been a no-sex kind of guy lately.'

Leah had one knee on the bed when he said that and paused in crawling towards him. Brandon took his hands from behind his head and sat, one impossibly long leg bent. She moved closer.

'Really,' she said, not making it a question. She believed him.

'Yeah. Um ... bad break-up,' he said by way of explanation.

'So you've been celibate?'

She pushed him back on to the pillows and straddled him, his cock thrust upwards between them. She stroked it as she spoke, watching his face but relishing the feeling of smooth hot skin under her palm.

'I didn't try to be, it just happened that ... way ...'

'Despite your downstairs neighbour who wants you to go to bed with her?'

He groaned, pushing upwards into her hand. 'I didn't want to sleep with her.'

Leah smiled as she pulled the condom from the package and smoothed it down over his delicious prick. 'Why not?'

'Because I wanted to be with you,' Brandon said through clenched teeth.

'Well,' she said with a sigh as she raised her body high enough so she could lower herself on to his erection, 'now you are.'

26

Leah hadn't forgotten the time-stopping magic of two bodies joining for the first time, but it had been a long time since she'd felt it. Her eyes fluttered closed at the sheer assault of pleasure as he filled her. When his hands moved to her hips, she opened them to look into his eyes.

He was looking into hers.

For one sparse second tension speared her. What on earth was she doing, fucking a near-stranger? One with whom she still needed to work for one more day?

When he thrust slowly, experimentally, the thoughts didn't disappear ... but they did get shoved away. Brandon's fingers tightened on her hips as he pushed deeper inside her. His cock was long and thick and lovely, and it filled her so completely she bit her lower lip against a moan.

Leah put both her hands on Brandon's chest. The flesh beneath her palms was warm. Smooth. She skidded them over his nipples, those twin dark discs she'd already fantasised about sucking. When her fingernails scraped the sensitive skin and he drew in a sharp breath as he thrust upwards, she smiled. She pinched them both, but not too hard.

Brandon let out another breath, his brow furrowing, but after a second he closed his eyes. His head tipped back into the pillow's cradling softness.

Leah circled her hips as she pushed with her hands to lift her body a couple of inches. She bent her elbows and let her breasts brush his chest. Her nipples, taut and aching already, teased his, and he opened his eyes. He licked his mouth, but his hands never left her hips and he didn't stop his slow sweet thrusts.

Leah had never been a fan of nipple play for herself. She didn't like them sucked or tweaked or, God forbid, clamped. Now, however, as she moved her breasts teasingly over Brandon's chest, the sensitivity in her nipples that had always kept her from enjoying too much stimulation didn't seem as overpowering. Each light touch sent a shiver through her. Her lips parted so she could sip in the air.

She pushed upwards again and pinched his nipples, watching the way his jaw clenched when she did. 'Do you like that?'

'Yes.'

Brandon's cock slid impossibly deeper inside her, and Leah wondered if he'd known he liked it before she did it. She wasn't the first woman he'd ever fucked or gone down on, not unless he was the boy genius of cunnilingus. No, he'd had experience. But despite his reaction to everything she'd asked of him so far, Leah doubted he'd ever played the sort of games she had been toying with her entire sexual life.

She loved this slow fucking, the absence of frantic thrusts, the pressured rubbing and stroking. Brandon's fingers tensed and relaxed on her hips as he thrust inside her, his cock-head hitting her G-spot each time until a liquid heat built inside her.

Brandon had snagged his lower lip with his teeth in concentration. Sweat gleamed on his upper lip and along his hairline, but he wasn't moving faster.

It could have been too intense, their slow and silent fucking, but Brandon's smile gave Leah permission to tip her head back and let out a deep throaty laugh. When she looked back at his face, his smile had grown a little bemused, but hadn't disappeared.

'You have a sexy laugh.' His voice was a little rougher than usual, a little deeper, a little lower. A little out of breath.

Hearing this evidence of his arousal, Leah settled herself firmly on his prick and stopped moving. She clamped her knees tight against him and laid her hands flat on his chest, her palms covering his deliciously sensitive nipples.

'You're not going to ask me why I laughed?'

She watched his tongue slide out to stroke along that luscious lower lip.

'I assumed it was because you were happy.'

Such a simple answer, which caused such an uprush of emotion in her.

'Is that why you think I'm with you right now?' she murmured, rocking on him but not moving enough to give him room to thrust. 'Because you make me happy?'

Now his hands left her hips and travelled up to caress her breasts, palming the nipples but not tweaking them. 'It wouldn't be a bad reason, would it?'

'No, Brandon,' Leah said as her back arched when he touched her. 'It most definitely would not.'

'Good,' he said and slid one hand down between them to anchor his thumb against her clit.

She drew in a breath at the direct pressure there, but she didn't start moving again. He was still achingly hard inside her, the head of his prick nudging her cervix. So far he'd only gently thrust; if he really let go and pounded into her Leah imagined, with regret, she might be wincing instead of writhing. She knew her body's limits well, but he didn't. She might want him to fuck her fiercely, but she didn't want to walk bow-legged the next day.

But he was still beneath her, his thumb pressing as slowly and exquisitely as he'd thrust his cock into her before. He was clearly patient. He was giving her control.

Leah's clit pulsed and her body jerked. Brandon eased the pressure. 'Too much?'

'No.' She shook her head. 'It feels good.'

She ran her hands up and down his chest without leaning forwards. She traced his ribs, then the concave dip of his belly, firmly muscled. She circled a fingertip around his navel.

Their frenzy had abated but not her urgency. 'I want you to fuck me so hard,' she murmured and delighted in the way his eyes widened ever so slightly and the brick-red flush crept up his throat. She swore she felt him throb inside her.

But when he shifted, Leah shook her head. 'But not yet.'

Some part of her was still waiting for him to get mad, to move ahead no matter what she said. To force himself on her – not a rape, but the simple, sheer force of his need taking precedence over hers. What he wanted replacing what she did.

So she waited, tense, for him to shake his head, or start fucking upwards inside her, to give over to the desire she saw clearly in his eyes and felt in every straining muscle of his body.

Brandon didn't relax. She didn't think either of them could at this point, not with their bodies joined so intimately and their pleasure so prominent.

He didn't relax, but he didn't move either. He nodded. His thumb circled, echoing the earlier motion of her hips.

He couldn't know her reason. The fact he didn't even ask, just gave her what she wanted, removed her last bit of hesitation. Leah sighed and rocked her hips forwards under his skilled touch.

His thumb slid over her clit, so wet it was like a ball bearing coated in oil. And still he was slow, steady in his touch as though he had an eternity to please her.

She wasn't going to last an eternity. She was barely going to last another few minutes. Leah's whimper leaked from behind her teeth and Brandon groaned at the noise.

'Like this?' he asked, looking first to where his thumb was working its magic and then into her eyes.

'Yes. Like that.' Leah arched again, still not moving on his cock but only shifting her weight to press her hips forwards and back. She tensed and released her inner muscles against his cock and strained to focus on the bundle of nerves behind her pubic bone as well as the tight hard button of her clit being so skilfully massaged.

'Slower.' She gasped the word.

He slowed.

White noise crept from the corners of her mind to fill up every space of it. She would speak. He would do. She would have what she wanted. What she needed. Whatever it was, Brandon was ready to give it to her and she wasn't going to question or fear it. She couldn't. All she could do was squirm on his cock and against his hand as the sweet, sweet tension built inside her.

Her heartbeat pulsed in all her secret spots. The steady thump of it sounded in her ears. She put a hand on her chest to feel it pound under her palm. Between her legs she felt it the most, not only in her clitoris but inside her too. A hundred thousand nerve endings sparked and fired with arousal.

Filled by his erection and with the barely moving pressure of his thumb on her clit, Leah hovered on the edge of orgasm. She breathed deep with it, gave over to it. Gave in to it and him.

'Stop.' Leah held her breath.

Brandon stopped.

Muscles leaped and jerked in her thighs and ass and lower belly. Each breath she took moved her body the smallest amount against the pressure of his thumb on her. There was no question she felt the throb of his cock inside her this time, no imagining it. It was real.

'Oh,' she said, and opened her eyes. 'Oh ... now.'

She didn't know how he did it, only that in seconds he'd used one arm to push himself up while the other held her tight. He sat up without dislodging her from his lap and used both hands to smoothly shift her legs to wrap around his waist.

He was already kissing her, his hands hot on her ass and grinding her on to his prick, when she came the first time. Face to face, his mouth devouring hers, Brandon lifted her up and down as he thrust. Her engorged clitoris rubbed his belly with every thrust and Leah didn't care if he was slamming into her, it felt too good to stop.

She could smell him, taste him. Feel his breath on her face, his hands on her body, his cock inside her. Her body strained, reaching for more, more, her orgasm only the tip of the pleasure waiting for her.

Brandon moaned into her mouth. Leah's entire body shuddered at the sound, that fucking sound, that deep, low, throaty fucknoise sending her over the edge again.

She was the reason for that noise. His body was being overtaken by pleasure because of her touch, her kiss, her cunt slick and slippery and grinding down on his prick, as she used her thigh muscles to move her along with his thrusts. She was the reason he was shuddering now, and why his hand had come up to tangle in her hair and tug her head back so he could mouth her throat. So he could press his teeth there, and, oh yes, oh fuck yes, she put her hand on the back of his head to urge him on and he used his teeth on her sensitive skin, biting and sucking just over her pulse.

Leah came again, this time with a shout.

Sweat slicked their bodies. It only made it easier for him to move her up and down on his prick. Those big hands held tight to her ass. He kissed her again and she held his face to keep his mouth on hers.

He said her name against her lips, the rest of his words lost in the frenzy of their kisses. It sounded like a plea. She sucked his tongue for another second before breaking the kiss to nuzzle into his ear.

'Yes, baby,' she whispered. Two orgasms had left her pleasantly fuzzed but capable of real speech, not just a string of inarticulate groans.

He turned his head to bring his mouth to her ear. 'I'm going to come . . .'

He wasn't exactly asking for permission. Not exactly. But at sound of his voice, the yearning there, her body tightened around him again. Her nails dug into his back. Her clit bumped his belly as they thrust, and inside her the liquid heat had built until she thought she might explode.

'Yes,' she said into his mouth. Her hand slid up his back to anchor in the hair at the base of his skull. She pulled, hard, fingers tangling, and when he moaned she started to come again. 'Come with me, Brandon . . .'

He jerked and shuddered when she said his name and she had time to delight in knowing he had such a potent trigger. His arms came around her, holding her close in an embrace surprisingly tender considering how she was riding him as hard and fast as they both could move.

His breath stole over her face when he kissed her again. Then he buried his face in her shoulder and cried out her name. The final waves of her orgasm washed over her as he spent himself inside her. Breathing hard, they clung to each other, glued by sweat.

Even with her legs cramping and his erection softening inside her, Leah didn't want to move.

27

Brandon didn't think he could move. At least, not until his left knee began muttering and his right calf started to cramp. He took one more deep breath of the tang of sweat and sex from Leah's skin and leaned back to look at her.

'Cramp,' he said.

'Right now?' Concern flashed over her face and she made to get off so immediately that he barely had time to get a hand between them to lock the base of the rubber so it wouldn't slide off when she did.

'In another minute, if I don't move,' he explained as she moved to his side. With a hand on his dick ... his cock, he thought with a smile, to keep the condom from sliding off, Brandon swung his legs over the side of the bed. He pointed his toes carefully, first one foot and then the other, stretching his muscles to keep them from locking up on him. He glanced over his shoulder at Leah, then stripped off the condom as he leaned forwards to hook the waste can with one finger. A nest of tissues already littered the bottom, but he threw a few more in on top. When he tested his legs again, it seemed safe enough to stand, but he didn't.

'I'm going to use the bathroom,' he said.

Amusement flickered in her eyes and she leaned forwards to kiss his shoulder in a gesture he wasn't expecting. 'You don't need to ask my permission to go. I'm not that harsh a mistress.'

He hadn't been asking permission, just letting her know because girls could be squeamish about bathroom stuff.

Something in her tone though stopped him from getting up just then. Or maybe it had been the kiss to his shoulder. Or maybe he didn't want to move away from her just yet.

'I know you're not,' he told her, and brushed her hair over her shoulder.

Leah's smile thinned a little when he did that and, he couldn't figure out why. She let him kiss her mouth though and, when he paused in the doorway to look back, she'd been watching him. He closed the door, more for her benefit than any modesty on his part. He used the toilet, ran some warm water in the sink and splashed his face and crotch, but hesitated before using the last towel hanging on the rack. The Hilton had a green policy of only replacing linens during a guest's stay at the guest's request. Leah must not have requested fresh towels every day.

Before he could decide if he should drip-dry or use a washcloth instead, the door creaked open. Leah, still naked he was glad to see, came in. Spotting the water running in the sink, she looked at him. Then the towel.

'Here,' she said. 'Let me.'

She grabbed one of the unused washcloths from the rack and ran it under the warm water while he watched, not sure what she was planning. She squeezed it gently, but it was still soaked when she pressed it to his belly.

Brandon jumped at her touch, and she shushed him with a small murmuring admonition that made him want to laugh ... but he didn't. In order to laugh he needed breath and her touch had stolen it away.

Looking up at him, Leah moved the cloth over his belly and thighs, wiping away the stickiness of sweat and the residue of her arousal. She moved between his legs, her touch gentle as she wiped the cloth slowly over his cock and balls, too. She put her foot between his, nudging to get him to widen his stance, and though he felt foolish he did it because looking into her eyes, her hand on his cock, he was pretty sure he would do anything she wanted.

She cleaned him thoroughly but swiftly and then ran the cloth under the warm water again and passed it over all the places she'd already covered one last time. Water pooled in his pubes and ran down his thighs and calves and feet. It tickled, but again he didn't laugh.

Leah put the cloth in the sink and took down the last towel. Looking up at him again, her head tilted sideways so she could see his face and, with a quick glance, also his body, she crouched in front of him on the bathroom's terry-cloth mat. She didn't kneel, just bent her knees more gracefully than he ever could have. Her hair fell forwards over her face as she looked at the towel in her hands.

His mouth dried at the sight of her there.

She used the towel with the same quick efficiency to dry his feet and legs. She moved upwards, standing, and dried between his legs and, finally, his belly.

It was the most sensually arousing experience of his life. He couldn't get hard again so soon, not after the mind-blowing sex they'd just had, but nevertheless arousal coiled in the pit of his belly, behind his balls. He let out a slow shuddering breath.

Leah tossed the towel on to the counter and leaned back against it, her legs slightly spread and her hands gripping the faux marble. 'Your turn.'

He took the cloth and ran the water, keeping his eyes on his hands so they wouldn't shake. He squeezed out most of the water, but when he turned to get down in front of her, his knee sent out a warning, loud and clear. Try it, buddy, the old soccer injury said. You'll get down, but you won't get up.

Leah must have seen his wince because she put her finger under his chin to lift his eyes to hers. 'I don't want you to hurt yourself.'

Brandon nodded and slipped an arm around her waist to draw her closer as he let the warm damp cloth slide between her legs and up over her belly. Leah tilted her head back to look up at him, and her mouth curved in that secret smile again. He wanted to know what she was thinking, but was a little afraid to ask. He was pretty sure she was the sort of woman who wouldn't have any problem telling him.

'Very nice,' she murmured when he'd cleaned her as thoroughly, if not as neatly, as she'd done for him. She gestured for him to put the cloth in the sink, then took both his hands and settled them on her hips as she hopped on to the counter and drew him between her legs.

Maybe he could get hard again after all.

Pressed against her like that, an interested but not yet ready prick against her soft warm flesh, Brandon understood without question why Viagra had been invented.

Leah slid her flat palms up his chest, stopping at his nipples. She rubbed them a little with her fingertips, and they pebbled as his skin broke out in gooseflesh. Brandon shivered, but not from cold.

'You like that.' Her smile teased him again.

'When you do it, I do.'

Her lips rounded. 'Good answer.'

He laughed and moved to kiss her. She didn't move towards him, but she didn't pull away. He stopped a breath's distance from her lips, patient when he had to be, until she slipped her arms around his neck and kissed him. Her tongue slid into his mouth, then out again. She tasted so sweet, his body stirred in a valiant effort.

Without breaking the kiss, Brandon tightened his grip on her and lifted her from her spot on the counter. Leah let out a cry and clung to him as he turned, but a second later she relaxed in his grasp and beneath his mouth. He kissed her as he walked, praying the bed would find them before the floor did. His knee twinged but held. He lowered her on to the bed and crawled up after her, his mouth finding whatever spot he could.

When she lay on the pillows with him beside her, Leah put a fingertip to his lips to stop his kisses. 'Brandon.'

'Yes,' he said and waited for her to kick him out.

'I'm going to ask you something and I want you to tell me the truth.'

'Why would you assume I'd lie?' he asked bluntly, not to be a jerk but because he'd already given her multiple orgasms and he figured he was entitled to a little trust.

'I didn't!' She looked a little shocked.

Brandon rolled on to his back, one arm behind his head, to stare at the ceiling. She didn't say anything. After a few seconds, he turned his head to look at her. She'd sat up and pulled a pillow on to her lap and was squeezing it.

'I'm not a good liar,' Brandon said. 'You can see a lie all over my face, or so I've been told.'

A smile twitched her mouth but she didn't quite give in to it. 'By who?'

'My mother, first of all,' he said. 'And about half-a-dozen girlfriends. So I'm inclined to think they're right.'

'Ah.' She nodded and chewed the inside of her cheek. 'Well, I'm sorry. I didn't mean to imply you'd lie. I just wanted to be sure you'd be honest.'

He sat up too, mirroring her position with the other pillow. 'I will be. But you have to be honest with me too.'

She gave him an assessing look. 'Is that what you'd like to do? Trade secrets?'

'Do you have some?'

'Everyone has secrets, Brandon.' She looked at the pillow in her lap. Her hair fell forwards over her face and shoulders, so long it brushed the pillow where her hands twisted together.

He couldn't think of any he had, but the playful, sensual mood was dissipating and threatening to turn into one of 'those' conversations. 'You can ask me anything,' he offered gamely. 'Go ahead. Just like Truth or Dare.'

She looked up at him then. 'So, if you don't want to tell me the truth, I get to give you a dare?'

He laughed. 'I'll tell you. Go ahead. Ask me what you wanted to.'

Her shoulders rose and fell as she took a deep breath in through her nose and let it seep slowly from her mouth. 'I want you to tell me how you felt when I told you to leave.'

He didn't ask which time. He knew what she meant. But he didn't have an answer he could articulate. Not right away.

Leah studied him. 'Were you angry?'

He shook his head. 'No.'

'Hmm.' She tilted her head and sucked her lower lip for a second, which drew his attention inexorably to her mouth. 'Don't you think you should have been?'

'Do you want me to have been angry?' His knee couldn't take the cross-legged position any longer so he stretched out his legs, then lay on his side with his head propped in his hand. He kept the pillow in front of him though, because she still had hers, and this was the sort of conversation where nakedness wasn't a plus.

'I want to know what you felt, that's all.'

'I wasn't angry. I was disappointed. I was surprised. But I wasn't mad.'

She plucked at the pillow's white case, then held out her fingers like she was examining her manicure. Brandon had seen girls do that before. It meant she didn't want to look him in the eye.

'How about you? What did you feel like when you told me to go and I did?'

'I liked it.' The answer came out of her almost before he'd finished asking the question. She gave him a challenging stare, which was better than her avoiding his gaze.

'And the list,' he said after a few seconds in which neither of them spoke. 'You liked giving me that list.'

Leah lifted her chin. 'You liked that too.'

'I could've cut diamonds with my dick that day, Leah.'

She laughed and he was glad. 'Really? I couldn't tell.'

He reached to trace a circle on the part of her knee peeking out from the pillow. She had tiny sharp stubbles there he hadn't noticed before. He doubted she'd appreciate him pointing them out, even though he liked feeling the prickles under his fingertips.

'What do you like about it?' Brandon didn't need to think too hard to guess. He'd met her ex, that frigging punk. She'd told him, that first night, that Mike had liked to tell her what to do. Brandon figured she was just getting a little payback – with a different guy, but how could he complain?

'What do you?'

'When you tell me what you want, I don't have to guess,' he said pointedly. 'It makes my job a heckuva lot easier.'

He'd put it that way deliberately, the part about the job. He wasn't completely clueless. He couldn't pretend to guess at all her issues, but her asshole ex-boyfriend was a big part of them. Brandon wasn't going to imply what had just happened was anything other than what she seemed to want it to be: sex, plain and simple. Except there hadn't been anything plain about it and it didn't feel simple either.

'Do you always get a hard-on that could drill brick when someone gives you a list?' Her tone was light, but her eyes weren't teasing.

'No. Just you.'

Her gaze travelled over his face. 'I believe you.'

'I told you, I'm not a good liar.' He wanted to let his fingers drift higher, to the inside of her thighs. He wanted to find her slippery heat. Instead, he took his hand away.

She noticed, her eyes going to her knee and then to his face, but she didn't comment on it. 'I like knowing I've provided you with everything you need to know in order to please me. It gives you no reason to disappoint me.'

'Me? Or any guy?'

She pulled the trigger of an imaginary gun. 'Bingo.'

That stung, a little, that she was making a point of him not being special. 'Is that true?'

'You think I'd lie?'

'It wouldn't be the first time I've been lied to by a beautiful woman.'

Everything that had been open in her face shut down. 'Just because you don't want to believe it's not true doesn't make it a lie.'

Brandon didn't move, though it took a lot of effort not to get up and get dressed. Walk out. It was probably what she wanted anyway.

Well, screw that.

'From what I can tell, you didn't boss your ex around.'

Her mouth thinned and anger flashed in her eyes. It was better than the blank look she'd given him a moment before. 'That's none of your business.'

'It's my business when he comes to where I work and threatens me,' Brandon said matter-of-factly.

There was no hiding her surprise and anger now. 'He did that? What did he say?'

Now he sat to lean against the headboard. 'He told me to back off. You're his.'

'Well, I'm not!'

He shrugged, deliberately. 'Hey, if I'm just a stepping stone, that's cool.'

It wasn't.

'Or if I'm just a reason to make him jealous –'

'That's not it at all!' Leah slammed the pillow from her lap on to the bed and got up.

She was so gorgeous it almost hurt to look at her. Brandon had been with women who had perfect bodies, not an extra ounce of fat or a stretch mark or a wrinkle or blemish anywhere on them. They'd been the ones who wanted to make love with the lights off or who threw on a robe the second they'd finished. Leah didn't bother.

Naked, she turned to face him, her hands on her hips. The pose emphasised her sweet curves. He made no effort at hiding his interest either, as he looked over her. Beneath the pillow his prick was thinking about round two, even if his mind was trying to convince him to cut his losses and get the heck out of there before it got ugly.

'What else did he say about me?' she demanded.

'He said he loved you and wanted you back.'

She pointed at him. 'You're lying. I can see it.'

'He said he was going to get you back.' He was doing his best, he really was, not to let irritation get the best of him, but he wasn't quite able to keep from frowning.

She saw it. 'Tell me what else he said, Brandon.'

He'd known her for three days and she already knew how to lead him. He couldn't force himself to hate that. So, moving slowly and deliberately as he'd done just about everything else that afternoon, he got out of bed.

If she could argue naked, well, he could too.

'He said you liked to get on your knees and suck his cock.' He watched her face carefully when he said it and, though he could see his words affected her, she didn't flinch.

'What else?'

'He said . . . you liked him to tie you up and spank you.'

Her chest rose and fell with her breathing, getting faster.

A flush not unlike the one that covered her when she came rose up her chest and her throat. His own heat swept through him when he saw the mark he'd put there with his teeth.

'Do you want to know the truth about me?' she asked in a voice trying to be cold and impassive and failing by only a fraction. 'You want to know my secret?'

He nodded, watching her.

Leah lifted her chin. 'The first time I ever actually had an orgasm during sex was with a boy I'd tied up in a barn.'

It wasn't quite what he'd expected to hear, but he didn't interrupt.

'I'd had lovers before him. I'd had orgasms by myself. But it wasn't until . . .' She faltered, then drew herself up and looked him squarely in the face. 'It wasn't until I put the ropes around his wrists that I realised a boy could make me feel the way my own hand could.'

Sweat broke out on his upper lip as she spoke and Brandon licked it away. Leah watched him. Her voice got lower, huskier, as she talked.

'Those ropes wouldn't have held him if he'd really wanted to get away,' she said. 'But knowing that he wasn't trying to get away, knowing he was getting off on letting me do whatever I wanted . . .'

He'd tensed without realising it, but he stayed still, not daring to move towards her.

'I could never forget it. I could never forget how it felt to have someone so totally under my control, willing to do whatever I wanted, however I wanted it done. I never saw him again after that summer, but I knew what I wanted. The problem was finding it.'

His throat had gone dry, so he swallowed. 'I find that hard to believe.'

She crossed her arms over her breasts. 'Well, it's true.'

'I didn't mean that you were lying,' he said. 'Just that I find it hard to believe a woman like you couldn't find whatever she wanted.'

Her head came up at that and she stared into his face. 'I found glimmers of it. Is that a better answer?'

'Don't you think a lot of people are looking for something and mostly only find glimmers?'

'Unless they're lucky,' she said.

He reached to twine a strand of her hair around one of his fingers. She put her hand over his and squeezed it before pushing it gently away. She turned and went to the window, where she stood hidden by the curtain and looked out.

'Mike made it very easy for me. He knew what I liked in bed and he gave it to me. He liked playing games.' She glanced at him over her shoulder. 'Probably not the sort a guy like you would know.'

'I'm from Iowa,' Brandon said. 'Not another planet. I have the internet, Leah. I'm not naïve.'

She turned to face him. 'Really? I'm not talking about fuzzy handcuffs and blindfolds, Brandon. Or a French maid's outfit. I'm not talking about some late-night soft-core flick on Skinemax where the women never take off their stiletto pumps when they fuck. I was his slave.'

'I don't believe that either.' He shook his head.

'That's what he called me.'

'That might have been what he called you,' Brandon said, 'but that's not what you were. Not really.'

'No,' she said after a second or two. 'No. Not really.'

They stared at each other for a very long time, until he found his voice.

'I like knowing you've given me everything I need to know to please you.' He was glad for the words she'd given him to use, so he didn't have to search for his own. He was certain he wouldn't have found them. 'If it takes a list, then it takes a list.'

Her voice was heavy with sarcasm. 'So you can do your job? Take care of business?'

'No,' Brandon said with a shake of his head. He wanted to convince her but didn't know how. 'Not for my job.'

Leah drew in a hitching breath and turned away again. He hoped she wasn't crying. He didn't want to make her cry. He wanted to take her in his arms and kiss her, and not just because the sex had been so great.

He wanted to please her.

He wanted to hate that about himself too. The desire to make a woman happy had caused him no end of trouble in the past. But he couldn't find it in himself to hate that desire.

He could think of only one thing to do right now. One thing he could give her. So he went to where he'd left his pants. His belt came free with a single tug, the leather making a smooth thwap as it left the loops.

At the sound, she turned, her mouth open. The flush deepened. Brandon slid the end of the belt through the buckle but didn't hook it, making an easily adjusted noose.

He held it out to her.

'Use it.'

28

For one awful string of moments he was sure he'd made a mistake. Standing with the belt held out to her, but Leah not taking it, Brandon wished he'd at least put on his briefs. He felt more than naked now. He felt horribly vulnerable too.

But then she let out a small strangled moan and took a step towards him. She didn't reach for the belt, but hearing that sound sent the heat ratcheting through him again. He hadn't screwed up. Not this, at least.

'You don't know . . .' She couldn't seem to finish.

'I don't know,' Brandon said. 'But I'm willing to find out. OK?'

It was like gentling a colt, his hand offering a treat she badly wanted but was afraid to get close enough to take. Only for the time it took for him to breathe in and out five times though. He knew because he'd counted each breath.

'I liked that, when I told you to get on your knees for me, you did it without a second thought. And when I told you to leave, and you did . . .' She drew in a long slow breath and plucked the belt from his hand. 'I fucking loved it.'

He couldn't help noticing once more how much smaller she was when she stepped up to him and ran the belt, looped around her fist, over his belly. There was nothing small about his prick though when she touched him. She looked up at him and she was smiling. The hand not holding the belt smoothed down his back to rest on his ass as she pulled him closer, until their bodies pressed together.

'I love that you could break me with one hand but you don't even try.'

'I wouldn't ever try to break you, Leah.' He stroked his hands down her hair and let his fingers tug it gently so she tipped her head back. 'Unless, you know. You wanted me to.'

She laughed, but her eyes glistened suspiciously. 'I don't want to scare you.'

'I'm not scared.' His heart had set up a ferocious pounding, but not from fear.

Leah shook her head so her hair moved back and forth over his hands, now planted on her shoulder blades. 'Oh, Brandon. I don't even know what to say.'

He raised an eyebrow. 'You didn't seem to have any trouble before.'

She buried her face against his chest. 'You're making this so easy for me . . . I don't know what to do . . .'

'Hey.' He tipped her face up so she had to look at him. She was biting her lip and he ran a fingertip over it to part her mouth so he could kiss her. 'Maybe you shouldn't think so hard.'

She broke the kiss. The hand holding his belt came up between them and used the other to take his wrist. She put some space between them and gave a low murmur of approval at the way his cock sprang up between them. When she crossed behind him, still holding his wrist in one hand and trailing the leather across his flesh, Brandon tensed.

Was she going to hit him with it?

Would he even like that?

She traced his spine with the belt, then down lower, over his ass. His cock wouldn't have just drilled brick, it would have pulverised it. When she let go of his wrist to stroke his ass, then lower, into the ticklish spot just above his thighs, he couldn't stop the groan from leaking out between his clenched teeth.

'Spread your legs wider apart.'

The confidence was back in her tone, and his balls throbbed in anticipation of what that meant. He did. Her hand slipped between them to caress his balls from behind and he ducked his head, eyes closed, not sure what the hell was going to happen but only knowing he wanted whatever it was.

Her fingers toyed with the sensitive skin between his balls and ass before withdrawing. He heard the snick of leather being slid between her hands and tensed again, but she laughed and stroked a hand down his back to pat his butt.

'I'm not going to hit you.'

Relief flooded him. She laughed again, lower, and came around the front of him. She kept a hand on him at all times, and every place she touched came alive beneath her fingers.

'You have such a delicious cock,' she said.

He opened his eyes. Her gaze danced with mischief. She stroked him from base to head, her fingers circling his shaft and lingering at the top before she let go.

One touch and he was ready to pop.

'I loved it when you were on your knees for me, licking my pussy.' She licked her mouth.

'I did too.'

'Were you hard for me that night, Brandon?'

He nodded, not trusting his voice.

Her hand came back to steal up and down his prick and then lower to cup his balls again. 'As hard as you are now?' She squeezed, gently, and he moaned.

'When I ask you a question, I expect an answer.' She said it in a no-nonsense voice, not mean but matter-of-fact. 'I like hearing your voice when you're struggling not to groan.'

'Yes. I was this hard for you. Tasting you made me hard.'

She hadn't done anything with his belt yet but hold it in one fist. The anticipation was killing him. She wasn't going to hit him with it, and he couldn't pretend he wasn't glad ... but was she going to tie him up with it? What?

'I want your face buried in my pussy right now,' she breathed.

Hearing the slight shake in her voice made his cock even harder, though a minute ago he'd have said that was impossible. He was already moving but her hand on his chest pushed him back into place. She slapped his hip just lightly with the belt.

'If you get on your knees right now, will it hurt you?'

'I'll be OK,' he told her, already tasting her.

She slapped his hip with the belt again. It didn't hurt. Didn't even sting. But he stayed still.

'Don't lie to me,' she warned.

'Yes,' he admitted with a sigh. 'It would kill my knee. But I don't care.'

'Well, I do. I told you before I don't want you to get hurt.' She shook her head, frowning. 'And from now on, if I ever ask you to do something that will hurt you or make you uncomfortable, you have to tell me.'

He opened his mouth to reply but she put a hand over his lips before he could.

'This is not a joke,' she told him. 'I have no intention of making you call me mistress or putting you over my knee or putting you in my panties. Those are not my kinks. But if you ever put yourself in a position where you could be harmed in anyway, even if it is to please me, I will never forgive you.'

He didn't need an advanced degree to figure out this was important to her. He cupped her face. 'I won't. I promise.'

She turned her face, eyes closed, to kiss his palm. But when she looked at him a moment later, the serious mischief glittered again in her eyes. She stepped back, the belt slapping lightly into her palm.

'Put your hands behind your back.'

He did, crossing them at the wrists and grinning. 'Good?'

'Very good.'

She wasn't going to hit him, and she wasn't going to make him kneel, and she was clearly getting into this. Which, of course, turned him on. He wanted her to be into this. He wanted her to go with what worked for her. There was nothing sexier than a woman who knew what she wanted and how to get it, and Brandon intended to do his best to make sure he gave it to her.

He wasn't prepared, though, for the lightning bolt of lust that speared him when she used the belt to secure his wrists. His bad knee actually almost buckled as a throb of desire uncoiled in his gut, but he recovered quickly. She tugged the loop tight, but not so tight he couldn't have pulled free if he wanted.

Brandon didn't want to.

'Has anyone ever tied you up before?'

He wouldn't have answered if she hadn't made it clear she expected him to reply even through a mouth that felt filled with sand. 'No.'

'Never?' She moved back a few steps so she didn't have to tilt her head to look into his eyes. 'Not even with a scarf or a ribbon?'

He shook his head. He'd never been so aware of the way his arms angled when his hands were behind him, or how the centre of his lower back felt against the backs of his hands when they were behind him.

And it wasn't, just like she'd said, that he couldn't get free if he wanted. It was that he could loosen the bonds she'd placed on him. He just didn't want to.

'Do you know how fucking sexy that is?' She shook her head. 'God, that makes me so wet.'

She put a hand between her legs and stroked herself with a shiver, then lifted her fingers to show him the wetness gleaming there.

'You are so beautiful,' she added, and that broke a laugh from him. 'And you blush. That is so adorable, I can't even tell you.'

'Great,' he rasped. 'Adorable. Just what every guy wants to hear when he's standing with his hands tied behind his back and a flagpole in the front.'

Leah laughed, the low throaty sound sending a thrill through him. 'You are gorgeous, but you know that, don't you?' She didn't wait for an answer. 'You've got those big, strong hands and those long, long legs.'

She stepped closer, running a hand from his knee and up his thigh to settle on his hip for a moment while she leaned in to rub her cheek along his chest.

'These sweet delicious nipples. Do you know how much I want to lick them?'

He hoped like all heck it was a question she didn't expect him to answer because, when she closed her mouth around one, he couldn't have said a word. Leah sucked gently on one nipple, then the other. The sensation went all the way to the soles of his feet with a pit stop at his balls.

When she bit down, gently but firmly, his hips bucked. His cock rubbed her soft, soft skin as her hands gripped his hips to keep them still. For an agonising moment he was sure he was going to embarrass himself by spurting all over her, but he managed to keep himself under control.

She stepped back. 'Nobody's ever done that either?'

'No.'

'But you like it.'

'Yes.' God, yes, he did.

Smiling, she leaned in to nuzzle his chest, kissing and licking and occasionally nipping her way down his body until she was on her knees in front of him. He must have looked surprised, because she laughed as she circled her fingers around the base of his prick again.

'Did you think I wouldn't want to taste you too?'

'I didn't –' He hadn't thought, couldn't think, couldn't do anything because she had taken him into the moist inferno of her mouth.

His instinct was to put his hands on her head, but he'd forgotten for the moment how she'd used his belt to tie him. His arms jerked and Brandon moaned when he realised he couldn't do anything but take what she was giving.

Leah swallowed his dick, then drew back to suck gently on the head. One hand followed the path of her lips and tongue while the other cupped and stroked his balls. Brandon bent his knees slightly to keep his balance, something unexpectedly more difficult without the free use of his arms.

'Spread your legs wider,' she murmured. 'Steady.'

He did and she engulfed him again. He'd had head before, but not like this. She didn't slobber or gobble or daintily treat his penis like something that might bite back. She made love to his erection without ignoring any part of it and, when her hand took over to stroke while her head dipped lower so she could tongue his balls, Brandon discovered he did believe in heaven, after all.

She lifted her face to him and got to her feet, wiping her mouth with the back of her hand. 'You taste good.'

'Thank you,' he whispered, panting.

She yanked the chair from the desk and turned it around to face him. 'Sit.'

He sat, glad he hadn't fallen instead. Leah moved between his open thighs. Standing, her breasts were inches from his mouth. She cupped one and lifted it to his lips and he opened eagerly to suck the nipple between his lips.

He wanted to hear her moan, but her breath only rasped in her chest as he licked and sucked each nipple she fed him. Her hand moved between her legs. She shuddered.

He wanted to be the one making her shudder. 'Let me use my mouth on you. Please.'

Her free hand slid around the back of his neck to tangle in his hair. She tightened her grip. His erection jerked when she tugged.

'What did I tell you?' She shook her head, sounding stern but husky. 'I don't want you hurting yourself.'

'Sit on the desk. Pull the chair closer,' he said around his urgency.

Her gaze flicked that way, then back at him. 'How badly do you want to use your mouth on me?'

If he'd been able to use his hands he'd have taken hers and put it on his dick, but as it was he could only lick his mouth and hope she saw his need in his gaze.

'I want to feel you come again,' he said.

'Get up.'

He stood. She yanked the chair around again, closer to the desk, then pushed his shoulder so he sat as she hopped up on it. With her ass just resting on the edge and her legs spread, he could lean forwards to reach her.

She giggled when he did, and he paused. His gut had turned to hot lead, his dick was so hard it almost hurt and he kept having to forcefully remind himself not to breathe so fast or else he'd hyperventilate, and she was laughing?

Determined to wring more than a giggle from her, Brandon licked the seam of her pussy. Her laughter turned into a very satisfying moan, and then a strangled cry when he found her clit and sucked it gently. She was so wet already, so hot, when he thrust his tongue inside her he expected it to burn.

Incredibly, she was already coming. He felt the beat and pulse of each spasm on his lips as he kissed her pussy. She cried out and jerked when he licked her again and, mindful that it might be too much now, he didn't do it again. He kissed her though, softly, and looked up at her with a grin he knew was smug but he didn't care.

Panting, she looked down at him with glazed eyes. Her breasts heaved, her pretty nipples so tight he wanted them in his mouth again. She swallowed and drew in another, slower breath, then sat up.

'I'm going to call you Titanic,' she said.

He didn't know what to say.

'Because you're so good at going down,' she told him, and laughed again.

It was his turn for the laugh to become a groan when she whipped open the condom package and sheathed him before he even knew what she was doing. She must have had it hidden behind her. With a hand on his penis to guide it inside her but her eyes never leaving his, Leah straddled him and sat on his lap.

They were face to face again, though the chair and the floor under his feet made it easier to move inside her than the bed had. Not that he had to move at all, because she rode him. Her hands dug into his shoulders as she pushed off the floor to lift and lower herself. Faster. Harder.

The chair creaked.

She cried out.

Her cunt clutched at his cock and he wasn't going to hold back much longer. Leah kissed him, her tongue stabbing into his mouth in the same rhythm as his penis inside her. She broke the kiss with a gasp to look into his eyes, her pupils wide and dark.

He was going to come. It boiled up from his balls, surging, that inevitable feeling of flying and falling, the clutching tightness in his gut that suddenly let free.

With a tug she loosened the belt from his wrists and he put his arms around her. They clung to each other, rocking the chair back on two legs as she pushed and he thrust and they both came together, shuddering and shouting at the same time.

Leah had buried her face in his shoulder. Brandon could only hold her, the sweet weight of her on his lap like something precious he wouldn't give up. She shivered and he stroked a hand down her back. She shivered again, her shoulders quivering.

She was crying.

Oh, no.

'Leah?' He pushed her gently but held her in place so there was no way she could fall back. 'What's wrong?'

She wasn't sobbing, but tears filled those beautiful blue eyes and spilled down her cheeks. She swiped at them and tried to get off his lap, but he tightened his arms around her and refused to let her. She fought for a second before relaxing.

'Nothing's wrong,' she said.

'Then why are you crying?'

She shook her head as though she had no answer. Yet something was wrong, clearly. Something she might not want to say. So he did the only thing he could think of to do.

He kissed her.

'I –' she said, her gaze naked and the tears still glimmering there.

Before she could finish, someone pounded on the door.

29

Brandon looked startled, then guilty, and Leah realised it was still only early evening on a day he was supposed to be working. She swiped her eyes quickly and got off Brandon's lap. By the time she grabbed up her robe and tossed it on, she'd wrestled herself under control.

She couldn't believe she'd cried. What a fool. But it had all been so overwhelming, so emotionally ... not devastating. Fulfilling. Ecstatic. She'd always prided herself on being able to keep a tight hold on her emotions, but it had been too much. He'd given her too much and she wasn't ready for it.

'Go into the bathroom,' she said quietly as she tied her robe around her waist.

Brandon looked at her without moving for a minute, then got up and went into the bathroom without another word. Leah lifted her chin and set her jaw. He could be angry, now?

Clutching her robe closed at the throat, she opened the door. She expected to see Kate maybe, or a housekeeper. Improbably but possibly even Dix.

The man on the other side of the door looked as though he hadn't slept in days. About three, to be exact. Shadow stubbled his lean jaw and hollowed cheeks, but it was a fashionable scruff. There was nothing trendy about the circles under his eyes though.

'Mike,' Leah said wearily. 'What the hell are you doing here?'

'I had to see you.'

'How did you even know what room I'm in?' If the front desk had told him, she was going to have to complain.

'I tipped the maid.'

She sighed, shaking her head, and didn't move aside to let him in. 'She could lose her job for that, Mike, if I make a fuss.'

'I don't care.' The stubborn set to his jaw was entirely too familiar. 'I had to see you.'

'You don't care. You never care about anything but what you want.' Leah sighed and rubbed the spot between her eyes.

'Are you going to let me in?' His tone had changed, gone softer. Wheedling. This, like his set jaw, was also too familiar.

Leah didn't mean to glance towards the closed bathroom door, but couldn't stop her gaze from going there briefly before she looked at Mike. 'No.'

Mike put his hand up on the door jamb and leaned just like he thought he was in an ad for *GQ* magazine. 'C'mon, Lee-lee. Let me in.'

'Don't call me that, Mike. Go away. I told you, it's over. I have nothing to say to you.'

He inched closer. She was tempted to slam the door in his face, but didn't. She stood up higher though, and looked him in the eye, which seemed to surprise him.

'You can't really mean it.' He reached to toy with the collar of her silky robe and let his fingers run down all the way to the tie at her waist. He seemed distracted by the hint of cleavage and expanse of thigh the robe showed off, or maybe he was simply unable to meet her gaze.

'I do really mean it.' She softened her tone and waited until he looked up at her. 'I do.'

She'd been trying to be nice. It proved to be the wrong tactic. He honed in at once, not on her words, but on her voice. Typical, she thought, watching the gleam in his eyes. Still only paying attention to what he wanted, not what she offered.

'Nobody else can make you feel the way I do.' Mike moved closer, confident now when it seemed she was giving in.

Her laughter set him back a step. 'Oh, I'm convinced of that.'

She knew him too well to believe he understood what she meant. All he heard was acquiescence. She sighed when he rallied and pushed past her into the room.

She didn't cower or shrink from him, just watched him strut into the centre of the room as though he owned it. He looked around, his gaze catching sight of the chair and the discarded belt. His head whipped around, his eyes narrowing and lips thinning. His strut turned to a stalk and he snatched the belt up from where she'd tossed it after pulling it from Brandon's wrists.

At home, in the house she'd bought but of which he'd claimed himself king, Mike brandishing a leather strap would have meant she'd have dropped to her knees, eyes downcast, hands in her lap. He was a big fan of ritual and pomp, of terms such as 'master' and 'slave' and fetish wear. It had been fun at first, all the little tricks and details he'd taught her. She hadn't known in the beginning his education had come from pulpy porn novels and internet chat rooms. Only after she'd done her own research into a world for which she'd always yearned but hadn't believed really existed did she discover so much of Mike's sexplay and BDSM experience was cookie cutter and surface only.

'You've been a very bad girl,' he said and, incredibly, gave her a leer. Leah didn't move when he crossed to her and grabbed at her wrist. 'Why don't you let me give you what you deserve?'

When he took her hand and put it on his crotch, Leah

didn't even give her next action a second thought. She squeezed. And squeezed. And then some more.

'Shall we play a little game?' she said conversationally, keeping her tone light. Bored even. 'I'm sure you've heard of CBT, Mike? Since you are the master and all.'

He grunted, face paling, but didn't squirm away from her.

'Cock and ball torture,' Leah continued with another, harder squeeze. 'Are you into it?'

Mike gasped, 'No.'

Leah let him go. 'Me neither. When I said it was over, I meant it. Please go.'

Mike straightened, both hands going to his crotch to rub and rub. He swallowed hard, cheeks still pale underneath the stubble. He didn't go though, and she was just about ready to get angry when his sad small voice stopped her.

'But . . . why?'

A small sound from the bathroom reminded her they weren't alone. Brandon was probably stewing in the bathroom and Mike wanted an explanation why she'd ended nearly two years of what must have been domestic bliss for him? Leah didn't have the energy.

'I thought you loved me,' Mike said.

Oh, shit.

'Mike . . .' Leah couldn't even continue. 'Mike, listen . . .'

He shook his head and straightened up. 'How long have you been fucking him?'

The accusation startled her into asking, 'Who?'

He shook the belt at her. 'Whoever this belongs to!'

'None of your business,' she began, and he cut her off.

'You sure as hell didn't waste any time, did you? It's that punk kid, isn't it? That twink?'

Leah had never felt threatened by Mike. Their games had been played and she'd played a part she'd thought she wanted, but she'd never really worried he'd hurt her. He was selfish, self-absorbed and arrogant, but he wasn't abusive. So now, when he fisted the belt in his hand and moved towards her, she didn't flinch.

She laughed.

Mostly it was because the thought of him calling Brandon a twink – a twink? Wasn't a twink some sort of hairless-chihuahua-with-hands type of boy? Brandon was so far removed from being a twink all she could do was shake her head and chuckle.

'It is him!' Mike scowled.

'It's none of your business, Mike,' she cried. 'Now get the hell out of here! And, by the way, I didn't love you.'

'Lying bitch!'

She merely shrugged, refusing to give him the satisfaction of an answer.

With a growl, Mike slapped Brandon's belt across his open palm, hard.

The bathroom door flung open. Leah and Mike both turned. Brandon, a towel wrapped around his waist and one fist keeping it closed, didn't even give Mike a chance to yelp before he had the other fist wrapped in the front of Mike's shirt. Mike didn't exactly dangle in Brandon's grip – that would have made it a movie-perfect moment – but he did stumble while Brandon held him upright.

'Get the fuck out of here,' Brandon said in a voice as deep and dark as the bottom of a lake.

He'd said 'fuck'.

Leah's knees went weak.

Mike seemed to be having the same problem, because he fell over his own feet when Brandon shoved him back. He dropped the belt. The buckle clinked on the floor. Mike gave Leah a sneering, angry look, but Brandon had already grabbed Mike's upper arm without waiting and marched him to the door.

He let go of the towel to open the door and pushed Mike through it. The towel fell over the door jamb and into the hall, but Brandon didn't bother picking it up. Bare-assed, he tossed Mike out after it, then shut the door firmly and turned to her.

Leah had watched this all with a little gasp, her cheeks flushing. She'd put a hand over her mouth to hold back the flurry of semi-hysterical giggles threatening to fly out. Without saying anything to her, Brandon pushed past her and found his clothes. She turned as he pulled up his briefs with a snap of the elastic and bent for his trousers.

'Brandon,' she said, but stopped herself when he held up a hand.

He wouldn't look at her. Even in profile, he looked pissed. He grabbed up his pants and shook them out, not paying attention to the jangle of change as a few quarters and pennies flew out on to the carpet.

'Brandon,' she tried again, stifling the stupid laughter that had nothing to do with humour. 'Look at me.'

He stopped, his pants still in one hand. He turned. He looked more than pissed off, he looked furious.

'You're laughing. At me.'

The last bits of laughter died in her throat. 'No, I'm –'

Again he held up a hand and turned, disgust clear in every line of his face. He pulled on his pants, his feet still bare, and stuffed his socks in his pocket as he stepped into his shoes. He sat on the chair to tie them, and that he'd make the effort to do that when he wouldn't take the time to put on his socks gave her such an insight into his character she wanted to cry again.

Leah shivered, though the room was warm, and wrapped her arms around herself. The slippery silk robe rode higher on her thighs when she did that and she untucked a hand to pull it down. She hadn't minded being naked with him before, but this was different.

'I'm not laughing at you,' she whispered.

He stood, ignoring her, looking for his shirt. When he found it, he thrust his arms into it and misbuttoned, let out a low curse and rebuttoned while she watched in silence. His tie went in his other pocket.

'Look at me,' Leah said. 'Please.'

He did, finally, his brow furrowed and mouth set into a hard unfriendly line. His hair had fallen over his forehead in a dark curl she wanted to brush away. He flinched from her when she tried, as though he thought she were going to slap him instead.

Leah tucked her hands under her arms again, willing her teeth not to chatter. This wasn't going how she'd planned. 'Brandon, please.'

He shook his head, hard. It was killing her that he wouldn't speak. He shoved his shirt into his pants.

He was going to leave.

It might be easier that way, but it wouldn't be better. She sighed and rubbed her arms through the silk. She kept her distance, the fact they'd fucked so raucously seeming much further away than she wanted it to.

'I'm sorry,' Leah said.

He paused, just barely, before finishing with the shirt. She thought he'd head for the door, but he didn't. He ran a hand through his hair. He put his hands on his hips. He looked up at the ceiling and blew out a gust of air from his pursed lips. And finally, he looked at her.

'Why were you crying?'

His question took her off guard. She didn't answer right away, just backed up a step. She didn't have an answer, actually. Not one she could articulate, just like that.

'I wasn't –'

He shook his head again, and this time Brandon was the one who laughed. 'No. See? I'm not an idiot, Leah. Maybe you think I am. But I'm not.'

'I know you're not an idiot!'

His look said he was weighing her and finding her lacking. 'Why were you crying?'

Because for the first time as long as I can remember, I felt like someone fitted me.

Because when you gave me that belt, you gave me what I'd been looking for.

Because this all turned out to be too much, too soon, and none of it at the right time.

'I wasn't crying,' she said and looked straight into his eyes.

He might not be a good liar, but she was.

For a split second those broad shoulders slouched, but so fast she wouldn't have noticed if she hadn't been trying to imprint everything about him in her brain. Once he walked out that door, it would be the last time she'd ever see him like this again, she was sure of that. He wouldn't want to come back, and she would be unable to let him.

She wasn't ready for any of this. It didn't matter how good the sex had been, or how sweet his mouth and hands, or how hard he'd made her come. It didn't matter that he'd been willing to give her his trust, or that he hadn't judged her for admitting what she wanted. None of that made a difference in the end, when the truth was she'd just broken off a long-term relationship with someone and there was no way in hell she was going to get tangled up in something else right away. Not even if it meant missing out on something that felt so right she couldn't believe she'd ever settled for anything else and thought herself even close to satisfied.

'I'm going to ask you one more time,' he said quietly. 'Why were you crying? Was it something I did?'

'No,' she told him, and knew there was no hiding the lie all over her face. 'It wasn't anything you did.'

It was everything he'd done.

He really couldn't hide anything. Every emotion flickered in his eyes as he stared at her. Hurt. Anger. She wanted to deny the glimpse of shame there too, but couldn't.

Without a word, Brandon bent and picked up his belt from where Mike had dropped it. He didn't put it in his pocket, and he didn't slide it through the loops and buckle it. He didn't even curl the leather into his palm and carry it out with him when he left.

Instead, he pressed it into her hand and walked out of the door without another look back.

30

The cab carrying Kate to Dix's suburban home drew down a side street as Kate finished leaving a voicemail for Leah. Apparently, Band Boy was making everything all right, in a sweaty naked sort of way.

She hadn't been at the afternoon sessions and when Kate had cruised by Leah's door the noises on the other side kept her feet moving through the lush carpeting in the hall, heading to the stairwell and downstairs.

Nervousness fluttered in her stomach, little leaves skittering across the sidewalk on a windy day, as they pulled into a driveway. Absently, she handed the driver some money and dragged herself from the back seat and headed up the walk to the front door.

The house wasn't what she'd expected. It was, for wont of a better word, homey. Comfortable. A glider swing occupied the front porch, the yard was manicured but clearly people lived here. The neighbourhood was upper middle class but filled with families. Bicycles leaned against the garage of the house across the street and she caught the tops of large play sets over back fences.

She'd expected a pristine palace of white and chrome and she got, well, the 'burbs. Her nervousness battled the smile she fought as she knocked on his door.

He opened some moments later looking relaxed and ridiculously sexy. Not like the man she'd seen so far. This man was in his element, totally at home. He wasn't supposed to have complicated layers.

'Right on time. Come in.' Stepping back, he waved her inside and she found herself standing in a hallway with coat pegs on the walls and pictures of the last fifteen years of his life as a father.

Pure joy on his face, picture after picture showed him on vacations, at the seaside, at baseball games, cooking out, doing all that suburban-dad stuff dads did. What the hell could she do with that? This side of him was disarming and yet slightly repellent, because she didn't think she could compete with it, wasn't sure she even wanted to or whether it was right to. Fuck. She'd never been in a place where she simply had no idea what to do before.

He stood behind her, his body pressing to her back. He smelled good, felt even better. 'That's Adrienne, the taller one. She just finished her school year and she'll be a sophomore in high school this fall. The other one is Kendall, she's a year older so she'll be a junior.' The pride and love in his voice were unmistakable.

'They're beautiful.' It'd been an automatic response but it was true nonetheless. They had his eyes, wide and green, and the tilts of their mouths indicated they had the bullshit streak their dad did.

She kept on into the heart of the house, her attention snagged by the part of her lover she'd only had the faintest of glimpses of. He'd spoken of his daughters before on many occasions but seeing him be a father was different. More real.

'You're so quiet. It's making me nervous. Tell me what you're thinking.'

Turning to him, she drew a big breath. 'It's, um, strange to see this part of your life. I'm just taking it all in. They're gorgeous girls, you're clearly an involved dad. That's a wonderful thing.' She shrugged. She certainly couldn't remember any times when her dad had come to any of her soccer games. She froze as she caught a photo of the whole family.

'Ah, yeah. That's Eve, their mom. Kendall got an academic award, her grandparents – Eve's parents – took that photo.' He moved her away from the wall and into the kitchen.

She'd known Eve was blonde and small, but shit. The ex was tiny. Fragile looking. Perfectly coiffed and artificially blonde. Kate didn't care about that so much, oh, so she did, fine. But it was the fact he had a picture of a woman he'd been divorced from for seven years on his wall. Kate understood his kids, they were his first priority, but she didn't plan to share a man like that.

'You're bothered.' It wasn't a question.

He handed her a glass of wine and she sat at his dining-room table and looked out over his large backyard. The pool beckoned, surrounded by lounge chairs.

'Not by pictures of your kids.'

'It occurs to me we have a lot to talk about. So settle in there, Kate. Let me get the food on the table.'

He took his luscious, faded-denim-covered ass and sauntered from the table. Bare-footed, he padded into the kitchen and she watched, sipping the wine as he brought food back to her. His hair was freshly washed and without the usual product to keep it in place. A lock of it fell across his forehead. His T-shirt was thin and hugged against his body nicely. Just the barest sliver of tanned, taut belly showed when he leaned to put the salad near her.

This part wasn't hard to get used to. Having a handsome, successful man bring her dinner certainly wasn't a punishment. All the other stuff though began to crop up at the edges of her fantasy. Damn that reality.

'I'd planned to eat out back but it's still too hot. Maybe later we can go for a swim.' He sat and nodded in her direction. 'Dig in.'

'I didn't bring my suit and your neighbours wouldn't appreciate skinny-dipping I'm sure.' She dished up some salad and forked some prawns and chicken on to her plate.

'Speak for yourself. I think I'd receive several thank-you cards from my neighbours if they caught sight of you naked and wet. Lots of divorced dads and teenaged boys around here.' He grinned and tucked in.

A nearly comfortable silence hung between them for a few minutes as they ate.

'So did you get everything handled regarding Carlina?'

'Yes. After taking a peek into her hard drive, we found all sorts of things. She's been planning this departure for at least five months. We even know where she's gone to work. I had a long talk with their HR person today about what the confidentiality clause means. I don't think they're very happy about it, but that's not my problem. Leah and I will work to get the rest of the forms signed and dealt with next week.'

'Good. The sessions went well this afternoon. Roger and Bob are douchebags but your team, other than those two, are strong.'

'OK, enough work. Let's talk about us.'

'Let's do the dishes first.'

He snorted but didn't argue as she helped him put away the leftovers and clean up the dirty dishes.

'Now, into the living room with you. You've stalled quite enough.' He gave her a gentle shove towards the living room and she grabbed her wine.

Once they'd settled in, he turned to her on the comfortable, overstuffed couch and gave her an assessing look. 'Let's just be blunt, all right? I said I was done playing games and I'm going to have to trust you are too. I want you. I want us to be together. I enjoy your company. I respect and admire you and I want to fuck you all the time we can manage it.'

Part of her thrilled to hear it. The rest of her, though, was another story. 'I have concerns.'

'And they are?'

'They're legion. But the big one is professional. We work together, Dix. Your dumb secretary already tried to fuck me over. I work hard to keep walls between my private life and work. She called my boss. That's a problem.'

'I'm sorry about that. But come on, Kate. That's a one-time thing. She's nuts and that had nothing to do with work, that was her being vindictive and crazy.'

She frowned a moment. 'Bullshit it had nothing to do with work! I let you get me off in a parking garage. She caught me with my hand down your underwear. If we'd kept it private it wouldn't have been an issue at all.'

'She didn't see anything. She got the jist of what happened but she didn't see anything. I was blocking her view. But OK, we already decided to keep our frolics in private from now on. The whole thing wasn't about you, it was about Carlina and her obsession. We'll handle it from now on. Next?' He waved her concerns away like smoke.

'I worry people will believe I got the job with Allied because of my relationship with you.'

He laughed. 'Kate, you got the job because your best friend is the HR director.'

'That, Charles, is networking. You know as well as I do that that sort of connection is acceptable. No one will think less of me for that. But if they think I got it because we're having sex, suddenly I'm undermined.'

'We don't work with each other. Not for the same employer and after you leave tomorrow you'll pretty much be done with Allied unless we have further need for your specialised services. In which case, we still won't be working for the same employer. I know it's harder for women in this field. I have daughters, I'm sensitive to how it is. But you're making up reasons to keep me away.'

'Hey, oh look! Condescending asshole is back! How very nice of you to understand how it is. I'll put a gold star on your picture.'

Dix narrowed his eyes at her. 'So why don't you share with me then? Tell me what the fuck crawled up your ass to make you such a paranoid bitch?'

As he'd suspected, the dig goaded her enough to finally tell him what the hell happened.

'Back when I was an undergrad, here at Penn State by the way, I interned with an elected official. It doesn't matter which one.' She waved away the question before he could ask. 'His aide and I had a thing. A mutual thing. He wasn't married, I wasn't married. He was only ten years older. We were discovered in a compromising situation after an event. Not having sex but enough to make it clear we were intimate. I was frozen out. They couldn't fire me, not when they weren't sure if I'd file some sort of sexual harassment charges. Which I'd never do, for God's sake, I told them it was consensual and never on-site. But that didn't matter. It was an election year and, while he was a stud for fucking the hot young intern, I was just the hot young intern. And apparently a liability because of my vagina.

'Soon enough the story got back to my faculty advisor. The funds for my position for the fall suddenly dried up. They didn't need me at the office any more.' She took several gulps of her wine and he retrieved the bottle and topped it up for her. She nodded her thanks. 'Anyway, now the aide in question works in Washington, making half a million a year last I heard. Meanwhile, I was advised, quite off the record you know, that it might be wise if I took the spot I'd been offered at the UW law school. My references had dried up but when they heard about UW they all couldn't wait to tell them how great I was.'

'Christ, Kate. That's a bundle of fucked up.'

'Yes, yes it was. And so my parents, who by the way are still friends with the elected official in question, were spoken to. Disappointed, they came to me and urged me to get out of town. To start over and to keep my legs closed.'

Well, he could see how that would make her extremely wary about relationships with co-workers but the situation was not the same.

'I'm so sorry. I didn't mean to condescend. But you have to see there are no corollaries between what you and I have and what happened to you before. We're equals working for two different employers living in two different cities. We won't see each other in a professional capacity after tomorrow very often, if at all again. I'm just another lawyer living in Harrisburg. If it makes you more comfortable we can just say we didn't start dating until after tomorrow.'

'I don't know what to think. Or feel. Or want.'

'Bullshit, Kate. You know what to want. You want what you want.' He shrugged. 'That's not the complicated part. Wanting is easy.'

'What is it you want?' She threw her hands up.

'You. You and me. Is that so awful? Do you not want that too? Tell me honestly.' Shit, he hadn't even imagined she wouldn't want a relationship too. He knew she did.

She looked at him, not speaking, for some time and finally nodded. 'I do. I do but, Dix, I gotta tell you, there are big things between us.'

'Well, we just said we could deal with the work issues, right?'

She sighed. 'If we take it really slow and very carefully. I think we can. I'm uncomfortable with it, but not so much I don't want to try.'

'Then what?'

'The thing with your wife.'

He sighed. 'What thing, beauty? I'm divorced. I have been for seven years. You're the first woman I've wanted a relationship with in all that time. That should tell you something, shouldn't it?'

'You're still her husband without the fucking. Her picture is on your wall.'

Her jealousy made him want to smile but, seeing the look in her eyes, he decided against it. 'I haven't been in love with Eve for at least nine years. Probably ten. But my daughters live here half of the time, I can't excise their mother from their lives.'

'I have no place to feel one way or the other about it.'

His amusement dried up. 'You're starting to piss me off. I thought you said you were done playing games. Of course you do and clearly you have an opinion on the issue. My kids come first. I won't apologise for that. I've always been clear about it.'

'Shut the fuck up. This isn't about your kids. You just let yourself think that. I respect that your kids come first. They should come first. Ugh, never mind! This is a mistake. Call me a cab. We had this very nice thing, don't spoil it by ending it on a fight.' She began to stand and he grabbed the waist of her skirt and pulled her back to the couch.

'You're not going anywhere. God, why can't you just talk to me about it then? What is your issue? Be specific. I'm a big boy, I can take it.'

'Fine. The last time we spoke on the phone before I came out here, remember that?' She paused as he nodded. 'We're hot and heavy, I've got a vibrator in my cunt, you're telling me unbelievably filthy things as you're jerking off and then your cell phone rings. It's your ex's number but, OK, your daughters are there so you answer it. And what happened? Were your girls in need of you? No. You ended our call and why? To go over there because she can't open a jar. Since you want me to be honest and all, I have to tell you how fucking pathetic that is. On both your parts.'

Ouch.

'She's not like you, Kate. She's always been coddled. Am I supposed to just abandon her because we're divorced?'

She blinked quickly. 'You're the ... that's the stupidest thing I've ever heard! Oh my God! See, this is why we can't be together. Abandon her? If she was going through chemo and you needed to be supportive, I'd stand behind that. If her car was out of commission and she needed help getting your daughters around until it got fixed, I can be OK with that. I can't, *will not* accept a nearly forty-year-old woman who can't open a jar and who calls her ex-husband over to open it. That's patently absurd and you cooperating with such ridiculous delusions is worse. It's wretched, Dix. She needs to grow the fuck up. You're not her father, or her husband.'

'Where is all this coming from? Why didn't you say any of this before?' Confused anger slid through him. And also the feeling she was right. Which made him defensive.

'Because before you were the guy who flew out to fuck me for a few days. Now you want that to change. You want a relationship. You want my opinion, and guess what? I'm not helpless. If you ask for it, I'm going to give it to you. Welcome to having a woman in your life who's an adult. Scary, huh?'

He pushed up from the couch and began to pace. 'Smart ass. She's not a threat to you.'

She actually rolled her eyes at that. 'Of course she isn't. Not in the way you imagine it, no.'

'Then why flip out because her picture is on my wall? You're here with me now, not her. It's you I want in my bed, at my side. You I imagine lounging by the pool as I grill. I've even thought of how I'd introduce you to my kids. I can't get you out of my head. I want you there.'

'You're a romantic, which is pretty damned hot, I'll admit.' She stood, moving to him, standing so close that each time she took a breath her breasts touched him just slightly. 'But you're wilfully blind. That is not hot.'

'What are we fighting about?'

'Dix, darling, we're fighting because you're not letting go. And because of that, I need to.' She moved past him and went for her bag.

'What are you doing?'

'I'm going to call a cab. I'm going back to the hotel and you're going to continue to be on call for a woman you supposedly left seven years ago.' She pulled out her phone and he grabbed her wrist. 'I care about you. More than I should. But not so much I can't see you have a lot of thinking to do.'

'This is stupid. Stop psychoanalysing me, damn you. I want you. I need you. I don't want my ex-wife. This isn't some episode of a network drama.'

She turned slowly, one eyebrow rising. 'Are you saying I'm dramatic?'

'I'm saying there isn't an issue here. You're using it to keep me away.'

'Now who's psychoanalysing? Hmm? I readily admit I want you. It wasn't easy for me to get to that point but here I am. I'm willing to do the work to have a relationship with you. But I'm not interested in your ex-wife. I don't date married men. That's what's keeping you away. Not anything more than that. But it's a big deal. Your security blanket.'

Discomfort nettled. What the hell did she know? She'd never been married. Didn't have kids or know the responsibility of trying to raise them between two households. She had no right to be so glib about his life.

'You don't have any right to be so flip about my kids.'

She started to speak but shook her head instead. 'I'll see you tomorrow.'

'You're not just going to walk away from this thing we have.' He pulled her to his body and watched her pupils swallow the colour of her eyes. Not in fear, but in reaction to him, an echo of the ache he felt for her.

His mouth found hers taking a kiss without asking. He knew she'd give it, knew she wanted to.

31

Her bag dropped from nerveless fingers along with her phone. She needed her hands free to grab his shirt and yank it up and over his head. They panted when they had to break free even momentarily.

She should go. This wasn't going anywhere good and yet her body had no intention of listening to her brain. Her body yearned for his hands on it, yearned for his lips, for the words spilling from his mouth, heating, softening all of her.

Time slowed as he backed her down a hallway, her clothes fell off as they moved, joining his on the cool tiles. The only moments their kiss broke was when she gasped as he touched something particularly sensitive or when they needed to part to rid themselves of another piece of clothing.

His bedroom lay heavy with shadow, hung with his scent. The space was masculine like him.

He growled something unintelligible and dropped to his knees. His arms went around her hips pulling her pussy to his face. He inhaled her like he couldn't get enough. She knew the feeling as she made the supreme effort to drag enough air into her lungs to keep from passing out.

And then his mouth was on her, in her, as he yanked her hips forwards. His tongue slid between the lips of her cunt and colours exploded.

She reached blindly for something to lean on, to hold herself up as her balance became more and more precarious.

He pressed a hand between her thighs from behind, widening her stance, sliding his fingers back and forth across the super-heated flesh of her pussy, around her gate as his tongue worked magic on her clit.

Her muscles burned as she tried to stay upright and not drown in the sensation he created within her.

'Fuck, stop! I can't concentrate and I'm going to fall,' she gasped, yanking his hair to pull him back.

When he turned his face to her, the look he wore shook her deeply. Possessive, covetous, he needed her and he wasn't going to stop until he'd had his fill. It didn't frighten her, not that way, she was definitely on board with having sex with him right then. But it cut deep, scared her to be wanted so much when she wasn't sure she'd be walking away from his door as anything more than that woman he fucked for a few intense months.

'On the bed then, before I fuck you right there where you stand.'

'Is that supposed to be a bad thing? Except for us falling into a heap and possibly breaking something. That would be bad. We'd probably have to alert the paramedics. You're over forty, I hear your bones go all brittle when you're old.'

A savage grin split his mouth as he surged up, using the momentum to toss them both on to the bed just a few steps away.

'You're going to be sorry for that comment.'

'I'll only be sorry if you don't have condoms handy.'

'I have work to finish before we get there. But I knew you were coming over. I stocked up.' He shoved her thighs open and, with his gaze still locked to hers, he snaked his tongue out and tickled her clit with the tip.

Silently she widened her thighs, arching into his mouth. Want made her mute, need stole her words. His mouth on her was beautiful, lovely, wet and warm as he broke down her defences.

She didn't want to come almost as much as she did. Pleasure built up through her, filling her, riding her as he opened his mouth, grazing her clit with his top teeth, teasing her gate with his tongue.

He wanted her to come, she felt it in the way he did all the things he knew she loved best. There was so much more going on than the physical.

With a sigh, the walls against climax fell and it crashed over her. He rushed in, taking advantage, and part of her admired his absolute unerring dedication to making her his. Part of her loved being the focus of his attentions in that way. But the rest of her knew the issues between them would remain after the serotonin high wore off.

Lazily, still floating on endorphins, she grazed her fingertips through his hair as he kissed up the sensitive seam where leg met body, up her belly, over each rib on one side and then the other.

'Look at me, Kate.'

She opened her eyes and found his face just inches from her own. His eyes seemed to almost glow in the low light of the room. She smelled herself on his lips, it tugged low and deep, a mark of possession in a real sense.

'It's different with us. You know that.'

She did. But did it matter enough?

Instead she stretched her neck to kiss him, to taste herself on his skin. The kiss wasn't the ferocious one she'd expected but instead it was tender.

Using her body, she rolled to flip him on his back, moving to straddle him.

Dix looked at her above him, memorising each freckle on her pale shoulders, marvelling at the sweetness of her taste. Her weight was perfect on him.

A smile took her mouth, her sweet, tart mouth, as she

dipped down to kiss across his collarbone. Her cunt sat wet against his cock and he wrestled the depth of his need to shove into her body.

Her teeth scraped over his nipple while she played over the other one with the tip of her fingernail. He arched with a moan. Christ, that felt good.

'You do have sensitive nipples, Charles.'

He felt her smile against his chest and he snorted, giving her ass a lazy swat.

She continued to taste his sides, his belly, his hip bones and down his thighs. He watched, transfixed by her lips as she skated them past his cock. Her tongue flicked out, zinging sensation to the back of his knee. She got to her knees between his legs, pushing his thighs open. Her face was intent as her palms slid down his calves, kneading and caressing.

Back up again, back towards where he wanted her. A groan from deep within whispered from him when she nuzzled his balls, then licked along the seam and up the line of his cock. He'd let her call him Charles until the end of time if she'd just . . . yes! He sighed happily when she took the head of his cock into her mouth, swirling her tongue around it.

Reaching down, he cradled her head between his palms, the softness of it soothing even as her mouth began to devastate him.

'You were just rubbing your pussy all over me. Can you taste yourself?' he asked.

'Mmmm.' She moaned and he took it for assent.

He lost track of time to the suck and draw of her mouth. Every slick swipe of her tongue simply drew him in deeper until there was nothing but that, nothing but the way she made him feel and the way he felt about her.

Climax built, his balls drew tight and he pulled back on her head gently. 'Wait, I'm too close. I need to fuck you.'

She pulled back off his cock and blinked. 'I need you to come in my mouth.'

Christ. He shook his head a moment. 'What you do to me. Kate, beauty, to look at you, no one would ever imagine what a gorgeously filthy mouth you have. Talented too.'

She grinned. 'I'm quite proud of my vocabulary, counsellor.'

'I want to shove my cock in your cunt. Deep and hard until you make that little squeal that's part excitement, part surprise and a tiny bit fear.'

Her pupils widened and her breath caught. Good. He wanted her to be as ensnared by the chemistry and pull between them as he was.

'Don't you dare joke right now, Kate.' He flipped her on her back. 'I want to look in your eyes as I slide into you. I want to lean down and taste your lips at will. I want to fit in the cradle of your hips.'

She opened her mouth and then shut it.

He reached over, grabbed a foil packet and freed a condom, then dealt with it quickly so he could get back to the business at hand.

The head of his cock found her opening easily. She was so damned wet. Her thighs widened to allow him better access and he took it, using his weight to hold her just where he wanted.

He took his time as he entered her body, letting her surround him with the snug heat of her pussy. He wanted to possess her incrementally, so slowly she wouldn't even notice until it was too late. Skittish, this beautiful, intelligent woman. But he'd overcome that and probably really think hard about what she'd said about Eve.

But at that moment, the woman he loved was spread beneath him, willing and warm, open to him, giving herself up, and he wasn't going to think on anything but that.

* * *

Once he'd totally hilted within her, Kate could barely breathe at the look in his eyes. Intent. Like he saw right into her insides.

His gaze penetrated as deeply as his cock. She wanted to look away but it seemed cowardly to run from it. He knew her in a way no one else ever had. He bothered to know her and that meant more than most everything else.

He took her hands, entwined their fingers and held them against the pillows above her head. She wrapped her calves around his waist, resting her heels on his fine muscular ass. The man had a world-class ass. God knew he understood the power of a good thrust and the angle, brushing just so. The entire length of him stroked over her clit as she was held open by her position.

'You feel good. Like you were made for me.'

Why did he say stuff like that? Gah! Why couldn't he just talk dirty and fuck her? Why did he have to be deep and sweet and dig under her skin? Why did he feed that hunger she had no idea existed, that hunger for connection and understanding? The depth of it frightened her, made her wonder what the hell was wrong with her to not have known.

He dipped his head and kissed her, a playful tease of his lips against hers. Just enough to give her a taste but not to sate. She arched, stretching up to demand more and he laughed.

'Want more?'

'Yes!'

'Good. I like it when you need me.'

And his mouth was on hers fully, his tongue filling her mouth, his taste mixed with hers sliding through her system. She struggled to free her hands but he kept them in his as he continued to kiss her.

Her breath was his and he gave it back. Over and over, he breathed into her as he fucked into her. Pressing deep and retreating, his cock filling and emptying. At once it sated and left her bereft.

The enormity of it left her trembling as tears slid down the side of her face, the warm trail cooling against her skin.

Tenderness.

'Aw, beauty, you wreck me. I'm bare-boned and crazy for you.'

She held in a sob at the lyrical reference. Crash. Yeah, he'd crashed into her all right. She was the one wrecked, filled up with him until there was nowhere to hide. No way not to love him. Shit. Shit. Triple shit.

He smiled as she blinked. The tip of his tongue trailed over her temple, tasting her tears. 'You taste sweet. Beautiful. Raw. Give yourself to me. I'm already yours. You know you want to. I want you to. Wanting is easy, Kate. Remember?'

'But needing is hard,' she whispered and he nodded. Needing someone you loved was really hard. She'd never experienced it before and the brilliance of it was so sharp it nearly hurt. Certainly scared her.

'I know. But I'm here with you.'

He continued to fuck her, to make love to her with the same intensity and focus he showed with everything else. It was one of the things she'd first become enamoured of: his intensity. The way he threw his entire concentration into the things he did. And now he was focused on her and it warmed her even as she didn't want to be warmed. But it was too late.

Her orgasm wasn't fierce and hard, it was slow and consuming. Building with each slippery slide of the stalk of him over her clit. It took over, but not blinding, not giving her that respite. Instead all she could do was focus on his eyes as they looked right into hers, knew her and boldly dared her to deny it.

'Don't panic. Come with me.'

Her lip caught between her teeth as deep ripples of pleasure rolled through her muscles, pulling her adrift with only his weight to anchor her there beneath him.

He groaned and arched, rolling his hips and stayed deep as the jerk of his cock inside her told her he'd joined her.

He'd broken through. He knew it. Saw it in her face. Tasted it in her tears. Leaning down, he kissed her briefly. 'I'll be right back.'

He rolled off and made quick work of the condom before she got any ideas about leaving. She lay there on his bed, so very still, her eyes closed.

Easing back to the mattress, he gathered her to his side. He wasn't sure what to say. He knew what he wanted to say but he wasn't sure if she could hear it just then.

So he held her and their hearts slowed as she stayed relaxed against him.

'You want to take a swim? I'm sure the girls have swimsuits that would fit you.' He nuzzled her neck, liking her scent, tinged with sex and clean sweat.

'I'd feel so strange wearing one of your daughters' bathing suits.' He caught sight of her nose wrinkling. 'I mean, um, I know you and you'll get frisky and, just, ew.'

He laughed, surprised. 'You can wear panties and a tank top then. Come on, I want to see you wet in the moonlight.'

'I'm currently wet. Open the drapes and there'll be moonlight.' Her mouth curved into a smile but her eyes stayed closed.

'You're fuck drunk.'

It was her turn to laugh. 'Yes, I suppose I am. It feels good here. I'm lazy. I'd have to actually get up to go for a swim. And stay afloat and everything.'

'About what happens after the conference.' He hesitated

and just then his phone rang. 'Shit. Don't move.' Rolling over, he peered at the caller ID window and recognised Eve's cell.

'Oh just answer it already. She's with the girls,' Kate mumbled and he groaned.

'Hello?'

Kate congratulated herself for being such an adult. She'd known who it would be but, hell, the damned woman was with his kids and it could be something important. He couldn't drive two hours to the lake house to open a jar of something. Not without a limp anyway.

He sat up and turned on the bedside lamp. 'OK, calm down, Eve.'

The tone of his voice scared her. She snapped to attention and sat up, turning to look. He wrote something quickly on a pad as he listened carefully.

'I'm on my way. I'll be there as fast as I can. I'll have my cell on so call me if anything changes.' He listened for a bit longer and hesitated. 'Yes, of course. Me too.'

Kate quickly grabbed her discarded clothing and began to get dressed. Something was obviously up.

He turned to her after hanging up.

'What's happening?'

'It's Kendall ... there's an old tyre rope swing at the lake. She was using it, standing up, swinging out back and forth, but the rope must have frayed. It broke and she fell and hit her head. She's at the hospital now.'

'OK. Go. I'll call a cab to get back to the hotel. If you like I can wait at that little café down the road. It's not so late they'll be closed.'

'I'll drive you to the hotel.'

He looked so pale and nervous she nearly forgot he must have told his ex he loved her too or some such just moments before. She hugged him instead of slapping him.

'Don't worry about me. Is she all right? Can I pack you a bag or help with anything?'

He stopped and looked down at her, smiling. 'You're something else. She's got a concussion and some stitches. I don't know much more. Eve was upset. I'm sorry to run out on you.'

She grabbed her things and called for a cab as he quickly packed a bag.

'I have to go. I can't be there tomorrow but all the major legal stuff is over now anyway.' He hesitated and she shoved them both out of the door.

'The cab is on its way. I'll wait out here on this lovely bench. Go to your daughter, Dix.'

'Cab? Damn it, I told you I'd drop you at the hotel. I don't want you waiting out here like, well, like what you aren't.'

She rolled her eyes. 'Get moving. Your daughter needs you and you're wasting time. Go on. The cab company said ten minutes. It's really not that long to wait and five have already passed.'

He nodded, his mind clearly on his daughter as he kissed her, hugging her against him. 'At least wait inside. The door locks on its own when you close it.'

Before she could say anything else the cab pulled up and she breathed a sigh of relief. 'See, nothing to worry about. Go.'

A bit of his tension eased from his muscles. 'All right. I'll talk to you soon.'

The drive back was quiet, lonely after the way things had ended so abruptly. She was concerned for him and his daughter but she couldn't get that pause and the 'Me too' he'd given back to his ex out of her head.

Did he still love her? Kate doubted it and was inclined to believe his assertions he hadn't loved his ex in a long time.

But he was still so attached to her. Attached in ways she hadn't really examined openly until they'd begun to discuss it when she saw the picture on his wall.

Kate wasn't sure she was being fair about it. She had no frame of reference at all. It was new. Not the annoyance at the ex-wife, admittedly Kate had thought her a useless waste of skin after the pickle-jar incident. No, she had concerns about how she'd balance having an actual working relationship with a man like Dix when he was still so entrenched in Eve's life.

At the hotel, she walked past Leah's room but, though there was nothing but silence, she didn't knock. An ache crept into her gut as she dropped her bag just inside her hotel-room door. She wanted someone to help her get over her crappy day too. Wanted that sense of completeness she'd had in those moments just after they'd come. Despite her fears at whether or not things would work between them in the long run, as he'd held her and they joked back and forth so lazily, she'd been satisfied.

And now that she'd experienced it? Accepted it and knew how well it fitted? Now that was gone? The absence of such a fine thing hurt more than not having it at all.

32

Exhausted, Kate headed down to the restaurant to have breakfast with Leah. She'd tossed and turned all night. A few times she'd picked up her phone, wanting to call and check in on Dix to make sure he was all right. But he was with his family and there wasn't a place where she fitted. Not yet and maybe not at all.

As usual, she overthought herself into a horrible stomach ache and had to take medicine for it. Then she was wide awake and surfed the internet, checking LiveJournal fourteen times. She didn't bother turning on her instant message program. Leah would be asleep or getting laid so she wouldn't be online wanting to talk about *Nip/Tuck*.

By the time she caught sight of Leah, Kate had moved past wanting to talk about anything. She had to hold it together to finish up the morning session. She could lose it when she got back to her new condo. She'd spill when there weren't any bystanders but a bottle of Jameson and her best friend.

'Yo. Sorry I'm late.' She sipped the coffee already waiting at the table. 'Thank God.'

Leah raised a brow as she took Kate in. 'Rough night?'

Kate snorted and raised a brow right back. 'You're looking a bit blurry at the edges there too. Not to mention the noises I heard from your room when I walked past yesterday on my way out.'

Leah made an excuse about just being tired and wanting to get back to her own bed. Kate raised her concerns about that loser she'd been living with but Leah had given a funny little smile and assured her it was fine.

'Buffet?'

Leah nodded.

After they'd filled their plates, they ate for a while in silence. Both hoarding secrets. It was easy to see Leah had something on her mind but Kate knew Leah would tell her when she was ready.

'I'm so tired. Fuck, what a mess with Bitchface the psycho assistant yesterday, huh?'

Leah snickered and then sobered quickly. 'Yes. I tried to connect with Dix this morning but got his voicemail.'

'That little twit called the senior partner who supervises me yesterday. She told her Dix and I were having sex in a public place.'

Leah's brows flew up. 'What a bitch!' Leah lowered her voice and Kate leaned in close so she wouldn't be overheard. 'Were you?'

'Not when she came up. And you know it wasn't actually sex sex. Just sort of. It was so stupid. Soooooo stupid I can't believe I did it. I could have lost my job and everything I've spent years working for, Leah.'

'Wow, he's really got something with you, huh? To send your common sense right out your panties?' Leah shrugged, not judging, just as Kate knew she wouldn't.

'Thankfully, Chandra heard the crazy in Bitchface's voice and didn't take anything she said seriously. But,' Kate sighed, 'I don't know about anything else right now.'

Leah soothed her worry a bit and then tried to redirect the blame for the whole Carlina fiasco on to herself.

Kate wasn't having a bit of it and reminded her friend why she'd been hired and brought to the conference to begin with.

Of course, then Leah teased her about Dix. Kate so wasn't

ready to go there, so she teased about Band Boy but Leah's cold reaction and brush off of the subject led Kate to believe her friend wasn't ready to discuss matters of the heart either.

'All right then, let's get this over with.' Kate stood and Leah quickly tossed some money on the table. Kate sent her the stink eye but Leah dared her to really argue and she backed down.

'You still need a ride to the train station later?' Leah asked.

Kate needed the time alone. Time to think and, judging from Leah's voice, she needed it too.

'I've got it covered. A cab will do just fine.'

'Really?'

Kate laughed a moment. 'Really. Look, don't ask, don't tell, right? We'll both spill when the dust settles. I'm just two hours away now. From the looks of both of us, we have a lot to talk about.'

Leah paused and then squeezed her arm without saying anything else.

'I'm going to pack the last of my things. I'll see you in there in a few minutes.' Kate quickly walked away before she burst into tears right there in the lobby.

Right. Leah watched her friend go, then squared her shoulders. She had things to do too. First, conference room. Make sure everything was set, that everyone had what they needed for the final morning session. Sign off on the final billing. Then she could go.

Brandon was already there when she arrived.

Leah's heart, which had already been beating faster than usual, flew into her throat. She stopped in the doorway, her suitcase clutched in one hand since she hadn't wanted to leave it downstairs at the desk. He was on one knee, bending to plug the overhead projector into the outlet on the wall. She wanted to kneel behind him and curl her body around the curve of his back.

Brandon turned and stood. His expression was not impassive. She had to look away from his face so she didn't have to see his honesty. Leah set her suitcase on the table along the back wall and fussed with the handle to give herself a reason not to face him.

Her palms were sweating and, though her half-eaten breakfast sat in her stomach like lead, she reached for the plate of pastries and bagels she'd ordered. She took a napkin instead of food and crumpled it in her fists to dry them. She couldn't do much for the heat pooling in her armpits and rising up her throat and face. She swallowed heavily, wishing she'd had water instead of hot coffee that morning.

'Everything's all set.' His face might have shown his feelings, but his voice betrayed nothing.

Leah risked a look. 'Thank you.'

Brandon nodded. Today he wore a pale-pink shirt with grey trousers and a maroon tie. Black shoes, polished to a gleam. Her gaze went unerringly to his waist.

No belt.

He was looking at her when she looked at him. He'd seen where her eyes had gone. His chin lifted, that strong jaw clenched a little. But he didn't look away.

'Everything looks fine,' she said.

They weren't going to be alone for very long. The meeting was due to start in less than ten minutes and there were always a few who showed up early, especially when there was free breakfast. She only had to get through this next few minutes with him. She could do that.

'I have your paperwork in my office,' Brandon said. 'You'll need to sign off on it.'

Shit. She searched his face for any sign he was doing this to be difficult but realised it was more than likely he simply hadn't wanted to shuffle the papers along with him while he set up the room. She nodded.

'I'll be down in about fifteen minutes, then, OK? Once I get everything started here.'

Something shone briefly in his eyes. 'I'll be there. If you're sure everything here is set to your satisfaction.'

Leah refused to acknowledge that she noticed the way his voice got lower, or the way he was trying to pin her with his gaze. Or how good he smelled today. She refused to notice that too. With a sharp nod, she turned to fuss with her suitcase again.

'Would you like me to take that down for you?'

He wasn't standing too close. He wasn't offering something special. He was only doing his job, she thought. His tone polite, his manner sedate. Except she knew it wasn't like that.

She'd thought it would be easier today to deal with seeing him. She'd assumed he'd be snappish and angry or distant and cold. And there was distance there, no question, but he wasn't being an ass to her about any of this, though she knew she well deserved it.

She kept herself from swaying towards him only by clenching her fingers tightly around the suitcase handles. Truth was, she did want him to take the bag, not because it was too heavy or inconvenient for her to carry, but because she wanted to know he was doing it for her. Just because. She wanted to know he was making sure she was taken care of, and not only because she was a guest of the hotel.

'No. I'll take it down myself.'

She'd let a thousand strangers carry her bags for her. Open doors, park her car, mow her lawn, carry her groceries, plough her driveway. She'd never had a problem with allowing someone to serve her needs, had, in fact, as Kate had so aptly pointed out, been accustomed to snapping her fingers and having someone jump. So why now?

He stepped back from her with a small nod. 'Fine.'

It wasn't anything close to fine, but Leah kept her gaze poised slightly to the left of his face. 'I'll be down.'

She didn't watch him walk away.

Eighteen minutes later – she'd deliberately counted out three extra minutes – Leah knocked on Brandon's half-open office door. At his muffled reply, she pushed it open and went inside. And stopped, surprised.

'Wow. You've been hard at work.'

She wrinkled her nose against the scent of furniture polish and ammonia as she stepped through the door. He'd cleared off the stacks of folders and files she remembered had been scattered over every flat surface. A small lamp with a decorative shade that looked as though it had come from one of the rooms upstairs had replaced the flickering, industrial overhead lighting and, though none of the furniture looked new, he'd rearranged it to make better use of the small space.

'Heather's decided not to come back after maternity leave. She gave her official notice. I got her job.' He shrugged, standing behind his desk with a folder in his hand.

'Congratulations.' Leah set down her suitcase and reached for the folder. 'This is the paperwork?'

He gestured at the chair in front of his desk. He'd put a cushion on it at least. She sat as an excuse to put her attention on the work, not on him. She opened the folder and scanned the list of items printed there, ticking each one with her pen. Nothing amiss. She signed the last page behind a number fairly staggering in its amount, but, hell, she wasn't paying for it.

Leah stood and put the folder and his pen on his desk. Brandon had stayed standing. He made no move to take the papers or pen, even though it rolled off the folder and threatened to keep going on to the floor.

For a long minute neither of them moved. With only the desk between them, it wouldn't have taken much for him to reach for her or for her to slide across it and into his arms. But there was more than the desk blocking that route, and there didn't seem much of anything else to say.

He reached behind him and settled another paper on the folder in front of her. 'Management requests guests fill out a performance survey about their experience here. You can mail it in later. You don't have to do it now.'

With one fingertip he pushed the paper towards her. She took it without looking at it and folded it in half, then tucked it into her purse. 'I'll do that.'

'Just to let you know,' Brandon continued, 'if you've determined your satisfaction with my performance to be anything less than the highest rating, management considers that failure. So would I.'

She had to look at him then. 'I'll keep that in mind.'

She wanted him to smile, but he didn't. 'Thanks.'

'You're very good at your job.'

'I'm very good at a lot of things,' Brandon replied.

For that, Leah had no answer. She gathered her bags and the sweater she'd slung over one arm. 'Goodbye, Brandon.'

He didn't answer her. Or maybe she didn't hear him through the door she shut behind her when she left. Then she went home. Alone.

33

'So, Band Boy. Why the long face?'

Brandon had been staring into the bottom of his glass, contemplating the secrets of the universe, but he looked up at the sound of a familiar feminine voice. Leah's friend Kate slid on to the stool beside him and ordered a Scotch with water on the side in the no-nonsense tone of a woman who knew what she wanted and wasn't going to wait around for it.

He waited until she'd been served and had taken her first sip before he swivelled to face her. 'What is up with the Band Boy thing, anyway?'

He wasn't angry about it or anything. Just curious. Kate laughed a bit and took another drink before answering.

'That night we met you, we were noticing you from across the bar –'

'Yeah?' That bit of news should've made him happy, but it didn't quite manage.

'Yeah. And Leah was saying how she wouldn't mind taking a drink from that long tall glass of water, and I . . .' She bit her lower lip briefly before laughing again. 'Well, let's just say I thought you seemed a little more . . . innocent . . . than apparently you are.'

'She told you that?' He finished his pop and Jimmy, good guy that he was, had already slid another into its place. Brandon had been sitting there for a while.

'Not exactly. Don't worry, she didn't spill all your secrets.' Kate's sly grin didn't exactly reassure him. His dismay must have shown on his face, because she looked instantly contrite and patted his arm. 'Really. She didn't tell me anything embarrassing. I promise.'

He drank deeply before replying. 'But you assume there was something embarrassing.'

Kate shook her head. 'I don't assume that.'

Brandon shrugged and turned back to the bar to settle his glass in the series of wet rings from previous glasses. 'If it's all the same to you, I'd rather not bare my soul to her BFF, OK?'

'Ouch.' Kate set her glass down with a thump. 'Hey. Look at me.'

He did, reluctantly.

'You went after her yesterday, didn't you?'

Her perplexed look told him she really didn't know what had happened after. Knowing this did little to soothe him, but he nodded anyway. Kate smiled.

'Good boy.'

'I'm not,' Brandon said irritably, 'a boy.'

'You're a good man then.' Kate rolled her eyes but reached to pat his arm again. 'Don't be so sensitive.'

He gritted his jaw but relaxed it almost at once. It was too hard to sigh with his teeth clenched. He swirled the liquid in his glass, wishing it were beer. The bar in the hotel where he'd just been named full-time conference-services manager was not the place to get drunk.

Then again it hadn't been the place to have crazy, wild sex with a hotel guest either, and he'd managed to get away with that.

'I went after her,' he said under his breath. 'Stupid.'

'It wasn't stupid.'

He looked at her. She smiled and shrugged, then sipped from her drink. Brandon glared for a moment before sighing again.

'It wasn't stupid,' Kate repeated quietly. 'She's my friend. I know that makes my judgement suspect, but she wasn't just screwing with you. She's not like that. Whatever's going on with her –'

'Yeah. I get it.' He hunched over his glass and refused to look at her. 'I don't need it spelled out for me.'

Kate snorted lightly. 'I know. You're not stupid.'

'Yeah, and I was never in the damned band, OK?' He swirled on his stool, eyes narrowed, and pointed an accusing finger at her. 'I played soccer!'

Kate held up both her hands. 'Whoa, whoa, OK. Hey, there's nothing wrong with playing in the band, by the way. Slow down on the Guinness.'

'I'm not drinking Guinness,' he said.

'Me neither,' Kate replied. 'Should we remedy that?'

He didn't answer for a second. 'Why do you want to get drunk?'

'Do I need a reason?'

'Do you have one?'

'You really aren't stupid,' Kate said begrudgingly. 'But if it's all the same to you, I don't really want to bare my soul either.'

'Would it be one of those "men are pigs" sort of soul-baring conversations?' he asked. Ninety-nine per cent of the people he worked with were women. He knew how it went.

It was her turn to sigh. 'No. Unfortunately, no. But you can buy me another drink.'

He laughed, finally, and gestured at Jimmy. 'Right. How did I know it would lead to something like that?'

She laughed too. 'How did I know you'd offer?'

'Because I'm a good guy.'

'Who doesn't have to finish last.' Kate lifted her fresh glass to him and they tapped their glasses. 'You went after her once, go after her again.'

'Great. You want me to turn into a stalker?' He shook his head. 'No, thank you. Besides, I don't know where to find her.'

'Um, hello. I know where she lives.'

He looked for the secret to life in the bottom of his glass again. 'No thanks.'

Kate's cough sounded suspiciously as though it covered up the word 'pussy'.

'Yeah,' he said, still annoyed. 'Because I'm really going to just show up at her house unannounced. That won't freak her out or anything.'

'You could call her first.'

'Why do you care so much anyway?' He ran a hand through his hair in frustration, wishing for the hundred-thousandth time he understood women's brains.

'She's my friend. I want to see her happy.'

'How do you know I'm not some jerk who will just break her heart?' he challenged, throwing out another line he'd heard so often from the girls at work.

'Because,' Kate said patiently, 'you are a nice guy. And you gave her what she wants. And needs.'

'I thought you said she didn't tell you anything embarrassing.'

'She didn't. But you better believe I'm going to force it out of her, based on the blush on your face,' Kate said, giving him a once-over. 'It has to be pretty damned good.'

'It was pretty damned good,' Brandon said and pushed his half-empty glass away. He'd lost his taste for it.

'If you let her just walk away without even trying to get in touch with her, I will mock you mercilessly.'

He rolled his eyes, copying her earlier look. 'What, that's supposed to scare me?'

'It should.'

'Maybe I don't even want to,' he protested.

'You want to. You want to so bad it's like an army of ants gnawing at your brain –'

'Fine.' He cut her off and frowned when she smiled at him. 'You're right, OK? I'm crazy about her and I don't care that we only knew each other for a few days. Are you satisfied?'

Kate's smile softened. 'She's my friend. I want her to be happy. That's all. I think you could do that.'

'You don't know that for sure.'

'Nobody knows anything for sure!' she snapped and looked into her own drink, which didn't seem any more likely to offer up advice than his had.

'I'm not saying I'm going to go after her,' he said finally. 'But if you told me where she lives, I might think about it.'

'What do you have to lose?' She held up a hand. 'Don't answer that. I can't stand the puppy-dog eyes.'

He had to laugh at that. 'I don't have puppy-dog eyes.'

'Don't you know better than to argue with a woman?'

'Apparently, I don't.'

Kate finished off her drink but didn't ask for another. She sighed, her shoulders hunching just a little.

'Just say it,' Brandon offered.

She looked at him. 'What?'

'Men are pigs. It will make you feel better.'

Her smile took a moment to stretch across her mouth but, when it did, he felt a lot better.

'Not all men are pigs. That's the trouble,' Kate said.

'We're all pigs,' he offered. 'Really.'

Then they were laughing again, and it felt good to laugh even if he knew it was only a temporary respite from feeling like crap. Kate's sigh this time sounded marginally less melancholy and, when she reached to pat his arm, she added a little squeeze.

'It would be easier if that were true.'

'Sorry.' He reached for his wallet and pulled out a few bills, making sure to leave Jimmy a good-sized tip. It wouldn't be cool to stiff the dude just because the drinks here were way overpriced.

'Thanks for the drink, Band Boy. Sorry,' she amended, 'Soccer Dude. Go get her, tiger.'

Brandon groaned and buried his face in his hands, even though he was smiling.

'Fire ants,' Kate added. 'In your brain!'

'You're either a really, really good friend or you secretly hate her,' he said.

'The former.'

He scrubbed his hands through his hair again and stood. 'Sure you don't want to call me a pig?'

'I'm sure,' she said.

He held out his hand and they shook. 'Is there anything else I can do for you before you go?'

'Aren't you off work?' She raised a brow.

'Just asking.'

Kate shook her head as her phone trilled from her bag. 'God. You're perfect for her. No. G'wan ahead. Go bend it like Beckham.'

He didn't know so much about the perfect part, but he couldn't ask her more because she'd flipped open her phone and was listening intently. She hadn't even said hello. She dug in her bag, tore out a piece of paper and scribbled an address, which she handed him before waving him off.

He looked at the crumpled paper in his hand. He knew where Leah lived. It wasn't too far from him either. The problem was, should he really go to her, like her friend had said, or should he leave well enough alone?

34

They finally came for Kate in the bar some half an hour later to tell her the cab had arrived. About damned time. What was it about the end of conferences and the seemingly endless wait for cabs anyway? She sighed, she'd be cutting it close but she'd make it and it had allowed her to have that convo with Band Boy. Later on when she got home, Kate planned to call Leah up and demand an explanation.

Her phone rang as she'd been digging for her pad to write Leah's info down for Band Boy. Dix, or so the caller ID window said. She flipped it open and listened, absently scribbling the address and handing it to Brandon with a last admonition to get his ass out to find Leah.

'Hang on, I'm getting in a cab,' she said as she loaded in and the cabbie put her luggage in the back. 'OK. How's Kendall?'

'She's OK. Grouchy because they woke her up all night long.' He sounded exhausted and Kate heard feminine voices in the background and wondered.

'You sound tired.' Which was so obvious she knew she sounded ridiculous. But what else was there to say?

'It's been a long day. Everything finish up all right?'

God, small talk? Their easy rapport had wasted into this? Would he ask about the weather next?

'Yes, fine. I'm on my way to the train station now.'

'I have a pen here and some paper. You'll give me your number in Philly and your address?'

The only reason she let his bossy tone slide was because she felt sorry for him. And, OK, she was glad he'd asked. God she was such a girl. He'd turned her into a fifteen-year-old girl.

'Bossy.'

He laughed and it made her smile. She rolled her eyes at herself as she gave him the information.

'I'm going back to the house for now. I'll be back in town in a few days. We don't want to have Kendall on the road for a bit so we'll stay at the lake house until she's had the chance to rest up.'

She had no right to be mad. Of course he didn't want to subject his daughter to a two-and-a-half-hour drive the day after she was in the hospital overnight for a head injury. Still, sucktown.

'Oh, of course. Well, I'm sure I'll talk to you when you get back then.'

His frustrated sigh gusted over the phone. 'You will. You know that.'

He was hindered with what he could say. She got that, which meant, oh, fuck, who knew what it meant, and she was too tired to guess and utterly done with being fifteen again.

So she pulled up her big-girl panties and took a bracing breath. 'OK. I'm glad your daughter is all right, Dix. Get some rest, I'm sure you need it.'

'I'll be in touch.'

'I'll be in town. I have to go, we just pulled up at the train station and I've got to hustle.'

They hung up and she shoved too much money at the cab driver and headed to the train with her bags.

Dix settled Kendall into a bed and tucked the sheet beneath her arms, bending to kiss her forehead. 'Rest.'

'Dad? Are you OK?'

'Just worried about you.' He went to the door and closed it gently when he saw she was already drifting off.

They'd bought the lake house when Eve was pregnant with Adrienne. Kendall had been an infant still. They'd been so young. He'd wanted a family, wanted the tyre swing, wanted what he'd gotten and, over time, the family part had been great, but the wife, not so much. He'd been obsessed with work and she'd just, well, been.

She was waiting for him downstairs, he knew it. She'd listened to his phone call with Kate quite closely and had been very quiet on the drive back from the hospital. Adrienne was out with some of the other teenagers visiting the area so it wasn't a conversation he could avoid. And, frankly, not one he could afford to avoid if he meant to make something with Kate.

'She pretty much went right to sleep,' he said as he entered the kitchen, heading for the coffee machine.

'Good. While you're here you should take a look at the tyre swing and the dock might need some work too.' Eve sat at the table, so petite and lovely. Once she'd stirred him deeply but now, aside from her obvious beauty, she did nothing for him. He wanted Kate to understand that.

'I'll have the carpenter I used a few years ago for the shed come out and look at the dock. I'll look at the swing later. You should get some rest, you were up all night.' He sat with his coffee, across from her.

'So, who is she then?' Pretty blunt for Eve. She had to be angry to let go of that calm façade of hers.

'Her name is Kate.'

'You don't need to feel guilty, you know. I'm sure she understands your family comes first. Anyway, they always disappear after a week or two. I'm surprised you actually talked to this one while you were with us.'

Outwardly, her statement was fine but he knew what she really meant and it meant Kate was right too. He sighed and sipped his coffee.

'It's different. She's different. And I don't feel guilty, not in the way you imagine. She does realise my children come first. This is a woman who will be a regular part of my life, Eve. Eventually I'll introduce her to the girls.'

'Does she understand your commitment to your family, Charles?'

How come when Eve called him Charles it didn't amuse him? He was being unfair, the comparison wasn't fair but he couldn't stop himself from making it.

'I said she does.'

'What makes this one different? And you shouldn't drink coffee so late in the day, you'll have trouble sleeping.'

Were they even friends?

'Yeah. And it's different because she is. I'm ready to have a real relationship and she's someone I want that with. I'm sorry if that hurts you. I honestly don't want that.' He pushed the cup away, she was right about the caffeine.

'We've been divorced a long time. You've gone through a lot of women over the years. You think I didn't know?' She waved a perfectly manicured hand. 'I'm the only one you come back to. You should think about why. You're still in love with me and you can't admit it. It's why you haven't been with anyone seriously in all this time.'

And, pow, Kate was right. Christ. 'Well, see, part of that's true in a sense and it was brought to my attention recently. I don't come back to you though and I'm an ass if I gave you any false hope that we'd be back together. I've been happy for you when you had men in your life. I wanted to be sure the girls had stability. I don't hate you, I just don't want to be married to you. You and I aren't meant to be married, you said so yourself. We share two great kids and I never planned, nor do I ever plan, to walk out of their lives. You're part of their lives so naturally we're part of each other's life. But that doesn't mean I come back to you.'

She levelled a gaze on him and shrugged. 'If that's what you think. She's not here and, yet, you are. What does she think about that?'

'She told me I was still married to you without the fucking. At the time it pissed me off. But it turns out she was pretty right about it. She also shoved me out of the door when I got the call about Kendall being hurt.'

'She said that? In those vulgar terms? What kind of woman are you going to expose our daughters to?'

He stood and washed his cup out in the sink. 'Don't ever call my judgement into question when it comes to the girls, Eve. She's the kind of woman I'm in love with. I'm sorry if this hurts you. I am. We've been divorced for seven years. It's apparently partly my fault you haven't moved on so let me be totally clear. I'm not coming back. We've had what I've always thought of as an amicable divorce and have managed to work together on parenting. I'd like to keep things that way. But that doesn't mean we're still married and it doesn't mean I haven't moved on. You need to see other people, find happiness. You deserve it. You're a good woman. Beautiful, intelligent, you run a successful business, there are many men who would love to snap you up.'

'Just not you?'

He barely resisted hugging her. He wasn't an asshole, he didn't want her hurt. But he didn't want her holding out false hope either. 'I'm sorry.'

Kate hadn't spoken to Dix much over the last week. He'd been at the lake house and then at work. She didn't want to call him at home because she hadn't wanted to intrude on his private life, especially since she knew he had his daughters with him.

He'd left a few voicemails for her and she'd responded but ended up with his voicemail in return. Each message he left made him sound more and more frustrated and she totally understood. She was pretty damned frustrated herself.

Uncertainty wasn't a place she liked. She'd made the damned decision to love him and then all hell had broken loose and she'd been given way too much time alone to think.

On her way home from work she dialled Leah.

'Griffin.'

Kate smiled at Leah's businesslike clipped tone. 'Hey. Whatcha up to?'

'I'm about to hit Wegman's. What's up with you?'

'Just calling to check in, make sure we're still on for next week.' And how nice it was, Kate realised, to be able to see Leah regularly. Just to hang out.

'Of course, wouldn't miss it.'

'All right then. I'll let you go seeing as you're about to enter the nirvana of grocery stores.' She hesitated. She'd wanted to talk to Leah about the Dix thing all week long but kept hesitating. Stupid of her really.

Kate realised Leah had been talking and she finally burst out. 'God, Leah, what am I going to do about Dix?'

Leah laughed. 'I was wondering when you'd finally talk to me about it. Tell me.'

So Kate did, pouring out her anxiety, fear, anger and frustration. There was more than she'd thought but it came out easily when she was talking to Leah.

'I just don't know what to think. The thing is, it's all stupid. I mean, he's called even if it's just phone tag. I don't have any reason to think he's blowing me off but Pickles is still in the way. If he doesn't deal with the ex, I don't think we can make it work.'

'That's fair. I'm never going to be able to look at him without snickering now that I know about the pickle-jar thing. For now I think you need to cut the guy some slack and, if he doesn't show up to your place within the next few days to sweep you into bed, then you can cut his balls off.'

Kate grinned. 'You always say the best stuff. So, um, speaking of showing up at your place and all. Any Band Boy smack to share?'

Leah let out a suffering sigh. 'What did you do? Did you do something?'

'Look, he was all morose and you were so sad and I knew he wanted to go after you and you needed him to and all, so I gave him your home address and number. I'd say I was sorry but we'd both know I was lying so yadda yadda. He doesn't strike me as stalker material and he seriously has a jones for you.' Kate grimaced, waiting for Leah's response.

'Well, he didn't use them.'

Kate only barely stifled herself from showing any pity. Leah would hate that. 'Well, you could call him.'

'I could. But I'm not going to.'

Kate sighed at Leah's stubbornness. She unlocked the front door to her building, waved at the doorman and found her voice. 'Why not? It's been a week.'

'Only a week.'

'And a day even. Gah! Leah! A week can be a long time.' Yeah, really long. She sobered. 'Believe me.'

'I'll think about it, OK?'

Kate perked up. Clearly she'd need to put all her own angst into a campaign to get Leah to call Band Boy and jump his squeaky-clean bones until she sullied him. 'You know you want to. He's probably used like eight boxes of tissues and a lot of hand lotion just thinking about you. He's mopey. His mom keeps asking him why he keeps showering so much and hanging out in the basement with his Star Wars figurines.'

Leah snorted a laugh. 'Ew! OK, so not ew, but eight boxes seems excessive. Anyway, do you really want to go there? Because I'll go there about you and Dix and then we won't have anything to talk about at lunch next week.'

'Dude, if Dix is jerking off so much he needs eight boxes of tissues in a week, I don't think I'll be enough for him. But OK, truce. For now.' She got out of the elevator and saw him, Dix, finally, standing in front of her door. 'See you later. Call me if you want to talk.'

35

Kate hung up, amazed her legs still worked as she moved towards him, hoping her tongue wasn't hanging out. Had he looked this good the last time she saw him?

He smiled, looking her up and down. 'Hi. After leaving a dozen voicemails back and forth, I figured I'd come to you.'

His voice was so sexy. She couldn't help herself as she leaned towards him, slid her arms around his neck and tiptoed up to kiss him. Oh he tasted so good, smelled even better. The man was walking, talking delicious.

Dix caught her body, breathing her in, realising he'd been more nervous than he'd thought.

'That's a fine welcome.' He grinned as she pulled back and unlocked her door.

'Come on in,' she called as she sauntered past, carefully hanging her briefcase and purse on a neatly hung peg just inside.

He did, closing and locking the door behind himself. He looked around the surprisingly feminine and bright space.

'I . . . I guess I hadn't expected you to have girly taste.'

She turned and glared at him. 'Girly? Do you see any glass unicorns or big-eyed baby figurines with praying hands and puppies? Girly, humph.'

Laughing, he tossed his overnight bag just beneath where she'd hung her things. 'I meant, well, flowers and soft colours. Pillows on the couch.'

'You have pillows on your couch if I remember correctly. What does that say?'

'You're being argumentative, counsellor.' He moved to her and she rolled her eyes and headed down a hall. He followed, liking to watch as she peeled her suit jacket off.

'I'll have you know,' she said as she entered her bedroom, 'I get paid a lot to be argumentative.'

His mouth dried up when she shrugged out of her blouse and stepped from her skirt. 'Kate, stockings? My. So very sexy.'

She sent him a raised brow and hung her things up. She put her shoes neatly in the large closet and turned back to him.

'My boyfriend at work likes to bend me over his desk and fuck me. The stockings make it easier.' She paused with a smirk. 'Charles Dixon, why are you here? Why really?'

'I'm here for you. Isn't that obvious? How can I talk when you're standing there in a bra and tiny panties with stockings? It's beyond distracting. I haven't had you in a week and I'm dying.'

The line of her neck beckoned as she laughed. How pretty she was, so at ease with herself as she stood there. A shift had occurred since he'd seen her last. She wasn't hesitant with him at all, instead offering intimacy freely. Still there was a certain wariness in her features.

'Come on then. I'll put clothes on. We can order some Chinese food and have a beer. I've worked way more hours than I wanted to this week and today is the first day I've been home before eight at night.'

He looked at her bed. 'You don't have to get dressed you know. I mean, since I'll have to undress you all over again to fuck you.'

'Don't get ahead of yourself, Charles.'

Captivated, he couldn't look away as she slid her stockings down, one by one, and took them off. The tiny little dress she put on didn't actually cover much more but it wasn't as if he planned to complain.

'Your message light is blinking,' he said as he slid himself on to her couch. Very nice.

'I'm sure. I'm a popular girl.' She passed the machine and dug out a menu. 'So any preferences for dinner?'

'I like it hot.' He grinned and she laughed.

While she ordered the food he set his phone to ring only for the girls' numbers and put it on a nearby table. No interruptions for them tonight.

She pushed an ice-cold beer towards him before sitting.

Her scent teased him. 'How long until dinner arrives?'

'It'll be about twenty minutes. They're pretty close.'

He took several swallows of the beer and dropped to his knees before her. 'Enough time to make you come then.'

'We have a lot to talk about before we have sex, Dix.' But she hadn't moved. Instead she leaned quite comfortably back into the cushions and watched him, her head slightly cocked to the side. His hand lay against her thigh where the muscles remained loose. She was warm against his palm, familiar.

'We do. We will talk. I promise. But why get started only to be interrupted by the food?' As he spoke, he slid his fingers up under the dress and reversed, bringing her panties down and off her legs.

Her eyes seemed to burn as she watched him and he couldn't break his gaze even as he bent to kiss her knee and then up her thigh.

Her lips parted into a soft gasp when he slid his thumbs up through the furls of her cunt, spreading her juices around her clit.

'Wet already.' He loved that, it made him feel invincible that he affected her so much.

'It's the commute; it makes me hot. Oh God . . .' Her head

dropped back and his mouth met the place where his thumbs slid back and forth.

Her taste, Christ, her taste was so good. The flesh of her sex was salty sweet against the rasp of his tongue. He closed his eyes against it, the sharpness of his need for her, and simply let himself feel like he'd come home in her.

Slowly, slowly, he took long soft licks through her, meaning to take every moment of those twenty minutes.

It was more than a blow job. Dix's mouth worshipped her, paid homage to her body. Every movement of his hands, tongue and the slight scrape of teeth was reverent.

She wanted to arch, to get more, but he held her in place. His warning growl rumbled through her sex. She held a hand to his head, revelling in his hair between her fingers. Her other hand slid into the bodice of her dress and found a nipple.

The sharp pleasure of her fingertips tugging brought a moan from her and then from him. She dragged her eyes open to find him watching her, even as his mouth still worked against her sex.

He lapped at her like a cat and then flicked the tip of his tongue against her clit rapidly until her entire body began to vibrate.

God, it was too much. One of his thumbs played at her entrance, teasing in and out while the other played over her rear passage. All she could do was pant and moan while orgasm began to take over her body.

She came, with a hoarse gasp, her fingers tightening in his hair and on her nipple. Her gasp built into a moan so loud she was pretty sure her neighbours knew she was up to something naked.

On and on it went and he never backed off as climax reverberated through her body. She finally shoved at him because she couldn't take another second of it.

He pulled back and kissed her inner thigh. 'You're so gorgeous when you come,' he murmured, petting her mound gently as she slowly came back to herself.

The buzzer sounded and the doorman let her know the delivery guy was on his way up.

Dix stood and rearranged her dress. 'Sit here a second. I'll handle the door.'

She didn't argue.

Dix watched for a while as she ate and drank her beer before saying anything.

'How are you settling in? I like this place. It's a good building. The manly man in me is pleased the security is so good.'

She laughed. 'So good you and my parents got in.'

'Believe it or not, when I approached and started to ring you, one of your neighbours saw me and recognised me. He's one of the referees in the soccer league Adrienne plays for. He let me in. I didn't say who I was here to see, by the way. Not that I wanted to hide it, but I didn't know how you'd feel just yet.'

'Well, that's good. After someone in the building let my parents in, I sort of read the doorman the Riot Act about being extra vigilant with my visitors.'

'I take it you weren't happy to see them?'

'I was in Harrisburg at the time so I lucked out and wasn't here. We're, um, not close. Or rather they think we are, but I know we aren't. Sadly, they just live in Bala Cynwyd, so near enough to menace me on a whim. Anyway, my job is good, surprisingly so. My stuff arrived from Seattle and nothing was broken. How's things with you?'

'You're so easygoing right now I'm nervous.'

She laughed and popped the last of an egg roll into her mouth. 'Oh, come on, just say it already. I'm all mellow and full of serotonin and Chinese food. Add the beer and it's all good. What do you have to be nervous about anyway?'

'You're not worried?'

She snorted in a very unladylike fashion and it made him smile. 'Well, I'm not worried you fucked your ex at the lake house or that you've found an assistant who does her roots. I have concerns but you know what they are.'

'You can be very vicious.'

'What? Did I bring up pickle jars even once?'

He laughed. 'Man, you are! I didn't mean the pickle-jar incident, although I'll give you fifty bucks to never mention it again. I meant the roots comment.'

'Dix, darling, if you think that was vicious you don't know nearly as much as you think about women. There's so much I didn't say – to you anyway – about that bitch-faced cow you have no idea. Anyway, you're skirting the subject again.'

'Fine. The girls are good. We're finishing up with getting the new confidentiality and non-compete agreements signed company-wide and you were right.'

'Glad to hear it. Good. And, duh, I'm frequently right. Learn it now and save us both a lot of headache. What do you mean specifically?'

He put her plate to the side and took her hands in his. 'You were right about the situation with Eve. I did a lot of thinking that night as I drove to the hospital and while I was awake all night long. By the time Eve told me I still loved her and that's why I'd never committed to anyone in the years since we'd divorced, well, that was pretty much a big underlined "Kate was right."'

Kate's jaw tightened and her brows rose before a light came into her eyes just briefly. 'So you had a talk with her about this?'

'Is that hope I see in your face? Trust?'

'I told you already, Charles, I trust you. If I didn't, you wouldn't be here right now. Do *you* have trust issues?'

He sighed and drew her to the couch, snuggling her into his body. 'It's never been an issue because I've never had anyone in my life I felt a sort of possession over. I do with you. I want you and I want you to want me as much. But I don't feel as if you'd betray what we're building.'

Wow, he was so freaking self-actualised it sort of scared her. 'You know, I thought men were supposed to be all silent and broody and women had to pull teeth to get them to share. I am so turned on by the way you open yourself up. God, I'm such a freak.' She laughed and he kissed the top of her head.

'I'm forty-two. I've lived long enough to know what I want and to say so.'

'OK. So, in kind, it was hope you saw on my face. I, well, you know my concerns about your ex. I just don't want a third person in this relationship. Unless it's Gerard Butler, in which case, I'm on board. I'm not worried you'll want her back, I'm worried you never left. Not really. And I know without a doubt I cannot tolerate that. It's emotional infidelity. I can deal with stuff to do with your kids, but the pickle-jar stuff has to end. At this point I can't even go back to fucking you casually and not caring about pickle jars. I care about you too much to not be bothered by another woman having such sway over your concerns.'

He took a deep breath and she heard it through the wall of his chest along with the steady thump of his heart. 'I did leave, damn it! People keep saying how it was unclear but, fuck, I divorced her seven years ago! I haven't made a single romantic or amorous move towards her in longer than that. I've dated more women than I can count.' He paused when she pinched his side. 'Ouch. OK, so that was a dumb thing to say but, shit, I don't know why everyone is making it my fault.'

'I'm not making it your fault, Dix. But everyone thinks you're unclear because, despite divorcing her, you go on vacations with her, you open her fucking pickle jars, you mend things around her house and you treat her like she's still your wife. That's confusing enough to me and, well, Eve doesn't strike me as a super-modern woman.' Which came out way nicer than her mental dialogue about the woman. 'I'm guessing she just figured you'd fuck your way around town but as long as you checked her tyre pressure and changed her windshield wipers you were still her husband. And, you know, to be fair to her, that's what husbands do.'

'I'm a nice guy! How am I the bad guy for being nice? By changing those wiper blades my kids are safe.'

She pulled away to face him and rolled her eyes. 'Stop it! Stop making this about your daughters. Because, hello, when my car needs new blades, guess who changes them? Not my dad. Not my ex-boyfriends. I do. Because it's not that complicated. She's not a moron. She has all her fingers, right? You said her consultant business makes good money so if she's too stupid or simply doesn't want to change them she can afford to go down to the lube and tune or whatever and pay the twenty bucks. Like other parents do. This isn't about your kids at all. The point is, you never really left your caretaking role with her. Divorce or not.'

'So what is and isn't a problem with you? I mean, do I need to run everything past you now?'

'You're a tool.' She curled her lip. 'I know you're feeling attacked and defensive but don't insult me. I've said several times I expect you to care for your kids. But if your ex-wife thinks you're coming back to her after seven years of divorce, it's not an issue of my expectations. I've told you what I have a problem with, butthead.'

The anger on his face softened into amusement. 'Point taken.'

'What does she think? Did you tell her about me? About us?'

In that moment Dix saw Kate's vulnerability, saw what she'd been trying to hide. He kissed her just because he could. 'I did. She knew actually, heard my call and asked who you were. That's new and she picked up on it, I suppose. I explained you were different and also that there was no coming back for me. I'm not sure why divorce and seven years of me living away from her didn't seem clear enough, but you were right. It's partially my fault for not simply letting her stand on her own feet. I suppose she became one of my children, or maybe she has been since day one.'

This relationship thing was hard work. The woman he sat with and poured his guts out for would expect nothing less but everything and it felt right that she'd have high expectations. Like he was worth it. Funny that.

He took a deep breath and watched her as she simply, calmly took him in before nodding.

'OK then. So, um, are we, like, dating?'

'More than that, Kate. We're together. I did tell the girls I was seeing you. I told them I was in love with you and I hoped you felt the same. I'd like you to meet them before school starts. They're curious about you, I expect you are about them too. Or I hope you are.'

'You love me?'

'I'm usually smoother with the ladies, you know. But you've been unexpected in every sense. Got in under the radar and, before I realised it, yeah, I was in love with you.'

She furrowed her brow for a moment. 'I told my mother about you this week when she called to harangue me about ... whatever it was she complained of. I can't remember, it's all white noise. Anyway, she doesn't approve of you being divorced and you having kids means I'll die childless and alone and they'll steal from me if you actually do marry me and kick off. Just so you know.'

He paused and then began to laugh. 'OK, so I can see why you aren't close.'

'And you're too old and likely to become impotent and then you'll use Viagra and become a deviant. I should be so lucky that you'd just become impotent and won't want sex at all.' She snickered. 'I'm sure you can't wait to meet them now. My dad said nothing except when I asked if he took Viagra and became a deviant. Then he sputtered. It's about all you get from him. He likes to sputter. I just think full disclosure is good. I don't open their pickle jars and I'm going to tell you up front, I now expect you to change my wiper blades because, while it's not hard, I always break nails and it sucks. But I can open my own jars and if something breaks I can call a handyman.'

Panic ate at his insides as he struggled to pay attention to her meandering chatter about her parents. Did she love him or not? God, all he got from her in response to his declaration of love was a furrowed brow?

'I can see by that mildly panicked look on your face you're concerned about telling me you love me and I didn't immediately retort I loved you too.' She cocked her head and then launched herself at him, laughing. 'Of course I love you. Dumbass. Do you think I'd put up with an old, possibly impotent future deviant with a penchant for attracting crazy women who think you love them even when you don't touch them if I didn't?'

'You're such a romantic.' He laughed and pulled her snug against him.

'Practical too.' She ground herself against his cock. 'I'm here, you're here. Your penis is here. Kismet.'

'Should I take that to mean you'd like to have sex?'

'I need to grab it while I can, apparently.'

'Can't wait to meet your mom.' He stood and she stayed wrapped around him.

Kate held on as he walked down her hall and into her bedroom. Kate couldn't quite believe she'd just told him she loved him. He made her want to be softer in some ways, harder in others.

Instead of tossing her to the bed like he'd done before, he laid her down gently. She swallowed hard, her hand pressing to her lips.

Grabbing a pillow, she propped herself up to watch him undress. 'For an old guy you have such a gorgeous body.'

He grinned lasciviously as he tossed his shirt over his head and went to work on ridding himself of his pants, boxers and shoes.

She got to her knees and whipped the dress off and wriggled out of the panties.

'I need to taste you again,' he murmured as he climbed on to the bed.

'You already did. It's my turn.' She grabbed his cock, warm and hard in her hand.

'You can have your turn later. You should let the visitor have special privileges.' He tipped her back to the bed and followed, kissing her, his tongue sliding into her mouth with surety. She loved that about him, his confidence in his own sexual allure.

They stayed like that for some time, just kissing, slow and deep, the fire between them building and building. Finally his mouth moved from hers and touched her eyelids, her nose, her cheeks and along the line of her jaw.

She touched every part of him she could reach – the muscled planes of his back and shoulders, the dip of his spine just above his ass. His hair was soft against her palms, his neck muscles hard as she skimmed over them.

The slight shadow of a beard abraded the skin of her neck as she arched to give him access. His tongue laved the sensitive spot just beneath her ear, teeth sliding across the tendon where neck met shoulder.

'I can't get enough of you,' he said, his lips brushing over the top of her left breast. His tongue slid across the nipple, stroking a wet caress, leaving sharp sensation in its wake.

Some men didn't know what to do with a nipple. They twisted it like a radio dial a few times and headed for pussy. But Charles Dixon appreciated and understood the multitude of things nipples – hers especially – liked. He licked and nuzzled, nipped with his teeth, sucked hard and soft until she writhed beneath him, desperate to get contact against her sex.

He chuckled and relented, kissing down her ribs and across her belly before settling between her thighs again. He took her ankles and pushed her knees up and wide until she lay spread open wide before him.

It took her breath away just seeing the way he looked at her then.

'You've got the prettiest cunt, Kate. Swollen and pink, glistening with your juices. Your clit is hard, peeking from the hood, just begging for a taste.'

Before she could encourage him in that direction, he dipped his head and did just that. The flat of his tongue pressed against her clit, sliding from side to side.

He feasted as he held her wide, took every bit she had and turned it back, giving her more.

She grasped handfuls of the duvet in her hands to keep from yanking him bald.

One of his fingers filled her, then another. It wasn't enough, she needed his cock. Still, she gasped out her pleasure when he turned his wrist and found her sweet spot, stroking it as he fucked her that way.

'Oh God, more, please,' she begged.

A third finger joined and stretched her, his mouth opened over as much of her cunt as it could and she drew in a deep breath and bit back a cry when he made her come.

He let go of her ankles and grabbed her wrist, moving her hand to her sex. 'Play with your clit while I get a condom,' he said as he moved back.

She managed to open her eyes and watch him dig through a pocket of his discarded jeans, all the while sliding her middle finger over her clit ever so gently as tiny aftershock climaxes echoed through her.

'Why not let me suck your cock?'

He was hard enough he had to angle his cock to roll the condom on. He groaned as he looked up at her. 'Because I want to fuck you right this very moment. God, you're hot when you do that.'

She spread herself and raised a brow. 'This?'

'Later . . . Later you're going to masturbate while I watch. Now I'm going to have you.'

She flipped on to her belly, sliding her knee up and arching her back. 'This way?'

He groaned again. 'Christ, you're sexier than anything I've ever seen. That'll do nicely.' He moved in and she nearly whimpered in relief when the head of his cock brushed against her sex and began to slide inside.

Burrowing her arm between her body and the bed, she found her clit again, occasionally reaching down further to stroke over his cock as he pressed into and pulled out of her body.

His weight anchored her and the way he held her pinned brought her body up over her fingers with each plunge into her cunt.

Each thrust stroked her clit against her hand as his cock filled her, stretched, firing nerves and sending pleasure flooding through her body.

Every part of him felt good, the slide of his cock invading and retreating, the slap of his balls, the wiry hair on his thighs against the backs of her legs, the way one of his hands encircled her wrist, holding but not harming. His body on hers, possessing, warming. Little gusts of his breath stirred the wisps of hair on the back of her neck.

Her nipples slid over the cool nubbed fabric of the duvet. Her skin was hypersensitive to the differences in sensation surrounding her. It all added to the nearly overwhelming richness of what was happening.

This was fucking, raw, feral, rife with emotion, but it was more too. She wasn't scared. She'd already admitted to herself and to him that she loved him and now she'd have to trust he'd handle his ex and keep his promises. The man to whom she'd entrusted her heart and body, while arrogant, had proved to be honourable and true every time she turned around.

'Kate, I'm going to come. Then I'll rest and you can suck my cock all you like,' he whispered against the back of her neck.

'Mmmm, not a bad offer at all.'

She pressed her finger more solidly against her clit and tightened her muscles. He moaned in response and quickened his pace. She came in deep rolling shudders and shortly after heard his tortured whisper of her name as he joined her, pressing hard over and over and over again until he stilled and rolled off with a final kiss to the back of her neck.

When he returned, they snuggled for a while. 'I'm staying over and I think you should give me a key too.'

'You're very bossy.'

He snorted. 'You should know. Tomorrow morning let's go for breakfast and then you can help me pick up some new sheets for my bed. I have all sorts of domestic crap I need to do.'

'I'm touched you'd offer me pancakes before offering to share domestic crap.' She grinned into the skin of his side. 'Why is the hair under your arms so soft?'

'One of life's great mysteries I'm sure. Right up there with why I'm suddenly struck with how good your pussy smells when I'm right in the middle of a meeting and then I get hard and have to think about algebra for a while. Meet me halfway for dinner next week?'

Surprised by his change of topic, she laughed. 'Boy, once a girl lets you in, you just blow the doors off, don't you? But OK. I'm hanging out with Leah next Wednesday but we can meet up another day.'

'Since I've blown the doors off and all, why don't you come to my house next weekend? Stay over? The girls are with their grandparents for a few weeks. Then you can meet them next month. If you're OK with it.'

She took a deep breath and agreed. It wasn't that hard really. Just a nod and suddenly she was there. In a relationship with a man she loved. Cool.

36

Another week. Another trip to Wegman's. The automatic doors opened for her and Leah headed first to the store's prepared-foods section. She loved to cook, and when she was with Mike had made a practice out of perfecting delicious meals catering to his pleasure. The sensual delights of food had been one of the best parts of their relationship, mostly because the act of him feeding her had seemed submissive to him but had actually fuelled her fantasies of being catered to utterly.

In the past couple of weeks, though, with just herself to take care of, Leah most often opted to pick up side dishes and easily heated entrées from the store. The plastic containers went straight into the microwave and meant she didn't even need to wash dishes. It was a little bit hellish on her budget, but it was also an indulgence she permitted in lieu of other extravagances.

Tonight she was in the mood for sushi. The selection at Wegman's was impressive, considering it was a grocery store and Pennsylvania was an inland state. The spicy tuna looked good. So did the spicy salmon.

Leah put both packages in her basket. Friday night was date night, and she had no date. Wasn't that reason enough to treat herself? She picked up a few more items, and paid for her purchases, already looking ahead to an evening of quiet at home. Just her sushi and a good movie. Later, a hot bath and a new book.

The parking lot remained full, nearly every spot taken,

but she didn't mind the walk. With the sun going down, the day's heat had begun to dissipate.

She heard his voice before she saw him, a deep chuckle she'd imagined a thousand times over the past two weeks. She almost turned and fled before she could see him, but curiosity wouldn't let her. Hitching her canvas shopping bag over her arm, Leah walked around the back of a large SUV that had been blocking her view.

They were still about four cars away, but Leah stopped as suddenly as though her feet had gotten mired in the heat-softened asphalt.

'No,' he was saying with that laugh and, oh God, that smile. That brilliant, gleaming smile she wanted to be for her alone. 'No way.'

'Give it to me!' The tiny blonde made a grab for whatever he had in his hand. Her T-shirt swelled voluminously with the mounds of breasts too bouncy to be anything but real. She tossed her hair and took another swipe, but Brandon moved his hand out of reach.

'Nope.' His arm, impossibly long, stretched up, up and up, his hand cradling a package of something Leah still couldn't see. He put his other hand on the girl's forehead, holding her back without much effort, but gently, as she tried again to grab away the unseen prize. 'Forget it.'

He wasn't hers. Hadn't ever been. Yet there was no denying the way Leah's throat closed as her heart leaped into it, or the way her fingers tightened convulsively on the handle of her shopping bag as she kept herself from waving to capture his attention.

'You are so mean!' the girl cried. She crossed her arms, pouting, and even went so far as to stomp her foot.

Nice.

'I'm not mean.' Brandon's voice, implacable. 'Just taller than you.'

'What do I have to do to make you give them back?' The girl's tone turned wheedling, sounding like she'd done this often before.

Brandon, his dark hair hidden beneath a battered baseball cap, didn't relinquish the package. 'What are you offering?'

'A kiss.'

'Pah.' He laughed again. 'I've already had one of those.'

'You're such a jerk!' The girl sprang towards him, slapping at his broad chest.

She didn't look to be doing much damage, but Brandon swatted her hands away and lowered his arm to hand her the package. 'Fine. Take it. Blacken your lungs, see if I care.'

The girl grabbed the pack of cigarettes from him with a triumphant look, but then she paused. 'You don't care?'

Neither of them had noticed her before now, though if she wanted to get to her car Leah would have to go right by them. Unless she ducked back behind the SUV and went around the front of it to avoid him. She didn't. She walked, slowly, but with certain steps, towards her car at the far end of the lot.

'I ... ah ...'

'Jerk,' the girl muttered. 'You're always so mean.'

He looked contrite and snaked out one long arm to pull her closer to him. 'I'm sorry, Crissy.'

Crissy looked mollified. She tipped her face up towards him, her mouth pursed. She wanted that kiss. Leah couldn't blame her.

But Brandon didn't kiss the girl in front of him. He looked down at her, yes, and his big hands settled on her waist, but at the last second his attention swerved. He looked straight at Leah. Then he let go of Crissy, even took two steps back from her, his hands falling from her waist as though he'd never touched her at all.

'Hello, Brandon.' His name felt smooth and rich on her

tongue. She hadn't said it aloud in a long time, though the beat of its syllables had been on her mind often.

He didn't reply with words, just a nod. Crissy gave him an expectant smile, but he wasn't looking at her. He was looking at Leah, who kept her face carefully neutral despite the triumphant grin trying to leap on to her lips.

A few weeks might not have been long enough to mend a broken heart, but Leah's heart hadn't been broken. Not even bruised, really. If anything had taken a beating it was her sense of self, her understanding of what she wanted and what she did not. How could she have ever thought she didn't want him?

She didn't want a string of anonymous fucks, or an occasional play-date with some EmoGothSub boy she met on the internet who called her 'mistress' without asking if that's what she wanted and was really only interested in being tied up and stepped on by someone in stiletto boots. She wasn't interested in the 'scene', such as it was in Harrisburg, or even the larger D/S culture in Philadelphia. She didn't want what she'd had with Mike.

She wanted what she already had been lucky enough to find, but had been stupid enough to toss away because going after what she wanted in her personal life hadn't been as simple as it was in business.

She wanted Brandon.

'How have you been?' An innocuous statement with anything but an innocent intent.

Crissy looked back and forth between them, her face crunching into an extremely unflattering look. Brandon didn't notice. His attention had focused squarely on Leah.

'How's work?' she prompted. 'Still taking care of business?'

The ghost of his smile warmed her. The step he took away from Crissy might have only been half a foot, but it might as well have been a mile. 'Yeah. I guess you could say that.'

'It's good to see you,' she said finally.

He nodded again. 'You too.'

She drew in a breath that made her taller. Stronger. He gave her that, she realised, with nothing more than a nod. A glance. That smile. With Brandon she had been stronger, and two weeks had passed, but that hadn't changed.

'I'm going home,' she said quietly, not looking at Crissy, or the passing cars or the setting sun. Looking only at him.

She saw the gleam of understanding wash over his face. He really couldn't hide anything. Leah passed him by without even a second glance, though she felt the weight of his gaze following her and she was desperate to turn back to see him looking. She dug in her purse for her keys and her keyless remote. The welcoming 'boop, boop' of her car unlocking covered up her slow, hissing exhale as she let out the breath she'd been holding.

'Who was that?' she heard Crissy say, but Leah got into her car and closed the door before she could hear the answer.

Then she drove home to wait.

It took him two hours to get there.

Leah, her appetite replaced by anxiety, hadn't been able to eat the sushi after all. She'd showered and changed from her work clothes into a pair of soft cotton lounge pants and a tank top. She'd pulled her hair up on top of her head in a loose ponytail and replaced her workday make-up with no more than a dusting of powder and a smudge of eyeliner and mascara.

She opened the door as soon as he knocked. He took up more space than she'd expected, filling her doorway from top to bottom and side to side. He didn't move towards her, just waited for her to step aside so he could come in. They didn't waste their time or breath with trite greetings.

She closed the door after him. They turned to face each other. Leah meant to speak, to say something cool and collected. Witty, even.

'Oh, Brandon,' she said instead when he held out the flowers.

A bouquet of daisies and colourful wild flowers she couldn't name, tied with a wide bow of scarlet ribbon. She took them and pressed them to her face, her eyes closed so she wouldn't have to blink away sudden tears. They smelled like summer and anticipation.

She looked at him. 'I was crying that night.'

'I know you were.'

'Come into the kitchen with me while I put these in some water.'

She filled a vase and tugged the ribbon free so she could put the flowers in the glass container. The soft red satin coiled in her palm and she closed her fingers over it before facing him.

'I've spent a long time trying to make myself believe what I really wanted didn't exist or, if it did, I shouldn't want it. I fooled myself pretty well too.' Leah ran the ribbon through her fingers, back and forth, relishing the softness. 'Until I met you.'

He licked his mouth before he spoke, his voice husky. 'At least you knew what you wanted.'

Heat bloomed inside her. 'I'm sorry.'

'Don't be sorry.' He shook his head. 'I just didn't know. Now I do.'

'Well, that's something,' she said too brightly and looked into the puddle of crimson in her palm.

'Leah,' Brandon whispered, like speaking louder would have cost him too much, 'I want it with you.'

He was uncertain. She saw it in his eyes and every line of his face. But he was here anyway, offering himself the way he'd offered the flowers.

She reached for him and he was there. His mouth, as sweet and hot as she had been unable to forget. Her arms went naturally around his neck, the red ribbon dangling, as his hands settled on her back and he pulled her closer.

She broke the kiss to breathe. 'There's more to a relationship than hot sex, you know.'

He slid a hand up to cup the back of her neck, easing the pressure of her having to tilt her head to look at his face. 'I already know how you like your coffee. And bagels. I can't forget that.'

She laughed, slightly self-conscious and let him kiss her some more before she managed to say against his mouth, 'Are you sure?'

'Are you sure?' he murmured as he nibbled at her lips and moved along her jaw to nuzzle her throat.

'Not really,' she said with a sigh as his hand found her breast. 'But I could be persuaded.'

He chuffed lightly against her skin, then pulled away to look at her, his expression serious. 'I want to try at least.'

Leah hopped up on to the counter and drew him closer, between her legs. She wanted to be able to look him in the eyes. She put her hands on his face for a moment, holding him still so she could look at him. His flesh heated beneath her palms as he blushed, but he didn't look away. She let her fingers trail down the sides of his neck, over his shoulders, down to his chest. His heart thumped under her hand. The red ribbon dangled.

'Me too,' she said.

'I'm not wearing a belt,' Brandon said, smiling.

Leah held up the red ribbon with a grin of her own. 'That's all right. I'm quite convinced you're good at improvising.'

'Can we start right away?' His eyes gleamed.

'Oh yes, Brandon,' Leah said, pulling him closer as she slid her hand down to his wrist to wrap it with a loop of scarlet. 'Now.'

Visit the Black Lace website at
www.black-lace-books.com

LOOK OUT FOR THE ALL-NEW BLACK LACE BOOKS – AVAILABLE NOW!

All books priced £7.99 in the UK. Please note publication dates apply to the UK only. For other territories, please contact your retailer.

To be published in November 2008

THE NINETY DAYS OF GENEVIEVE
Lucinda Carrington
ISBN 978 0 352 34201 0

A ninety-day sex contract wasn't exactly what Genevieve Loften had in mind when she began business negotiations with the arrogant and attractive James Sinclair. As a career move she wanted to go along with it; the pay-off was potentially huge. However, she didn't imagine that he would make her the star performer in a series of increasingly kinky and exotic fantasies. Thrown into a world of sexual misadventure, Genevieve learns how to balance her high-pressure career with the twilight world of fetishism and debauchery.

THE NEW RAKES
Nikki Magennis
ISBN 978 035 234503 5

Fuelled by Kara's sexy performances, The New Rakes are poised for rock & roll stardom. And when Mike Greene, the charismatic head of a record company, offers the band a deal, it seems their dreams are about to come true. But Kara and Mike have history and this time he wants more than a professional relationship. Already in the thick of a love-hate relationship with her guitarist Tam, Kara's tempestuous affairs with both men threaten to spoil everything. Tangled in a web of sex, power and deceit, she finally has to choose between the limelight and true love.

To be published in December 2008

THE GIFT OF SHAME
Sarah Hope-Walker
ISBN 978 0 352 34202 7

Sad, sultry Helen flies between London, Paris and the Caribbean chasing whatever physical pleasures she can get to tear her mind from a deep, deep loss. Her glamorous life-style and charged sensual escapades belie a widow's grief. When she meets handsome, rich Jeffrey she is shocked and yet intrigued by his masterful, domineering behaviour. Soon, Helen is forced to confront the forbidden desires hiding within herself – and forced to undergo a startling metamorphosis from a meek and modest lady into a bristling, voracious wanton.

TO SEEK A MASTER
Monica Belle
ISBN 978 0 352 34507 3

Sexy daydreams are shy Laura's only escape from the dull routines of her life. But with the arrival of an email ordering her to dress provocatively, she wonders if her secret fantasies about her colleagues are about to become true. Unable to resist the new and more daring instructions that arrive by email, she begins to slip deeper into dangerous water with several men. But when her controller finally reveals himself, she's in for a shock and a far greater involvement in his illicit games.

ALSO LOOK OUT FOR

THE NEW BLACK LACE BOOK OF WOMEN'S SEXUAL FANTASIES
Edited and compiled by Mitzi Szereto
ISBN 978 0 352 34172 3

The second anthology of detailed sexual fantasies contributed by women from all over the world. The book is a result of a year's research by an expert on erotic writing and gives a fascinating insight into the rich diversity of the female sexual imagination.

Black Lace Booklist

Information is correct at time of printing. To avoid disappointment, check availability before ordering. Go to www.black-lace-books.com.
All books are priced £7.99 unless another price is given.

BLACK LACE BOOKS WITH A CONTEMPORARY SETTING

❏ THE ANGELS' SHARE Maya Hess	ISBN 978 0 352 34043 6	
❏ ASKING FOR TROUBLE Kristina Lloyd	ISBN 978 0 352 33362 9	
❏ BLACK LIPSTICK KISSES Monica Belle	ISBN 978 0 352 33885 3	£6.99
❏ THE BLUE GUIDE Carrie Williams	ISBN 978 0 352 34132 7	
❏ THE BOSS Monica Belle	ISBN 978 0 352 34088 7	
❏ BOUND IN BLUE Monica Belle	ISBN 978 0 352 34012 2	
❏ CAMPAIGN HEAT Gabrielle Marcola	ISBN 978 0 352 33941 6	
❏ CAT SCRATCH FEVER Sophie Mouette	ISBN 978 0 352 34021 4	
❏ CIRCUS EXCITE Nikki Magennis	ISBN 978 0 352 34033 7	
❏ CLUB CREME Primula Bond	ISBN 978 0 352 33907 2	£6.99
❏ CONFESSIONAL Judith Roycroft	ISBN 978 0 352 33421 3	
❏ CONTINUUM Portia Da Costa	ISBN 978 0 352 33120 5	
❏ DANGEROUS CONSEQUENCES Pamela Rochford	ISBN 978 0 352 33185 4	
❏ DARK DESIGNS Madelynne Ellis	ISBN 978 0 352 34075 7	
❏ THE DEVIL INSIDE Portia Da Costa	ISBN 978 0 352 32993 6	
❏ EQUAL OPPORTUNITIES Mathilde Madden	ISBN 978 0 352 34070 2	
❏ FIRE AND ICE Laura Hamilton	ISBN 978 0 352 33486 2	
❏ GONE WILD Maria Eppie	ISBN 978 0 352 34670 5	
❏ HOTBED Portia Da Costa	ISBN 978 0 352 33614 9	
❏ IN PURSUIT OF ANNA Natasha Rostova	ISBN 978 0 352 34060 3	
❏ IN THE FLESH Emma Holly	ISBN 978 0 352 34117 4	
❏ LEARNING TO LOVE IT Alison Tyler	ISBN 978 0 352 33535 7	
❏ MAD ABOUT THE BOY Mathilde Madden	ISBN 978 0 352 34001 6	
❏ MAKE YOU A MAN Anna Clare	ISBN 978 0 352 34006 1	
❏ MAN HUNT Cathleen Ross	ISBN 978 0 352 33583 8	
❏ THE MASTER OF SHILDEN Lucinda Carrington	ISBN 978 0 352 33140 3	
❏ MIXED DOUBLES Zoe le Verdier	ISBN 978 0 352 33312 4	£6.99
❏ MIXED SIGNALS Anna Clare	ISBN 978 0 352 33889 1	£6.99
❏ MS BEHAVIOUR Mini Lee	ISBN 978 0 352 33962 1	

❏ PACKING HEAT Karina Moore	ISBN 978 0 352 33356 8	£6.99
❏ PAGAN HEAT Monica Belle	ISBN 978 0 352 33974 4	
❏ PEEP SHOW Mathilde Madden	ISBN 978 0 352 33924 9	
❏ THE POWER GAME Carrera Devonshire	ISBN 978 0 352 33990 4	
❏ THE PRIVATE UNDOING OF A PUBLIC SERVANT Leonie Martel	ISBN 978 0 352 34066 5	
❏ RUDE AWAKENING Pamela Kyle	ISBN 978 0 352 33036 9	
❏ SAUCE FOR THE GOOSE Mary Rose Maxwell	ISBN 978 0 352 33492 3	
❏ SPLIT Kristina Lloyd	ISBN 978 0 352 34154 9	
❏ STELLA DOES HOLLYWOOD Stella Black	ISBN 978 0 352 33588 3	
❏ THE STRANGER Portia Da Costa	ISBN 978 0 352 33211 0	
❏ SUITE SEVENTEEN Portia Da Costa	ISBN 978 0 352 34109 8	
❏ TONGUE IN CHEEK Tabitha Flyte	ISBN 978 0 352 33484 8	
❏ THE TOP OF HER GAME Emma Holly	ISBN 978 0 352 34116 7	
❏ UNNATURAL SELECTION Alaine Hood	ISBN 978 0 352 33963 8	
❏ VELVET GLOVE Emma Holly	ISBN 978 0 352 34115 0	
❏ VILLAGE OF SECRETS Mercedes Kelly	ISBN 978 0 352 33344 5	
❏ WILD BY NATURE Monica Belle	ISBN 978 0 352 33915 7	£6.99
❏ WILD CARD Madeline Moore	ISBN 978 0 352 34038 2	
❏ WING OF MADNESS Mae Nixon	ISBN 978 0 352 34099 3	

BLACK LACE BOOKS WITH AN HISTORICAL SETTING

❏ THE BARBARIAN GEISHA Charlotte Royal	ISBN 978 0 352 33267 7	
❏ BARBARIAN PRIZE Deanna Ashford	ISBN 978 0 352 34017 7	
❏ THE CAPTIVATION Natasha Rostova	ISBN 978 0 352 33234 9	
❏ DARKER THAN LOVE Kristina Lloyd	ISBN 978 0 352 33279 0	
❏ WILD KINGDOM Deanna Ashford	ISBN 978 0 352 33549 4	
❏ DIVINE TORMENT Janine Ashbless	ISBN 978 0 352 33719 1	
❏ FRENCH MANNERS Olivia Christie	ISBN 978 0 352 33214 1	
❏ LORD WRAXALL'S FANCY Anna LiefSaxby	ISBN 978 0 352 33080 2	
❏ NICOLE'S REVENGE Lisette Allen	ISBN 978 0 352 32984 4	
❏ THE SENSES BEJEWELLED Cleo Cordell	ISBN 978 0 352 32904 2	£6.99
❏ THE SOCIETY OF SIN Sian LaceyTaylder	ISBN 978 0 352 34080 1	
❏ TEMPLAR PRIZE Deanna Ashford	ISBN 978 0 352 34137 2	
❏ UNDRESSING THE DEVIL Angel Strand	ISBN 978 0 352 33938 6	

❏ PACKING HEAT Karina Moore	ISBN 978 0 352 33356 8	£6.99
❏ PAGAN HEAT Monica Belle	ISBN 978 0 352 33974 4	
❏ PEEP SHOW Mathilde Madden	ISBN 978 0 352 33924 9	
❏ THE POWER GAME Carrera Devonshire	ISBN 978 0 352 33990 4	
❏ THE PRIVATE UNDOING OF A PUBLIC SERVANT Leonie Martel	ISBN 978 0 352 34066 5	
❏ RUDE AWAKENING Pamela Kyle	ISBN 978 0 352 33036 9	
❏ SAUCE FOR THE GOOSE Mary Rose Maxwell	ISBN 978 0 352 33492 3	
❏ SPLIT Kristina Lloyd	ISBN 978 0 352 34154 9	
❏ STELLA DOES HOLLYWOOD Stella Black	ISBN 978 0 352 33588 3	
❏ THE STRANGER Portia Da Costa	ISBN 978 0 352 33211 0	
❏ SUITE SEVENTEEN Portia Da Costa	ISBN 978 0 352 34109 9	
❏ TONGUE IN CHEEK Tabitha Flyte	ISBN 978 0 352 33484 8	
❏ THE TOP OF HER GAME Emma Holly	ISBN 978 0 352 34116 7	
❏ UNNATURAL SELECTION Alaine Hood	ISBN 978 0 352 33963 8	
❏ VELVET GLOVE Emma Holly	ISBN 978 0 352 34115 0	
❏ VILLAGE OF SECRETS Mercedes Kelly	ISBN 978 0 352 33344 5	
❏ WILD BY NATURE Monica Belle	ISBN 978 0 352 33915	£6.99
❏ WILD CARD Madeline Moore	ISBN 978 0 352 34038 2	
❏ WING OF MADNESS Mae Nixon	ISBN 978 0 352 34099 3	

BLACK LACE BOOKS WITH AN HISTORICAL SETTING

❏ THE BARBARIAN GEISHA Charlotte Royal	ISBN 978 0 352 33267 7	
❏ BARBARIAN PRIZE Deanna Ashford	ISBN 978 0 352 34017 7	
❏ THE CAPTIVATION Natasha Rostova	ISBN 978 0 352 33234 9	
❏ DARKER THAN LOVE Kristina Lloyd	ISBN 978 0 352 33279 0	
❏ WILD KINGDOM Deanna Ashford	ISBN 978 0 352 33549 4	
❏ DIVINE TORMENT Janine Ashbless	ISBN 978 0 352 33719 1	
❏ FRENCH MANNERS Olivia Christie	ISBN 978 0 352 33214 1	
❏ LORD WRAXALL'S FANCY Anna Lieff Saxby	ISBN 978 0 352 33080 2	
❏ NICOLE'S REVENGE Lisette Allen	ISBN 978 0 352 32984 4	
❏ THE SENSES BEJEWELLED Cleo Cordell	ISBN 978 0 352 32904 2	£6.99
❏ THE SOCIETY OF SIN Sian Lacey Taylder	ISBN 978 0 352 34080 1	
❏ TEMPLAR PRIZE Deanna Ashford	ISBN 978 0 352 34137 2	
❏ UNDRESSING THE DEVIL Angel Strand	ISBN 978 0 352 33938 6	

BLACK LACE BOOKS WITH A PARANORMAL THEME

❑ BRIGHT FIRE Maya Hess   ISBN 978 0 352 34104 4

❑ BURNING BRIGHT Janine Ashbless   ISBN 978 0 352 34085 6

❑ CRUEL ENCHANTMENT Janine Ashbless   ISBN 978 0 352 33483 1

❑ FLOOD Anna Clare   ISBN 978 0 352 34094 8

❑ GOTHIC BLUE Portia Da Costa   ISBN 978 0 352 33075 8

❑ THE PRIDE Edie Bingham   ISBN 978 0 352 33997 3

❑ THE SILVER COLLAR Mathilde Madden   ISBN 978 0 352 34141 9

❑ THE TEN VISIONS Olivia Knight   ISBN 978 0 352 34119 8

BLACK LACE ANTHOLOGIES

❑ BLACK LACE QUICKIES 1 Various   ISBN 978 0 352 34126 6   £2.99

❑ BLACK LACE QUICKIES 2 Various   ISBN 978 0 352 34127 3   £2.99

❑ BLACK LACE QUICKIES 3 Various   ISBN 978 0 352 34128 0   £2.99

❑ BLACK LACE QUICKIES 4 Various   ISBN 978 0 352 34129 7   £2.99

❑ BLACK LACE QUICKIES 5 Various   ISBN 978 0 352 34130 3   £2.99

❑ BLACK LACE QUICKIES 6 Various   ISBN 978 0 352 34133 4   £2.99

❑ BLACK LACE QUICKIES 7 Various   ISBN 978 0 352 34146 4   £2.99

❑ BLACK LACE QUICKIES 8 Various   ISBN 978 0 352 34147 1   £2.99

❑ BLACK LACE QUICKIES 9 Various   ISBN 978 0 352 34155 6   £2.99

❑ MORE WICKED WORDS Various   ISBN 978 0 352 33487 9   £6.99

❑ WICKED WORDS 3 Various   ISBN 978 0 352 33522 7   £6.99

❑ WICKED WORDS 4 Various   ISBN 978 0 352 33603 3   £6.99

❑ WICKED WORDS 5 Various   ISBN 978 0 352 33642 2   £6.99

❑ WICKED WORDS 6 Various   ISBN 978 0 352 33690 3   £6.99

❑ WICKED WORDS 7 Various   ISBN 978 0 352 33743 6   £6.99

❑ WICKED WORDS 8 Various   ISBN 978 0 352 33787 0   £6.99

❑ WICKED WORDS 9 Various   ISBN 978 0 352 33860 0

❑ WICKED WORDS 10 Various   ISBN 978 0 352 33893 8

❑ THE BEST OF BLACK LACE 2 Various   ISBN 978 0 352 33718 4

❑ WICKED WORDS: SEX IN THE OFFICE Various   ISBN 978 0 352 33944 7

❑ WICKED WORDS: SEX AT THE SPORTS CLUB Various   ISBN 978 0 352 33991 1

❑ WICKED WORDS: SEX ON HOLIDAY Various   ISBN 978 0 352 33961 4

❑ WICKED WORDS: SEX IN UNIFORM Various   ISBN 978 0 352 34002 3

❑ WICKED WORDS: SEX IN THE KITCHEN Various   ISBN 978 0 352 34018 4

❑ WICKED WORDS: SEX ON THE MOVE Various   ISBN 978 0 352 34034 4

❑ WICKED WORDS: SEX AND MUSIC Various   ISBN 978 0 352 34061 0

To find out the latest information about Black Lace titles, check out the website: www.black-lace-books.com or send for a booklist with complete synopses by writing to:

Black Lace Booklist, Virgin Books Ltd
Virgin Books
Random House
20 Vauxhall Bridge Road
London SW1V 2SA

Please include an SAE of decent size. Please note only British stamps are valid.

Our privacy policy
We will not disclose information you supply us to any other parties. We will not disclose any information which identifies you personally to any person without your express consent.

From time to time we may send out information about Black Lace books and special offers. Please tick here if you do _not_ wish to receive Black Lace information. ❏

Please send me the books I have ticked above.

Name ....

Address ....

....

....

....

Post Code ....

Send to: Virgin Books Cash Sales, Random House,
20 Vauxhall Bridge Road, London SW1V 2SA.

US customers: for prices and details of how to order
books for delivery by mail, call 888-330-8477.

Please enclose a cheque or postal order, made payable
to Virgin Books Ltd, to the value of the books you have
ordered plus postage and packing costs as follows:

UK and BFPO – £1.00 for the first book, 50p for each
subsequent book.

Overseas (including Republic of Ireland) – £2.00 for
the first book, £1.00 for each subsequent book.

If you would prefer to pay by VISA, ACCESS/MASTERCARD,
DINERS CLUB, AMEX or SWITCH, please write your card
number and expiry date here: ....

....

Signature ....

Please allow up to 28 days for delivery.